The ship gave a great shiver, as if a giant hand had seized it. Then it shot forward, in a blinding burst of speed. The landscape rushed by, and now Gerrard saw the portal, light swirling within it. As he gazed, he seemed to see a ghostlike parade of figures flitting through, escaping the dark prison of Rath. Above the portal, clinging to a rope that swung from the arch above the portal, was the slender, blond, boylike figure of Ertai.

"Slow down so we can get Ertai!" Gerrard shouted to Hanna.

"I can't!" she yelled.

Philip Athans has lived somewhere or another for his entire life. He has known many people, some of whom he is related to. A short attention span and various hobbies and interests occupy some of his time. After graduating from college he held a number of jobs including the one he currently holds, and which he will hold until he lets go or is pulled off.

Hannovi Braddock was born in Tucson, Arizona. In college, he changed his major five times, probably out of frustration that there was no major called Fantasy Studies. He finally settled for a B.A. in Humanities, which was the next best thing. He's the author of a MAGIC: THE GATHERING® novel from HarperPrism, *Ashes of the Sun*. He lives in Eugene, Oregon, where you can't swing a cat without hitting a science fiction or fantasy writer. (Not that Hanovi would swing any cat who didn't want to be swung.)

Miranda Horner lives in the state of Washington, where she edits projects for the DRAGONLANCE:® THE FIFTH AGE® roleplaying game. In her small amount of spare time, she loves to read, visit local areas of interest with her husband, play games, and write.

Kij Johnson has published short stories in various science fiction magazines (including *Asimov's*, *Amazing*, *F&SF*, *Weird Tales* and many others), for one of which she won the 1994 Theodore A. Sturgeon award for best short story of the year. She is the coauthor of a *Star Trek: The Next Generation* novel, *Dragon's Honor*. An original novel titled *The Fox Woman* is due as a hardcover from Tor Books in late 1999. She got involved in writing for MAGIC: THE GATHERING by generating flavor text for cards in the game. She figured that it make be a pleasant change to be allowed thousands of words in which to describe something.

J. Robert King, author of numerous books set in the shared worlds of DRAGONLANCE, RAVENLOFT®, PLANESCAPE® and MAGIC: THE GATHERING, has eluded Dark Knights on Krynn, roamed the dark forests of Barovia, battled Tanar'ri on the Outer Planes, and walked the planes of Dominia. When not doing these things, he lives in southern Wisconsin with his wife and two sons and an impressive collection of cigars.

Francis Lebaron lives in the Seattle area with his wife, daughter, a hamster, a fish, and a cat. While writing *Mercadian Masques* for the MAGIC: THE GATHERING novel line he comforted himself with the thought that humans will eventually outlive their fascination with computers and return to the saner and more civilized world of the fountain pen.

Michael G. Ryan gave up his dream of having the definitive Harrison Ford collection—Indiana Jones pinball machine and all—after he realized that Harrison Ford, by definition, has a better one. Now he's working on the definitive Michael G. Ryan collection (sans the pinball machine), though he still wears the Ford fedora.

Jennifer Clarke Wilkes, aka the "Goblin Editor," is a displaced Canadian currently living outside Seattle, Washington, where she is employed as a mild-mannered MAGIC: THE GATHERING editor. By night, she is a crusader for neglected games, a puzzle fiend, and a reptile groupie. She has the usual complement of cats.

Liz Holliday has written novelizations of the British television series "Cracker" and is editor of *Odyssey* a U.K. science fiction magazine. She lives in London.

MAGIC: The Gathering®

A World of Magic

THE BROTHERS' WAR
Jeff Grubb

RATH AND STORM
A Magic: The Gathering Anthology

PLANESWALKER
Lynn Abbey

MERCADIAN MASQUES
Francis Lebaron

RATH AND STORM

A MAGIC: THE GATHERING Anthology

Edited by

Peter Archer

RATH AND STORM
©1998 Wizards of the Coast, Inc.
All Rights Reserved.

Distributed to the book trade in the United States by Random House, Inc. and in Canada by Random House of Canada Ltd.

Distributed to the toy and hobby trade by regional distributors.

Distributed worldwide by Wizards of the Coast, Inc. and regional distributors.

First Printing: July 1998
Printed in the United States of America.
Library of Congress Catalog Card Number: 97-062372

9 8 7 6 5 4 3 2 1

8731XXX1501

ISBN: 0-7869-1175-1

U.S., CANADA, ASIA,   EUROPEAN HEADQUARTERS
PACIFIC, & LATIN AMERICA   Wizards of the Coast, Belgium
Wizards of the Coast, Inc.   P.B. 34
P.O. Box 707   2300 Turnhout
Renton, WA 98057-0707   Belgium
+1-206-624-0933   +32-14-44-30-44
                Visit our website at **www.wizards.com**

A Dark Room

The room was long and dark, lit only by a single, guttering candle. The bookcases that lined the stone walls, each loaded with leather-bound tomes, seemed to lean inward, menacing the slender figure who knelt by an open chest. Wild white hair straggled across his face, and from time to time he brushed it impatiently away. His eyes flickered uneasily about the room, especially toward the high vaulted window covered by heavy drapes. Through a gap in the curtains there flashed intermittently a harsh, ghastly light.

A muffled boom of thunder rumbled through the room, and a few books tumbled from the shelves. The white-haired man, surrounded by packets of papers, started and half-rose. Then, shrugging his shoulders, he returned to his documents.

So preoccupied was he that he took no notice when a small wooden door at the far end of the chamber swung open and a boy entered. Slight of figure with slender wrists, perhaps ten or eleven years old, he was clad in the brown robes of a student. Softly he advanced until he was directly behind the man.

"Master . . . ?"

"Whuff!" The older man started again, scattering papers and nearly upsetting the candle. "Don't *do* that, boy! Are you insane? You could be killed, sneaking about like that!"

He paused in his tirade to consider the boy more closely. "What are you still doing here, anyway? You should be in bed."

The boy shook his head, tears starting in his eyes.

"Don't be angry with me, Master. I was frightened by the storm, and I saw a light in here. One of the other masters was telling us of a fire started by lightning that burned down a great library, and I was worried. I couldn't bear for all this to be lost. . . ." His voice trailed off as he hung his head, sobbing openly.

"Nonsense! The storm? Just thunder and lightning. Nothing that will hurt anyone." The master's voice softened. "What's your name?"

"Ilcaster, sir."

"Well, Ilcaster, take it from me that this library will still exist long after you and I are gone. It can outlast any storm."

"But how, Master?" The boy gazed disconsolately about the room, most of it sunk in shadow. "Books don't last forever."

The master's hand lightly slapped his pupil.

"Books!" he said contemptuously. "Books are not the soul of the library."

"But Master, it's written elsewhere that a library without books is like a castle without walls, a monastery without monks, a—"

"The true library," interrupted the old man, tapping his forehead, "is up here."

"What do you mean, Master?"

"I mean, foolish boy, that what matters are the memories in our heads, not smudges of ink on paper."

Ilcaster wrinkled his brow. "I think I understand, Master. But then why preserve books at all? And why are you bothering with these?" His outstretched hands indicated the papers lying about them.

The older man grunted and bent again to his task. "Because although the library is the sum of memories, we need reminding occasionally. But these papers are perishable. Never forget that, lad. Now, as long as you're here, help me sort these. This part of the archives hasn't been touched in decades, and I want to clean it up."

The two figures bent over the documents, their shadows stretching over the floor to meld with the deeper darkness beneath the library walls. To Ilcaster it seemed as if the flashes of light were growing more frequent, and the deep-throated rumbles were louder than before.

"What's this?"

The white-haired man glanced over the boy's shoulder. "A flying ship. See, down there's her name."

"*Weatherlight*.. It's a pretty name."

"A fine name for a fine ship. But it's quite well-known. Didn't you read about her in *Early Dominarian Legends*?"

The boy hung his head, and even in the dim light the master could see he was blushing.

"For shame! The story of *Weatherlight*' is one of the great epic stories of the age."

"Well, *I* never heard it, anyway," observed the boy. "And I never heard of a sailing ship that could fly. Flying is for ornithopters."

"Ah, well then, naturally you know all about it." The old man returned grumpily to his papers.

Ilcaster saw he'd gone too far. "I beg your pardon,

Master. I didn't mean to disbelieve you. *Weatherlight*. No, I never heard of her. Who was her captain?"

"Gerrard Capashen. Though how he came to be captain . . ." The old man's voice trailed off and he glanced up at the gloom that surrounded them.

"Go on, Master. What happened to him?"

The master sighed and spread his hands in resignation.

"Very well. This was many years ago, but still thousands of years after the Brothers' War—you *have* heard of that, I suppose? In Argive Reckoning, the date of the Rath Cycle would be 4205, but the story actually begins some twenty-six years previous to that.

"Gerrard was an orphan, living in Jamuraa. He'd been given into the care of a warclan by his parents before their death, and raised by the Sidar Kondo along with his own son Vuel."

"Sidar Kondo—who's that?"

"The leader of the warclan."

"Why did Gerrard's parents abandon him?"

"They did not abandon him. They gave him over to the warclan for his own safety."

"Why? Who was threatening him?"

"Ah, well. As Gerrard grew older, he heard stories of a mysterious figure called the Lord of the Wastes. Some members of the warclan even claimed to have seen this strange figure. They said he was tall, with burning eyes, surrounded by a halo of flame that destroyed everything it touched."

Ilcaster nodded. "Yes, Master, I think I've even heard of those stories. So that's who was threatening Gerrard's life?"

"No, of course not. Those stories were so much superstitious nonsense. Halo of flame indeed!" The old man's eyes grew dim, as if he were looking deep inside himself, drawing forth memories that had not been recalled in a very, very long time. "No, the real enemy was someone much worse."

"Who could be worse than someone who burns everything he touches? Or . . . someone named the Lord of the Wastes?"

The old man scowled. "I'll tell you, if you'll be quiet and listen. For the moment, it suffices to say that Gerrard grew up knowing his parents were dead, murdered by some mysterious force whose true name he did not know.

"Gerrard was brought to the clan by a silver golem named Karn, a bequest from his parents. The golem was a marvelous machine that you might almost mistake for a living being. But even more marvelous, the golem carried within it a collection of magical artifacts known as the Legacy.

The old man turned over a paper. "I had a list here, somewhere," he murmured. "A list of the items that were part of the Legacy. Well, no matter. Here, boy. Sort through that pile and separate all the documents headed in red. You can do that while I talk.

"The Legacy had also been bequeathed to Gerrard by his parents. The origins of this collection were unknown to Gerrard or, indeed, to Karn himself. Nonetheless, the golem knew the collection was of supreme importance and that both Gerrard and the Legacy must be closely guarded until some far-off day of destiny.

"Gerrard and Vuel, the sidar's son, were close as blood brothers. They played together, learned together, and together they sampled all the pleasures and pains of growing boys. But as they neared manhood, Vuel grew jealous of Gerrard, an envy egged on by a mysterious fellow named Starke."

"Another mystery," said the boy, drawn by the story. Who was this Starke?"

"None knew at the time. He appeared from out of the desert and sought refuge with the warclan. At first he spoke softly and gently. But some noticed that he spent much of his time watching—watching the two boys. Some thought as time went on that Starke seemed to look with a special intensity at Vuel, as if he had some great future planned for the young man. And always he whispered in Vuel's ear, though what the young man heard from Starke he kept hidden from all, including both his father and Gerrard."

"Others might have resisted Starke's blandishments, but Vuel was jealous, quick to anger, sensitive to slights. Starke persuaded the foolish Vuel—who was also arrogant as only a young man can be—that Gerrard intended to steal his birthright.

"But Gerrard was innocent," interrupted Ilcaster.

The old man, in the full flow of his narrative, swung round and glared at the student, who blushed and pretended to study carefully an illustration on the manuscript before him.

"Yes," conceded the librarian, "Gerrard was innocent of the intentions Starke attributed to him. But Vuel believed the whisperings of the mysterious man, and in all Gerrard's actions he saw only plots against his rightful place in the clan."

The master paused, and Ilcaster, after a moment, said, "Perhaps Starke was working for the Lord of the Wastes. Or rather," he added hastily, "for the force that had killed Gerrard's parents."

The librarian nodded grudgingly. "That's an interesting guess. Whatever the case, Starke succeeded in turning Vuel against Gerrard and against his own father. His plot culminated during Vuel's rite of passage."

Ilcaster nodded. "I've heard of those. They're used in some societies to show passage to adulthood. Was that what this one was for?

"Yes, it was a ritual to which every sidar's son was subject. To succeed his father in the leadership of the clan, Vuel had to pass this test. Starke knew this and manipulated matters so that Vuel's life was threatened during the ritual. Starke also knew that Gerrard could not bear to see his friend in danger and would rescue him."

The old man sighed. "Gerrard performed just as Starke had expected, and Vuel was saved from death. But since he had disrupted the ritual, Vuel angrily accused his step-brother of destroying his chance to become warlord. Vuel brooded on the insult until finally, at Starke's urging he decided to steal the most precious thing Gerrard possessed—the Legacy.

"Karn became aware of this plot, though too late to prevent it. One night, when the clan slept, Vuel rose from his bed, gathered the pieces of the Legacy together, and carried them away with him."

Ilcaster looked puzzled. "But how could he steal them so easily?" he asked. "Wasn't Karn guarding them?"

"He should have been. But the golem ws deceived by Vuel, like both Gerrard and the sidar.

"Karn was aware of the theft almost immediately, and gave chase to the treacherous young man. His journey was long, for the golem could not travel nearly as fast as the sidar's son, and he lost the trail many times, but at last he traced Vuel to a remote village and there demanded the return of the Legacy."

"And did Vuel fight? I wouldn't have thought he'd have had much chance against a golem." Ilcaster asked, his tone skeptical.

"No, in ordinary circumstances Karn could probably have defeated Vuel easily. But the young man tricked the silver golem. During their fight, Karn was responsible for the death of an innocent bystander. Horrified, he stopped the fight, swearing that he'd battle no more lest others be hurt. And in that moment of weakness, Vuel used a piece of the Legacy called the Touchstone to deactivate the golem."

Ilcaster wrinkled his brow. "Used it? Did he use the magical power within it to destroy the golem?"

"No. He brought it close to Karn, where its power turned off the machine that was the golem. But just before his consciousness faded, Karn reached out and clutched the Touchstone, pulling it away from Vuel. All the latter's efforts were insufficient to pry it loose again, and Vuel was forced to flee the village, whose inhabitants had turned against him. In fact, the villagers believed Karn had liberated them from Vuel, and as a reward they placed the immobile statue of the golem in the village square, where it remained for years."

Ilcaster laughed delightedly, and the unexpected sound seemed to momentarily push back the gathering shadows in the room.

"A statue. That's wonderful. But what happened to the Legacy?"

"Vuel took it with him and scattered it, piece by piece, throughout the lands in which he traveled. Gerrard was left with only a single item of the Legacy, a necklace with an hourglass pendant. See, here's a sketch of it."

"It's beautiful."

"Yes, but that was all Gerrard retained of his birthright. Meanwhile, Vuel, having scattered the Legacy far and wide, launched a war against his father."

There was another rumble of thunder. Rain rattled against the windows. The librarian moved to one wall and checked the fastenings on the panes before resuming his story.

"Gerrard left the warclan. He did not know what had happened to Karn, his guardian from boyhood. Perhaps he felt abandoned, having lost both Karn and Vuel. In any event, he took up magical training under the tutelage of a maro-sorcerer named Multani. There in the caves where Multani lived, Gerrard met Mirri, a cat warrior, and Rofellos a Llanowar elf. For many years they were his closest friends."

"I don't understand," interrupted Ilcaster. "Why did Vuel still hate Gerrard so much?"

The librarian steepled his fingers. "He'd become obsessed—some might say he was mad. He was determined to blot out Gerrard and all who were near to him."

"Vuel, in his envious rage, pursued Gerrard. Multani learned of the threat in time and sent Gerrard, Mirri, and Rofellos away from the cave. When they returned some time later, they found the cave in ruins and Multani gone."

"Dead?" Ilcaster's eyes were wide.

The master shook his head. "None know for sure. Certainly the three companions did not know. But worse was to come. When they returned to the warclan's encampment, the site of Gerrard's youth, they again found a scene of ruin and slaughter. The warlord, Gerrard's adoptive father, was dead, and Gerrard's last tie to his past was broken.

Gerrard knew this must be the work of Vuel. The three companions left the cave and tried to make the best lives for themselves that they could, traveling the land as hired fighters. At last during their travels Gerrard, Mirri, and Rofellos met Sisay, a Jamuraan native and captain of *Weatherlight.*

"Sisay! But I thought you said Gerrard was the captain—"

A frown from the old man silenced the boy's eager outburst.

"I'm sorry, Master." The boy subsided and huddled close to the old man's feet, his eager face turned upward.

"Sisay was able to persuade Gerrard to join her. In point of fact, she won a bet against him; his payment was to join her crew."

"What was the wager?"

The scholar snorted contemptuously. "It was thoroughly foolish. Apparently the three companions were throwing knives in a low tavern of some sort. Sisay watched them for a time, then challenged Gerrard to a contest of skill. He accepted confidently and rejoiced when his knife struck the very center of the target. But Sisay, whose warrior skills had been honed by long years of training, split the haft of his knife with her own cast. Gerrard was humiliated before his friends, and sullenly he agreed to fulfill his part of the bet and enlist with her.

"Once he and the others were aboard, she revealed to him that she'd been searching for the pieces of the Legacy ever since Vuel scattered them. She asked for Gerrard's help, and he reluctantly agreed to give it."

Ilcaster's brow was wrinkled. "I must be missing a piece of this puzzle," he said. "Why was Sisay searching for the Legacy? What did it have to do with her?"

The librarian nodded. "Well you should ask that. In fact, Sisay herself had a mysterious birthright. Like Gerrard she was an orphan; her parents too had died under strange circumstances. Before they died, they had told her stories of the Lord of the Wastes."

"But you said earlier that was just a myth—"

"I know I did. Be silent, boy!"

Once more Ilcaster dutifully subsided, but his lower lip stuck out defiantly.

"It's true that the Lord of the Wastes is mythological," conceded the librarian. "Had they lived longer, I think Sisay's parents might have told her that. But they died too soon, and Sisay did not know the entire truth. In any case, her parents warned her that the only force that had the power to defeat the 'Lord of the Wastes' was the Legacy. They passed to her their most precious possession— *Weatherlight*—and charged her to go forth and seek out the scattered pieces of the Legacy. Sadly, during one of her many journeys on the ship, her parents died. But meanwhile Sisay had accumulated many of the bits of the Legacy and stowed them on board the ship.

"This, at any rate, was as much of her history as Sisay told to Gerrard and his companions. Gerrard sensed there was more, but she was not yet willing to reveal it to him.

"*Weatherlight*'s crew included a good many strange characters whom Sisay had picked up in the course of her adventures. Tahngarth, a Talruum minotaur, was first mate; the navigator was Hanna, an Argivian artificer. Then there was Orim, a Samite healer, Crovax, a nobleman, and Squee, the goblin cabin boy. Of course there were many more, but these are the figures who play particular roles in our story. Gerrard, Rofellos, and Mirri joined this band.

"They searched for some time before an urgent message drew them back to Crovax's home in Urborg. It seemed his estate was under attack by strange creatures from a plane called Rath."

"Rath!" The boy bounced excitedly. "Master, that's the very word written at the top of this paper. 'The Rath Cycle'!"

"Of course it's the Rath Cycle! Isn't that what I just told you?"

"No, Master. You said—"

"All right, *all right*! Never mind that." The old man rose and stumped about the room, his feet beating out an indignant rhythm on the stone floor. Just be quiet and listen.

"*Weatherlight* arrived just in time to turn back an attack by these creatures—Gallowbraid and Morinfen their names were. But during the fight, Gallowbraid slew Rofellos the elf. As Rofellos lay dying in Gerrard's arms, Crovax drew on the power of a cursed artifact that had belonged to his family for generations, and summoned Selenia, a guardian angel in the service of Crovax's family. With her help, *Weatherlight*'s crew beat back the attack. But when the battle was over, Sisay and Gerrard quarreled. Gerrard wanted to abandon the search for the Legacy, a quest he blamed for the death of his friend Rofellos. And nothing Sisay said to him could change his mind. Taking the hourglass pendant and Mirri with him, Gerrard left *Weatherlight*."

"Left!" the boy almost shouted. "But you told me he became captain."

"So I did. And so he did. The story doesn't end here. Now are you finished sorting that stack of papers? Good." The old man tied the bundle with a string and thrust it into a cabinet. "Now do the same for these two stacks."

The boy began gathering scattered packets, stacking them neatly by the old man's feet, and then paging through them. The master, glancing around the room as if to assure himself they were still alone, went on with his tale.

"Undoubtedly there was much bitterness on both sides in the quarrel. To Sisay, it appeared that Gerrard was simply abandoning his destiny in favor of his own selfish interests. To Gerrard, it seemed Sisay put some abstract commitment to the Legacy over the lives of those nearest and dearest to her.

"Other crew members were affected by the quarrel as well. Over the years he'd served on *Weatherlight* Gerrard had grown close to Hanna, the navigator who probably knew more than anyone about the ship. Her feelings were strong indeed, but she hesitated to speak them aloud to Gerrard. When he left, she felt hurt and betrayed.

"Tahngarth, on the other hand, seemed almost pleased to see Gerrard leave, as if the young man was confirming some estimate the minotaur had formed of his character. At any rate, Gerrard and Mirri left, and the ship sailed on.

"While Sisay and the rest of *Weatherlight* crew were continuing their journey in search of the Legacy, Gerrard traveled to Benalia, where he joined the Benalish infantry and became a master at arms. Mirri returned to Llanower to inform Rofellos's kin of the elf's death. And so the two friends parted.

"Meanwhile, Sisay had discovered a key part of the Legacy, an artifact called the Thran Tome. From this magical book she learned two things of tremendous importance.

"First, the Tome told her that *Weatherlight*, itself a part of the Legacy, could actually move between different planes of existence. This ability to planeshift was made possible by the crystal that powered the ship's engines.

"The Tome also told Sisay of a plane called Rath, the very place from which Gallowbraid and Morinfen had come to attack Crovax's estate. Though the Tome's entries were not entirely clear, Sisay concluded from them that Rath had some great importance for the future of Dominaria.

"Sisay also recovered Karn from the village where Vuel had hidden him, and the silver golem became a valued part of *Weatherlight*'s cargo of artifacts. Along with Karn, of course, she also found the Touchstone, still clutched irretrievably in the golem's grasp.

"And then Sisay stumbled onto a piece of terrifying information. Vuel, the sidar's son, Gerrard's deadliest enemy, had left the plane of Dominaria for Rath. In that dark place, he had become the ruler and had changed his name to Volrath. He brooded there in his great fortress, the Stronghold, planning Gerrard's destruction.

"All this Sisay learned from a native of Rath, Starke—"

"Wait a moment," the boy interrupted. "Wasn't Starke the same one—"

"That's right. Starke, the same man who had corrupted Vuel."

"But why would Starke help Sisay?"

"Because, although he'd helped Volrath to become the ruler of Rath, he was horrified when he realized for whom Rath had been constructed and who its rulers truely served."

"Who?" The boy's voice sank to a whisper, as if he feared the answer.

"Phyrexia." The old man's voice trembled, and as if in answer the light flashed outside and the walls of the library shivered. The old man cleared his throat and continued his story.

"Starke had undergone many changes over the years. Now he was trying to play both sides against one another. He'd tried to corrupt Crovax, playing on the love the young nobleman felt for the angel Selenia. Crovax—who had returned to his family estate after the death of Rofellos—freed Selenia, smashing the artifact that summoned her. He did this out of his great love for her, but in doing so he doomed both her and himself. Soon after she was freed, the angel was snatched away from Crovax through a kind of portal. The wiley Starke persuaded Crovax to rejoin *Weatherlight*, hoping to shape Sisay's ship into a weapon with which he might oppose Volrath's power.

"He had a more personal reason for his hatred of Volrath: the ruler of Rath had taken Starke's daughter Takara prisoner and held her as insurance against her father's good behavior."

"Hmpf!" the boy snorted. "Would have served him right if Volrath had got wind of his plan."

"Starke's plot was even more complicated than that. He knew that Volrath's great enemy was Gerrard. He needed a way to lure Gerrard to Rath where the young master-at-arms could confront and destroy Volrath. So he performed one last bit of treachery."

"What was that?" The boy, his packets forgotten, sat open-mouthed on the floor.

"Starke betrayed Sisay to Volrath. The evil ruler kidnapped her and stole the bits of the Legacy she'd so painstakingly collected. Then Starke revealed to the crew of *Weatherlight* who had kidnapped Sisay and begged them to find Gerrard, to force him to accompany them as they departed on their greatest mission: to travel to Rath and rescue Sisay!"

I

WEATHERLIGHT

Gerrard's Tale

Michael Ryan

The morning the minotaur arrived, Gerrard entered the training yard in time to see Torsten, the heavier boy, bat Javero's blade aside and drive the smaller boy down to the sand on the other end of the yard. Javero's sword flew from his hands, landing well out of his reach, and Torsten moved over him, between him and his weapon. Both young men were breathing hard under the blazing sun. Torsten's blonde hair was dark with sweat and grime, and Javero's hands were spotted with sword oil and blisters. Gerrard was silently proud of both of them for practicing while the others slacked off. It was still hours before exercises, yet here they were, devoted to the art of war. He remembered that feeling quite well.

"Good move," he called as he took his heavy set of keys from the belt below his vest and moved to the war chests along the wall, "but you want—"

"Master!" Javero cried out in terror.

Torsten kicked Javero once in the head, just above his ear—the sound of his boot heel on the thinner boy's skull made a hollow *thock!* that carried all the way across the open yard—before slashing down with his sword at his foe's throat. Javero rolled, and the blade cut sand, knicking his ear and drawing blood. Torsten stepped back, regaining his balance and bringing his sword back to attack position as Javero struggled to get to his feet. Blood bubbled from his wounded ear.

"It's too late. He can't save you," Torsten said, raising his sword again. He glanced across the training yard toward Gerrard. "No one can save—"

The keys caught Torsten in the throat like a claw, tearing open the soft spot of flesh beneath his Adam's apple. He staggered backward, one hand to his bleeding wound.

"Easy, Torsten," Gerrard called. From nowhere he had produced a longbow, and an arrow was already nocked on string and aimed at Torsten. The arrow's point glittered in the sunlight flooding the training yard. "It's six steps back or six feet under, whichever you prefer."

Torsten looked over at Javero, then back at the arrow pointed at him.

"Don't make me kill you, too, Master Gerrard," he rasped. He took his hand away from his throat and looked at the blood on his fingertips. "This is a private fight between Javero and me."

"It's ending publicly," Gerrard said, "with a corpse, if need be. I could kill you twice before you could even get to me, Torsten. You're a good student, but education isn't the same thing as experience. You should've been quick enough to catch those keys. Now take six steps back."

For a moment, Torsten hesitated, sweat beading on his forehead. Then he raised his blade and, with a defiant shout, turned on Javero.

Gerrard dropped his aim and let the arrow fly. It took Torsten just behind the left kneecap as his leg bent, driving through the muscle and carrying the arrowhead and shaft out the other side until the fletching caught in the wound. Torsten howled, falling forward; the shaft snapped behind his legs as he went down. He dropped his sword, and as the blade knifed into the sand, Javero grabbed its hilt. Raising it triumphantly as he stood over the heavier boy, he looked up in time to see Gerrard nock another arrow.

"It'll be the right knee for you," Gerrard said. "A shameful limp and no service in the Benalish army. I'll change your entire future with one easy shot if you don't put that sword down, Javero."

"He was talking to Lord Kastan," Javero protested, "the assassin recruiter. The albino. I saw them together at the bridges this morning."

From the ground, where he was already working the arrow out his leg, Torsten snarled, "You're a corpse."

"I don't care if he *is* Lord Kastan." Gerrard began to move forward, his arrow still at the ready. His dark beard itched from the sweat that ran down his face. "*I* could be Lord Kastan, and it wouldn't change this mess you're in. Now put down the sword."

Javero relented, tossing the sword into the sand and stepping back afterward. Gerrard let his breath out slowly. "Great. Now we're all in better shape. I'm armed and you're not."

He put his arrow back in his quiver then picked up both swords. "Did Kastan try to recruit you, Torsten?"

Torsten said nothing, but Gerrard held back and let the silence drag on until it became as hot as the sun above. Finally, Javero said nervously, "I've heard that some of the others were approached, too, not just Torsten."

"Lord Kastan will sew your eyes open before he kills

you," Torsten snapped at him, then looked at Gerrard. "I must see a healer, Master."

"You've got it," Gerrard said. He held up Torsten's blade. "Your sword stays, of course. You're out—you tried to kill Javero, you threatened me, and, if I were a gambling man, I'd bet you took gold from the assassins. That's not what I trained you for, Torsten. That's not what the Benalish military is about. You've shamed the nation, and you've disappointed me."

Torsten managed to get his weak leg under him, throwing to the sand the arrow that had struck him. He grimaced as he put weight on the leg and nearly fell. When he found his balance again, he was forced to lean heavily to his right, for the wounded leg refused to carry him. The blood from his throat wound was already drying to a dark red splotch like a birthmark. He glared in fury at Gerrard. "Then there's more disappointment in your future. You're not the only instructor in Benalia who can teach a man to fight, you know."

Gerrard shrugged. "I'm not the only one who can teach you to dance, either. But no one will now." He gestured at Torsten's leg. "You're done being a soldier, if you ever were one."

For a moment, Gerrard thought the young man might come at him. Torsten's lips locked, his hands clenched into fists, and his eyebrows met in a scowl. Then he swallowed, took a deep breath, and said, "But I'm not done being a killer."

He limped to the training yard's entrance, never looking back. Gerrard watched him go. When he had disappeared into the dark tunnel, Gerrard turned to Javero. The young man seemed to be having a difficult time catching his breath, but the panic was fading fast from his face. "Thank the gods you arrived when you did," he half-whispered. "I have always heard you are one of the best, Master, but I never thought I would so desperately need you to be."

"Being the best usually means proving it." Gerrard walked to his keys, picked them up, and turned back to the young man. "For Torsten's sake, I hope you're right about all this—and it looks like you are. But for the Benalish army's sake, I hope you're wrong. We have some things to talk about."

Javero nodded. "A few things, Master Gerrard."

The two of them retired to Gerrard's chambers below the training yard. The three dusty rooms lay in shadows, cluttered with trappings and trinkets from days Gerrard had just begun to remember fondly. He watched Javero move around the main chamber, handling various artifacts and weapons and asking questions. The young man had apparently forgotten the heat of the battle despite the blood that trickled from his ear to stain his gold earring. Gerrard let him explore; students never came down here, and Javero's curiosity kept him distracted while Gerrard considered the implications of what had just occurred in the yard.

"And what's this?" the young man asked, gesturing to a skin hanging on the wall above a row of shelves.

"The hide of a scarmithal," Gerrard answered absently as he sat down behind his disorganized desk. He wondered if Torsten had gone directly to Lord Kastan after the fight. "I was traveling with some friends along the coast of Denawa when we ran into them. If you wear the skin, it changes your shape into one so you can pass among the other scarmithals. Kind of a scarmithal spy's cloak."

Javero nodded, paused as if he might ask something else, then gestured at the pendant around Gerrard's neck. "I've seen you with that pendant before. What is it?"

Gerrard held it up and across the desk for him to see. The pendant was shaped like a small hourglass, hung so that it could be up-ended to run its sands while remaining on the chain. As Javero leaned closer to examine it, Gerrard said, "The last treasure of a life I abandoned."

Javero was about to speak again, but Gerrard gestured for him to be silent. This was old soil, heavily tilled—memories of *Weatherlight*, Captain Sisay, and the Legacy were as untouchable as the gods themselves, and nearly as unforgiving. They were part of a time Gerrard couldn't change and hadn't understood at the time anyway. Regretting it only made him relive it. Besides, there were far more important things to discuss than Gerrard's past life as a sailor of the skies.

"So Lord Kastan is trying to recruit my soldiers as his bloodletters," he said matter-of-factly. "Never mind that such behavior is treason in Benalia. Surely he knows who he's taunting by even trying. I'm not exactly known for my diplomatic skills. Every master-at-arms, ranking officer, and infantry drudge would raise swords over this if word got out. But Kastan is jeopardizing my career with this arrogance. I'm obliged to do something about it or risk my entire life in Benalia. I'll be damned if I'll learn about a cure *after* the plague."

Javero touched his wounded ear and said, "I guess I should have been thinking the same way, Master. Confronting Torsten was a mistake. And now he has reason to hate me."

"You should have come to me with this," Gerrard agreed, "or taken it over my head to Commander Alaric. If I can trust him, you can. But he'll still spit poison when I tell him that the assassins are headhunting in the army's ranks."

"Yes, sir. I know he will."

"You know he's going to want the names of the others, everyone who Lord Kastan tried to recruit. There'll be an investigation. The army has no tolerance for this sort of betrayal. That's why I got into it in the first place. But at least the army will protect you from Torsten and the others, so you won't have to sleep with a dagger under your pillow." Gerrard paused, then asked, "So who else besides Torsten?"

He watched Javero's eyes pan nervously across the room, pausing on each individual heirloom, and he knew then that the young man had yet another secret, poorly concealed. "If I were a gambling man, I'd bet you've been approached," he said softly.

Javero swallowed, clearing his throat and keeping his eyes averted, unable or unwilling to meet Gerrard's steady gaze. "Yes, Master Gerrard. But not by Lord Kastan."

"Then who?"

"There's this mercenary band of siege breakers at the docks," Javero answered. "They're just passing through Benalia. I met with their recruiter yesterday, and he told me about their group—where they've been, what they've been doing. You know, the adventures that happen to mercenaries."

"Adventure's just another way of saying your day started out badly," Gerrard said.

"No, no. You don't understand." Javero turned abruptly from Gerrard's desk, picking up an elaborate rod from the shelf beneath the hide. Gerrard watched while Javero held it up as if his master had never seen it before. "Our first day of training, you showed this to us. 'A weapon is only as good as the hand that wields it,' you said. And then you fired it. Tt was amazing, all that magic coming from this little artifact. We were all impressed, by both the rod and the wielder. There's a story behind this, yes? Some insane risk you took to find it, some amazing battle you fought to earn it. And here it is, the treasure that epitomizes that whole adventure."

Gerrard grinned. "It's called the Null Rod, Javero. You know why? Because it doesn't *do* anything. It's all flash. I use it for show. Bad example."

"Then your pendant."

Gerrard's grin faded, and he touched the hourglass absently. He sighed, scratching his thin beard. "You're knight material. I know you know that. But you have to see your training through. You want adventure? Put Benalish armor on, and it'll come at you tooth and claw."

Javero shook his head. "So I can fill out battle reports and serve as an 'honor' guard for every Benalish noble with a fat gut but a fatter purse? Sentry duty and parades just don't suit me, Master Gerrard. The army is restrictive to the point of strangulation. It's not service, it's servitude. There's got to be something more with the siege breakers."

"You'd be making a mistake," Gerrard said. "The army is as good as it gets, and I should know. I've been out there. I was first mate on a ship for years. I traveled all over the world. You know what it got me? Dead friends. Bad dreams. I fought as hard as I could, Javero, and I still ended up right here, in 'servitude' to Benalia. I'm not saying you'll be back, but I am saying you'll wake up somewhere down the road with blood all over your hands. And you probably won't know whose it is, even if it's your own."

Standing rigid, Javero smoothed his dusty tunic and said formally, "I'd like to be dismissed, Master." He paused and added, "I'm sorry."

Gerrard rose from behind his desk. This is it, then, he thought. Two in one day. "All right. I'll dismiss you if that's what you really want . . . but not without names. I'll protect the army's honor by keeping you in if I have to, but the door's open and your password out is the names of the soldiers Lord Kastan approached."

Javero took a deep breath and began to speak, just as Gerrard knew he would.

* * * * *

Gerrard went directly to Commander Alaric's quarters after Javero left the training yard, and he made his report about Lord Kastan. Alaric's chambers, even the dark and dusty entranceway where Gerrard waited to get his commander's attention, were immaculate compared to Gerrard's. Alaric was pure soldier: efficient, strict, orderly. He had been in the Benalish military for more than twenty years and had been one of the first officers to test Gerrard when he arrived in Benalia after leaving *Weatherlight*. Gerrard had heard him referred to by some of the knights as "the first dog of war," and it suited Alaric's character. He carried himself more like a mountain man than a soldier, moving through the streets of Benalia Port as if he were stalking prey. He was curt, opinionated, and firm, and when he talked, his thick steel-gray eyebrows drew together so tightly that his eyes vanished beneath them. Gerrard watched those eyebrows furrow as he finished his explanation of the morning's events and the list of the soldiers Lord Kastan had approached, according to Javero.

"This could well be running rampant throughout the military," Alaric grunted, rubbing his mustache. He passed Gerrard a bottle of wine he had taken from the cabinet and opened just before Gerrard's arrival, but Gerrard shook his head and put it down on the bare table between them next to his empty glass. "It could bring us down from within. It makes us vulnerable to defectors, spies, all sorts of other elements. Who else knows about this?"

"Just you and I," Gerrard said. "At least I hope so. What do you want to do, Commander? We could bring Lord Kastan in, put some pressure on him to flush out his contacts. The students who have been approached are all the sharpest swords. Lord Kastan is getting access to the training yards or the testing reports. Either way, we have a traitor."

"Kastan is an underground assassin. We'd never find him without being led directly to him. Besides, the traitor could easily have been Torsten or one of the other students."

Gerrard could tell the commander didn't believe his own words. It would drag some knight out of secret back-alley meetings and would spill blood money from hidden coffers. Only someone in authority could pass reports to the assassins.

"Watch your students," the commander said. "See if you can get a sense for what they've been offered. Come see me immediately if you learn anything new."

"And Kastan?"

"I'll personally look into finding Lord Kastan," Alaric answered ominously.

Gerrard grinned tightly. "What's the saying? 'Before an assassin learns of murder, he should first learn of suicide.' "

Picking up Gerrard's wine glass, Alaric retrieved the Vesuvan wine bottle and poured. He passed the glass to Gerrard. "No assassin ever put stock in *that* thought. Here. Borlean. Best in the Domains."

"No, thanks," Gerrard said, waving the glass away. "My drinking days are long past."

Alaric cleared his throat and set Gerrard's declined glass on the table before him. "In truth, boy, those days are about to catch up with you. The past arrived on a flying ship just after dawn this morning. *Your* past."

Gerrard stared at the dark wine for long moments. When Alaric shifted uncomfortably in his chair, Gerrard looked up, brushing his dark hair out of his eyes as he did so. "Why didn't you tell me this when I first walked in?"

"Because you were wild-eyed about this situation with the assassins," Alaric replied. "Because I didn't want to take the fire out of your belly. You, Gerrard, *are* the Benalish military. If any other master-at-arms had learned what you learned today, they'd have shrugged it off and gone on about their business."

"I believe in the army," Gerrard said quietly.

"Yes, and that's where I want your commitment. But I remember the things you said when you first came to us and signed on. I remember that same passionate commitment in your voice when you spoke of *Weatherlight's* captain. Sisay, was it? Sisay."

"If I sounded passionate, it was only because I was angry. Sisay had been keeping secrets from me. People died because of what she alone knew."

Alaric said gently, "And people will die now for what you know. That's the burden of responsibility. You can't just run away from it."

Gerrard crossed his arms defiantly. "Are you saying that I'll abandon Benalia now because I might be responsible for someone's death?"

Alaric got to his feet and drew himself up to his full and impressive height, any semblance of subtlety disappearing as he did so. "I'm saying that you turned away from *Weatherlight* crew when the situation became difficult. They've come looking for you. But you have a duty of honor to the present as well as the past now—this matter of the assassins grows within your very ranks. You're going to be pulled in two different directions, and whatever you choose is honorable . . . and dishonorable at the same time."

Gerrard stood as well. "So you waited to tell me about *Weatherlight* until after I'd committed myself to the assassin matter?"

"I have a vested interest in keeping you with us," Alaric admitted. He picked up Gerrard's wine glass and held it out to him. "I make no apologies for the things I do in the best interests of Benalia. Do you want that drink now?"

But Gerrard had already turned and passed into the

dark entranceway, banging Commander Alaric's door loudly behind him as he departed.

* * * * *

He stormed through the streets of the city town, dodging through the open-air market to avoid a patrol of guards whose names and handshakes were known to him. Old friends were both the first and last things on his mind right now. He didn't want to talk to any comrades from the army for fear that he would tip his hand about Lord Kastan and the assassins, but he also could not stop thinking about Sisay and *Weatherlight*. What did she want? It had been a long time since he'd leveled his accusations at her and walked off the ship, but a stirring in him made him wonder if maybe it had been too long. The old, familiar anger clenched in his belly—the things she had known about his past that he didn't, the things she hadn't told him until one of their own lay dying, the high-handed self-righteousness with which she had detailed his destiny to him, lecturing him about "responsibility," these all came back to him now. He could still see the disappointment in her eyes. He could see it in the faces of the others, especially Hanna's. A broken heart bled into the eyes, he'd heard, and Hanna was the only one who had cried for him as he left *Weatherlight*.

The minotaur was waiting for him in the training yard, as Gerrard knew he would be.

"You've grown taller, Tahngarth," Gerrard called out casually as he let himself in and crossed the sands to the towering minotaur who had been Sisay's closest ally. "So when does puberty end for minotaurs?"

"I've not grown," Tahngarth retorted. "You've shrunk."

Gerrard bent down and picked up Torsten's sword, brushing sand from its oils as he rose. "I bet I'm not the only human who rues the day the gods gave the gift of speech to cows."

He looked up at the minotaur. "Have I mentioned yet that it's good to see you?"

"I am here for a reason," Tahngarth said gruffly, tossing his dreadlocks back over his broad brown shoulders. A deep breath erupted as a snort, puffing out his great nostrils. "Sisay needs you."

" 'Need' can be interpreted a dozen different ways." Gerrard gestured for Tahngarth to follow him. The two of them moved to the south wall of the training yard, the tall minotaur's shadow stretching well beyond Gerrard's. At the wall, Gerrard knelt and unlocked one of the war chests where he kept the exercise swords. As he fished around inside for a sheath, he said, "So which way does Sisay think she needs me now?"

"She is gone, Gerrard. She's been taken prisoner to another plane, a place called Rath. The one who holds her is Volrath, and he means to kill her if we don't act on her behalf now."

"Dammit," Gerrard grunted under his breath, pulling a battered sheath from the war chest. He pretended to look it over, curled his lip at its condition, put it back, and continued to search.

Tahngarth said, "You know that after you bolted, we continued to seek out the pieces of the Legacy."

"Oh?" Gerrard pulled another sheath from the chest. "Don't you know that hunting for the Legacy is the same thing as pinning an archer's target to your forehead? Sooner or later, somebody gets killed."

"And by Torahn's horns," Tahngarth roared, "this time it might be Sisay!"

Rising, Gerrard faced the minotaur, glaring up at him. "Sisay knew the risks better than anyone. Last time, it was Rofellos who died. That elf was like kin to me, you know. And when Sisay finally admitted that she'd tricked me into looking for the Legacy—"

"You are the rightful heir to the Legacy's power," Tahngarth interrupted, shouting over Gerrard's protests. "She knew what you would not acknowledge, that your destiny lies in wielding the artifacts of the Legacy against all the evils that would destroy the world."

"Those same evils wiped out the clan that reared me," Gerrard countered. "My adopted father, the sorcerer who trained me, everybody I ever knew. All for the Legacy, a grubby little collection of mismatched artifacts. I walked away from the Legacy the first time because it was surrounded by death, and Sisay fooled me into looking for it 'for its financial value' the second time. Why would I come back to it now?"

"Because Sisay needs you. And because you walked away from your obligations, no matter how noble the reason."

Gerrard sheathed Torsten's long sword; the fit was tight. "That doesn't tell me a thing, Tahngarth. I've heard this 'you owe us' argument before. You're going to have to do better than that."

"You owe *her*. She is your past," Tahngarth said.

No!" Turning away from the minotaur, Gerrard hurled the sword at the war chest with surprising force. It banged loudly against the chest's upraised lid, the sound echoing across the large empty training yard. "Even the gods can't undo the past. Whatever I owed her was paid in blood—my clan's blood, Rofellos's blood."

"You have not changed a day," Tahngarth charged. "You throw things in a tantrum, but your horns are still as blunt as the day you walked away."

Gerrard said nothing.

"It's true that Rofellos died because of your choices," the minotaur continued. "He died because you chose to pursue the Legacy, your destiny."

"That's right," Gerrard said cynically, "and I'm not going to risk anyone that way again."

"Then Sisay will die because of what you choose to do

now. You will always find reasons for doing or for not doing. The reason for doing this," Tahngarth paused, his throat stiff as he raised his head higher, "is because *we* need you as well. Hanna has reviewed the pieces of the Legacy we have collected and says you may be our only hope of using them to reach Sisay in Rath. Do not let her die too. You could not save Rofellos. But you are Sisay's only hope."

At the mention of Hanna's name, Gerrard felt himself soften. He remembered all the time she had spent handling the artifacts as each new piece came aboard, her eyes alive with anticipation as the two of them uncrated some recently acquired relic. And he remembered sitting down with her and his friend Sisay, before the bad times, the three of them sharing wine and discussing the myriad implications of each artifact's power. Sisay had been his confidant. They had shared moments that none of the others would ever know about but that he would rather die himself than lose.

He sighed. "You know this is a trick, don't you, Tahngarth? Whoever took Sisay is probably counting on you to drag me kicking and screaming back aboard *Weatherlight*. You're going to put your hoof right in the trap."

"Then we will all put our hooves in the same trap, and we will all walk with the same limp."

Gerrard considered for a moment. "I have a . . . *situation* here in Benalia. It demands my involvement, too. I can't do both."

"Need overrules choice," Tahngarth said simply. "Sisay needs you."

* * * * *

The afternoon exercises were a blur. Gerrard offered a terse and unconvincing story about the absence of both Javero and Torsten, then let the other students leave early. He considered taking aside those he knew had been approached by Lord Kastan, but he was unsure of what to say. What price treason? A soldier's allegiance is to Benalia, and if it's not, why stain its army with your presence? Where does responsibility to oneself end and responsibility to others begin?

But *that*, he knew, was the real question, and he didn't want to ask a question to which he didn't already know the answer.

At sunset, he raked the sand, double-checked the war chest locks, and sat in the shadows as the light ran away from the training yard. He turned his hourglass pendant over to watch the sands trickle from top to bottom. Once, when he was younger, he had thought it novel to count the number of enemies he'd killed. In the middle of battle, the significance of surviving could easily be overshadowed by the excitement of killing. At first, when there were few, Gerrard remembered every one of them, their last looks of surprise or pain before he sent them to whatever followed life. He became uneasy with the realization that they were people. After all this time he could still see their faces, hear their cries for mercy. It was too late for any of them. But Sisay's was a cry for help he could still answer.

Well after dark, he locked up the training yard and went below to his quarters. The lantern in his entrance-way had gone out, and he paused to light it, fumbling for a moment with his flint in the blackness.

"I've brought you a present, Master Gerrard," a voice snarled from the darkness as the flint struck.

Gerrard turned slowly, the lantern's light rising behind him. His shadow jumped across the entranceway walls and into the main quarters where Torsten stood, his throat bandaged with a black circle of cloth, a dagger in one hand. In the other, he held a bloody head by the hair. As the lantern's light reached the skull and the shadows fell away, Gerrard could see the earring, speckled still with blood. Javero. His bulging eyes had been sewn open, frozen in a stare. The stitches through the eyelids looked like small spiders lined across the dead boy's face.

Gerrard met Torsten's stare coldly, swallowing his rage. Torsten pointed the tip of his dagger at Gerrard's chest.

"He was alive when I did it," Torsten said arrogantly. "But I'll spare *you* that indignity."

He tossed Javero's head to Gerrard's feet.

"You've got the ball bearings of a brass man," Gerrard answered. His sword was sheathed, but there were weapons all around the chamber. Swords, axes, pole-arms—he only needed a moment to reach one. "I'm a master-at-arms, Torsten, and you show up here with a dagger. Why didn't you come blindfolded, too?"

Waving the dagger, Torsten advanced. "I've been training with assassins, Master Gerrard," he said, "and assassins need only a dagger when they have poison."

He slashed with the dagger, aiming at Gerrard's middle. Gerrard backpedaled, throwing the lantern for effect and watching for his opening. As Torsten dodged left to avoid the lantern, Gerrard dove right, narrowly missing Torsten's backhanded cut as Gerrard rolled into the main chamber of his quarters. He knew better than to come to his feet. Instead, he lunged forward, under the table, reaching up under it as he did so to find the dagger he kept secured there. Behind him, Torsten grunted as he swung, cutting where Gerrard's throat would have been had he still stood.

Gerrard tipped the table as he rose, shoving it hard toward Torsten, who jumped back. In the entranceway, oil splattered when the lantern broke and ignited the curtain that served as door. The room began to heat quickly.

"You might as well be blindfolded," Gerrard said, displaying his own dagger, "because now we're even."

Torsten raised his weapon again. Gerrard flipped his dagger end for end, caught it by the blade, and threw it at Torsten's sword hand. The knife rolled sideways in flight, then buried itself in the back of Torsten's hand from knuckle to knuckle instead of from knuckle to wrist. Torsten wailed with surprise and pain as the blade drove through to his palm. His own dagger flew from his grip. Instinctively, he reached to catch it with his uninjured hand. The blade sliced neatly across his palm as his hand closed around it.

Realization set in as he met Gerrard's knowing gaze.

"Good catch," Gerrard said.

Torsten began to tremble, dropping the poisoned dagger and looking wildly around the room. He teetered as if he might fall, shook his head as if to clear it, then scratched absently at the bandages covering his throat wound. Taking a step further into the room, he snatched the elaborate rod from the nearest shelf. He pointed it at Gerrard.

"I remember this," he said thickly, licking his lips, eyelids fluttering erratically. "From the first day of training. Powerful magic."

"It's only as good as the hand that wields it," Gerrard said.

"Yes," Torsten seemed to drift away for a moment, swaying on his feet again, "and I'm good."

"No," Gerrard answered. "You're dead."

"Maybe. But I'll take you with me." Torsten pointed the rod and twisted the grip. A magnificent blast of yellow light exploded from its core, roaring out the barrel and enveloping Gerrard. The quarters around them were momentarily bright as day. The rod hummed loudly as it unloaded its magic on the room. Just as suddenly, the magic went away, leaving the two men standing in the dimness of the chamber as they were before. Gerrard smiled.

"I bet you wish you'd gone for a *real* weapon," he said.

Torsten groaned, dropped the Null Rod, and sank to the floor. His knees drew up to his chin, and he wrapped his arms around them. Gerrard kicked the poisoned dagger away before he knelt next to him. The young man's breathing was quickly becoming ragged. Angry red blotches were already spreading over both of his cheeks.

"Where's Lord Kastan, Torsten?" Gerrard asked. "You know where he hides, where I can find him."

Nodding, Torsten stared up at the ceiling. His eyelids had stopped fluttering. Now he stared as blankly as the eyes in Javero's decapitated head. "I don't want to die alone."

"I'll stay with you until you pass," Gerrard said softly. "But before you go, tell me where Lord Kastan is hiding."

* * * * *

Commander Alaric tore a strip of bread from the loaf and passed it across the table to the albino, who accepted it with a gracious but awkward nod. The albino's long white hair whispered over his shoulders as he moved. Despite the late-night shadows dancing all around Alaric's quarters, the albino seemed to shine, as if the feeble light from the lanterns set him aglow.

"No tasters tonight," Lord Kastan sighed, smiling. He sniffed the bread. "I come ill-prepared."

"You'll notice I'm not serving Vesuvan wine," Alaric said, sharing his guest's smile. "I seem to have mislaid my only bottle. Oh, now I remember. It isn't Borlean, it's Vesuvan."

"Just as well. I've been told it goes down rough, like poison." Kastan's smile faded. "Do you think he knew?"

Alaric shook his head and smoothed his gray mustache. "He was upset about this *Weatherlight* matter. He was simply too distracted to drink."

Rubbing his fingers as if they were cold, Kastan said, "Better, perhaps, if you had encouraged him to rejoin the ship. Save us this bloody business."

"Then he would remain a wild card. He could return at any given moment to raise rebellion against the officers. And he would, too. He's thick with the knights. They'd march against us, for certain. It would be civil war in Benalia." Alaric bit off a mouthful of bread, chewed slowly, swallowed. "It's better this way . . . provided your boy's up to the job."

"It's not the boy who needs to work, just his dagger," Kastan answered. "With a touch of stealth, we'll get poison to Gerrard's heart one way or another."

Gerrard stepped out of the darkness of the entranceway and into the lamplight. Alaric choked on his bread. Leaping quickly to his feet, he dashed around the table to stand between Gerrard and the albino assassin.

"I didn't want to disturb your conversation, Commander," Gerrard said tightly. "I'm glad I waited."

Alaric put his hand on his sword. "This is an unfortunate surprise," Alaric admitted. Behind him, Lord Kastan rose quietly, turning to face Gerrard.

"This would seem to be the day for them," Gerrard agreed. "I *was* seriously considering staying—I figured the Benalish army couldn't be corrupted as long we were vigilant. But that was before you sent Torsten after me."

Alaric darted a look at Lord Kastan, the commander's eyebrows knitting in annoyance. "Never send an assassin to do a soldier's work, eh?"

"In your command, what's the difference?" Gerrard snapped. His hand dropped to his sword's hilt as Alaric reached for his own blade.

"Perhaps," Lord Kastan said, his voice barely rising above a whisper as the two men went for their weapons, "the time has come for a bargain."

Gerrard stopped, as did Alaric.

"A command position of your own," the albino suggested; he looked to Alaric for support, who nodded curtly. "You work closely with the soldiers. Even without reports, you know who has talent."

"And there's always gold," Alaric added.

"How much gold?" Gerrard asked. He moved into the room, putting the table between them. He stopped near Alaric's cabinets.

"Name a figure," Alaric said.

"There are conditions."

Lord Kastan began to speak but Alaric cut him off. "Then name them! You have us by the sword buckle. What do you want?"

"First, no more assassins are recruited from my ranks. I don't care what the other masters-at-arms do, but nobody gets drafted out from under me." Gerrard waited for both men to nod before continuing. "Second, you clean house among the officers. Lord Kastan recruits from without, not from within."

Kastan grimaced, but Alaric said, "It will be difficult, but if it buys your silence, then so be it."

"Well then," Gerrard said, opening the cabinet and reaching inside, "that just leaves one more thing. Let's drink to our newfound alliance."

He put the bottle of Vesuvan wine and two glasses on the table.

"After you, gentlemen," he said, grinning. "Should I be thinking of a toast? Or maybe an epitaph?"

"I should have known we would do this the hard way," Alaric said, drawing his sword. "You're a bastard, Gerrard. And a stupid one at that—we're two against one. I've no doubt you can take one of us, but the other one will gut you."

Gerrard drew his own blade. "I brought a guest."

The minotaur had to bend to get through the door, but he rose to his full height once within the main chamber.

He hefted his own two blades expertly, crossing them. Tahngarth snarled something in the language of the Talruum minotaurs, and his lips frothed with his fury.

Gerrard gestured at Lord Kastan. "If he moves, cut him down. The knights should be here any time now. They'll deal with him if he's still alive."

The albino stared up at Tahngarth, taking in the minotaur's broad muscular chest and furious stare, then quietly sat down again at the table.

"You summoned the knights?" Alaric asked.

Gerrard nodded. "When Torsten told me where to find Lord Kastan, I thought it might be a good idea to make sure he ended up in the proper hands. In mine, he'd probably end up dead."

Alaric turned his sword over in his hands, glaring at Gerrard while he did. "You've killed me, boy. When the knights arrive, my career ends. Twenty-two years in the Benalish military, ground under your boot."

"Your *own* boot, I would say," Gerrard mused. "You were my friend once, though, Commander. So here." He slid the bottle of Vesuvan wine toward Alaric. "I'll say it was Lord Kastan's doing. You'll die with some semblance of honor."

Alaric stared at him, then down again at his sword. "If I fight my way out—"

"They'll still figure out what you've done," Gerrard finished. He pointed at Tahngarth. "You have only his silence if I'm alive. Cutting your way out of this won't save you unless you think you can kill both of us. I'd bet on *us*, if I were a gambling man."

Slowly, Alaric put his sword down on the table, reaching for one of the glasses with a firm hand. He then poured the dark Vesuvan wine into the glass.

"Before you practice murder," Gerrard said as Alaric lifted the glass to his lips, "you should first learn of suicide."

Commander Alaric nodded. "A hard lesson learned, boy."

He drank quickly.

* * * * *

They had gathered for Captain Gerrard on *Weatherlight's* deck, thirty sailors strong in the morning's first light. Tahngarth introduced him to those who had joined since his departure, many of whom had already heard of his exploits. Gerrard accepted their compliments as well as their uncomfortable stares. For every one of them who thought him a hero, he knew there was one who thought him a coward. It was entirely up to him to change their minds.

At the end of the line, he bent to greet Squee, the goblin cabin boy who had been so enamored of Sisay when he first came aboard. The goblin shook his hand awkwardly, then hid nervously behind Tahngarth's knees. Gerrard looked up into the minotaur's unreadable eyes.

"You're first mate, Tahngarth," he said.

"Again," Tahngarth snorted. "Always a first mate. For the captain's record, *I* was captain from Sisay's abduction until this moment."

Gerrard grinned. "Two steps up, one step back. Don't feel too alone. You and I'll both get demoted when we get Sisay back."

The minotaur bowed his head for a moment, closing his eyes as if in prayer. He let out a great breath through his nostrils, shaking his nose ring. "I have been afraid to say 'when.'"

"I'll tell her you said so," Gerrard said, moving on, "when she comes up that gangplank."

Finally, he came to the last crew member. The two stood uncomfortably facing one other while Tahngarth and the others drifted to their stations to prepare for sailing. Hanna smoothed her blonde hair behind each ear, adjusted the various tools on her work belt, and shuffled her feet once. She's still beautiful, Gerrard thought. He looked out at the sails, let his eyes follow the goblin across the deck, and listened to the sounds of port life drifting to the ship from Benalia. Finally he said, "I missed you, Hanna."

She half-smiled, then caught herself and straightened her expression. "Welcome back aboard."

"Thanks." He paused, wondering what he could say that would change things. Instead he said, "Tahngarth tells me we're going to need a wizard to get to Rath." When she nodded, he added, "He also tells me you know someone who can help us."

"In Tolaria," she said. "I can navigate us there."

"So why did you decide to come back, Gerrard?" she suddenly blurted. "Let's face it: you've been running away from the Legacy since the day you first learned of it. It never really meant anything to you, did it?"

"You're right. It doesn't mean a thing to me," Gerrard said softly. "If it gets me what I want or what I know is right, I'll use it, but if it doesn't, I'll forget about it. We can just toss it over the side when we reach Rath. I'm back for you, for Tahngarth, and for the rest of the crew. And most important, I'm back for Sisay."

"Well," Hanna said, bemused. She cocked her head as Tahngarth shouted her name from the foredeck. "Benalia made an adult out of you despite yourself, I see."

"It was a bloody battle," Gerrard said, grinning, "but one of us had to lose."

"The anchors beckon, Captain." As she turned away, Hanna gestured to the necklace dangling from his throat and the object at the end of the chain. "What happened to the hourglass you used to wear?"

Gerrard's grin faded. He held up the blood-flecked

gold earring, looking at Hanna through its circle. "I'm leaving it behind," he said solemnly. "This is just about as valuable, I think."

The ship set sail for Tolaria.

Here ends the Tale of Gerrard

believe them—because they are a reminder to us that memory goes on even longer after we are dead.

"Did they have an easy time finding Tolaria?"

Ilcaster's question broke in abruptly upon the librarian's thoughts. "Hardly that." The master shook his head sadly. "Nothing about their voyage was easy, and throughout all their troubles, they remembered Sisay in the clutches of Volrath and could only imagine what tortures she might be suffering.

"Their first stop, though, was not in Tolaria but in Llanowar."

"I remember Llanowar," the boy said eagerly. "That's where whats-her-name was from." The master looked at him blankly. "You know—the cat person."

"Ah, yes, Mirri. She was not, in fact, from Llanowar, but Mirri had gone there after she and Gerrard parted. But now *Weatherlight*'s captain needed the help of and old friend."

"How did he persuade her to come with them?"

"With difficulty. During the journey, Gerrard settled, somewhat uncomfortably, into Sisay's cabin. He used the time to examine the journal of his former captain and shipmate, as well as the Thran Tome, which he received from Hanna. From these documents he realized for the first time the importance of *Weatherlight*. He also discovered a spell that could overcome the effects of the Touchstone, the device used to immobilize Karn, though the value of this was not immediately clear to him.

"Gerrard wandered around the ship, renewing his acquaintance with its features. Making his way through the hold, he saw the pieces of the Legacy Sisay had collected in the time after he had left *Weatherlight*. Then, to his utter amazement, he came upon a silent, motionless figure standing upright, shining in the dim light. Karn.

"Using the spell from the Thran Tome, Gerrard reactivated his old friend and guardian. Though Karn had stood motionless for years, his mind had frozen at the precise moment of his deactivation. He was in anguish at the thought of having been responsible for the death of an innocent. Brokenly he told Gerrard of his resolution to never again take a life."

"Just a minute," interrupted the boy, skepticism in his tone. "Do you mean Karn would *never* take a life? Even if somebody was threatening to destroy him?"

The librarian nodded.

"What about if someone were threatening to kill Gerrard?"

"A good question, boy. I'm glad you're paying attention. In point of fact, it was the very question Gerrard himself asked. The golem thought long and hard, but in the end he replied that his decision was absolute: even Gerrard's fate could not overcome his choice. He would never knowingly take a life—not merely a human life, but the life of any creature."

Ilcaster considered, chin in hand. "I think that was a mistake," he said at last. "I mean, I don't think he should have gone around killing people, but everybody has to defend themselves if they're being attacked."

The master shrugged. "It was, nonetheless, his decision. And Gerrard was so overjoyed to see the golem that he did not, perhaps, fully understand what a profound change had come over his old protector. He greeted him joyfully and introduced him to the rest of the crew.

"And all this time, while Gerrard renewed his friendship with the silver golem and his familiarity with the flying ship, *Weatherlight* steadily drew closer to Llanowar."

Tahngarth's Tale

Hannovi Braddock

In the corridors of my birth—the labyrinths of Talruum—the priestesses burned shrine lamps for the gods and goddesses. Near the hearth of my family, before our doorway hung with beads of red, green, and blue, two lamps burned. One was for Kindeya, goddess of learning, and the other for Torahn, god of judgment. When I was still so young that I only dreamed of having horns, my mother spoke thus to me: "Tahn, every day you see the two lamps burning outside of our home. Turn your heart to Kindeya's lamp, my son, to learning. And turn away from Torahn. Leave justice to the gods who see more than we do."

She sought to bend me from the nature of my clan, but I was born Three Beads. As was she. In the end, justice meant more to her, to me, to all our clan than the peace of Talruum. And so there was rebellion within the halls. War.

That is not the story I wish to tell. I only mean to make it clear that the fires of judgment burned hot in me, and that was why I, of all the crew of *Weatherlight*, did not want to ask this Gerrard to return to our ship.

I stood watching him as we sailed over the forest mists of Llanowar. It was hard to judge the age of humans, but I knew they got their beards later than minotaurs grew their horns, and Gerrard already had a beard the first time he joined our crew. He was not then a child, nor was he one now. I could grant him no excuse of youth. Indeed, he wielded a sword well, and had an accurate hand and eye with the throwing knives he wore. He had accomplishments born of practice, born of years.

But he had not yet grown wise.

"Blast these clouds," he said, gripping the railing with his strange human hands. (And why did the hands of Hanna and Orim not seem strange to me? They were also human. But I liked them.) He squinted as if that would give him a clearer view of the land below. The low-hanging mists let us see only the ground that was directly beneath us. "There must be a place to land here somewhere."

"We waste time," I said. I did not speak his language well, so I kept my utterances short and simple. Perhaps he thought me simple, too. "Sisay needs us."

"We need Mirri first. I thought I'd made that clear."

"She left us," I said. "As you did."

He turned to look at me. "I'm back," he said, as if that were proof enough to banish my doubts.

"We don't need her."

"One more time, Tahngarth," he said as if he were explaining to a child, "Captain Sisay is captive in Rath. We don't know how to get there. We can't possibly find the place until the ship's Thran crystal is encoded for it. I don't have magic enough for that. Mirri was always better with magic than I—"

"So is any mud wizard. So is any kitchen sorcerer."

His jaw tightened for a moment, then he laughed. "You touch a truth there," he said. He patted the knives that were strapped across his chest. "I was ever the better master of a blade."

I pointed off the bow. "There," I said. I turned and shouted across the deck, "Hanna! Fifteen degrees to starboard!" Behind the window glass of the bridge, she signaled that she had heard me. *Weatherlight*'s sails extend sideways from amidships, and they rippled as Hanna adjusted our course.

Some have said that *Weatherlight* looks like a flying fish. I have never seen a flying fish. I would say instead that our ship is like a goblin's throwing dart with white bat wings.

"Ahead slow!" I called.

"Tahngarth . . ."

"What?" I glared at him.

No doubt he was about to remind me that he was the master of *Weatherlight* now. But he held his tongue.

The engine had been humming quietly. Now it dropped to a whisper. The mists began to break beneath us as we flew over the meadow.

"Hanna, take us down!" he ordered.

"Belay that!" I shouted. He gave me a sharp look, and I said, "Captain Sisay would circle first." Indeed, Hanna was already steering a wide arc around the clearing. Far edges of the meadow were still obscured by mist, but there was a strange shadow near the trees. I pointed at it.

"Is that a funeral mound?" Gerrard wondered as we approached. "A barrow?"

It did look like a mound of dirt, one shaped to look like a man lying on his face: rounded back of the head, the ridge of spine along a broad back, and the powerful curve of buttocks. Mist obscured the legs, but beyond that the heels jutted up.

In what I thought was a trick of the mist, the shoulders seemed to swell, then settle.

We were flying toward the head. Now I could see a green-clad rider approaching the mound.

"Llanowar elf," said Gerrard. "Mirri's as good as found. Didn't I tell you—"

"Look," I said, pointing at the mound. I thought it had moved again.

"Hanna!" Gerrard called. "Take us down!"

The whisper of the engine grew softer still. As we slowed, Hanna tipped the bow up to keep us aloft. We began to descend, still on a course toward elf and earth mound.

The rider's horse was skittish, shying sideways half a step for every step forward. The elf unslung a bow from his shoulder and set fire to an arrow tip. With a warrior's ululation, he loosed the missile. Flame arced through the air and landed with a hiss in the crown of the muddy head.

The rider turned his mount. For a moment, both horse and rider seemed frozen by the sight of *Weatherlight* descending. Then the mound shifted behind them. The horse's nostrils flared, and it raced across our shadow toward the trees at the far end of the meadow.

I heard a rush of indrawn air, and the bushes near the giant head stirred as in a wind.

The head lifted itself up from the ground.

White eyes stared from the earthen face. Below was a cavernous mouth, one shaped for a perpetual howl of hunger. Roots dangled from its lips.

"Milk of the Mothers!" I cried in my own tongue.

Great muddy arms moved, fingers clutching at the ground. With a sound like a mudslide, the creature shook its hill-sized shoulders. "It's an aboroth!"

"Hard about!" Gerrard shouted. "Full thrust! Hard about!"

The engine hummed, then rose to a loud whine. The ship pitched to portside. I heard the goblin Squee yelp in surprise below decks. Gerrard lost his footing, snatched at the handrail, missed, and would have gone sliding across the deck. I grabbed him by the collar.

The ship righted. Astern, the ground rumbled. The giant was on its feet. *Weatherlight* shook as her engine thrusted and we picked up speed.

The aboroth took one tentative step, then a more confident one, and then another. On its fourth step, it began to run. Toward us.

We were overtaking the rider, and Gerrard said, "We don't need to be faster than the monster. We just need to be faster than the elf." He looked at the aboroth. It had covered half the distance to the forest in a few strides. "In that race, my bet would be on the dirt, if I were a betting man."

"It's not chasing the elf," I told him. For the blank eyes were upon us, not the rider. Near the first trees, the monster passed the elf, almost stepping on him.

The monstrous fingers reached for the sails of *Weatherlight*. The claws looked like the tips of lightning-shattered trees. They almost snagged us. . . .

Then stopped.

War cries had erupted from the forest below. Elvish warriors, mounted and afoot, came streaming into the meadow. Something stirred among the trees, making the canopy ripple.

"War machines," I said. Even as we sped away, they grew before our eyes, these machines of tree trunks lashed together with vines. The vines rippled and twisted and tugged at the trunks. As muscle moves bone, thus did the vines haul the tree trunks and articulate them. It was like watching a scaffold that builds itself. The machines took the shape of headless, legless golems, and then the battle receded into the mist.

The engines were still shrilling. Gerrard shouted, "Reduce thrust! Level off!" But Hanna could not have heard him above the whining engines. I signaled the orders to her. *Weatherlight* leveled, and the engines dropped to a hum, then a whisper.

My hand still gripped his collar. He said, "Thanks for catching me, but you can let go now."

"When you order a maneuver, think of the ship. How it will move," I said, releasing him.

"In short," he said, grinning, "hold on!"

I did not return his smile.

"What did you call that thing?"

I told him of aboroths, how some years they grow up out of the soil near Llanowar villages. When they awaken, they live but a short while, but in that time, they wreak havoc. It is the custom of the elves to assemble for battle near the ripening aboroths, to provoke them as they wake and lead them away from the villages. If the aboroths can be occupied with battle long enough, they shrink and die. When I was done, Gerrard said, "Where did you learn this?"

I chose my words carefully, like choosing a blade. "From the elf Rofellos," I said. Then slowly I added, "He told me such things as friend is wont to tell friend."

Gerrard gave me a long look. "Rofellos was my friend, too."

"Is that why you made a mockery of his death?"

Anger burned in his eyes. "Rofellos was my friend ere he was yours! You understand nothing!" His hand touched the haft of his sword.

"Have a care where your hand strays," I told him. And even though I knew his accomplishments as a man of arms, I insulted him by turning my back—and came face to face with Orim. A fringe of brown hair peeked from beneath the headdress she always wore with its blue agal. Her eyes, like her hair, were brown and somehow soft.

I do not know how it is that anyone, minotaur or

human, can frown with anger and yet show gentleness in her eyes. But that was her expression. There was always, in her dress and in her manner, a softness to Orim, though she was a Samite woman born of the hard deserts.

"A word with you," she said in the minotaur tongue. For one whose mouth was not shaped for the language, her accent was excellent. Most minotaur-speaking humans— and they are rare—know only the Hurloon dialect. Orim knew the inflections of Talruum. She spoke well enough to make me long for home.

"Then follow me," I said. I stomped back to the bridge and took the controls from Hanna. As much as Orim was outwardly soft, Hanna's manner and dress were trim and efficient. She tied her hair behind her like a warrior. In fact, she could handle a sword, but she was an archaeologist and our navigator. I told her, "Go help him who has not the eyes for it find another meadow."

Hanna looked out at Gerrard, who was at the railing again, peering into the grayness. "He is unaccustomed to seeing the world from the air," she said.

"He is unaccustomed to many things," I said, "loyalty among them."

Hanna went to the hatchway. She said, "We need him."

When she was gone, Orim said, "With your iciness to Gerrard, you freeze Hanna, too. You know of her feelings for him."

"No," I said, "I do not. She may have felt something for him once, before he left us. But I do not know what she feels for him now. She must have her doubts."

"You have more than doubts, Tahngarth. I heard how you attacked him with the memory of Rofellos. Gerrard left us because the death of his friend had wounded him."

"Did the death of Rofellos not mark me as well? More than that. Rofellos sacrificed himself for the sake of this ship and crew. To abandon *Weatherlight*, as Gerrard did, was to abandon the memory of Rofellos, to rob his death of meaning."

"Do you think Gerrard a coward?"

"I could forgive a coward. He is something more dangerous to us. He is unreliable. And his first command is that we should come to Llanowar to recover his friend, Mirri. Why? We might find conjurers of her equal for hire in a hundred ports. And she is every bit as unreliable as Gerrard."

"Tahngarth, Gerrard is heir to the Legacy. He is, by rights, master of this ship and its contents, even more than Captain Sisay is."

"How can such as he have so much importance?" I bellowed. "How? Sisay is bold! I would follow her into the Corridors of Pain where Torahn gores the wicked ones! But Gerrard . . . The man has not the will to face reality! He resists what must be!"

Orim smiled. "Tahngarth, even as I would begin to speak to you, you say the very thing that must be said. Now there is nothing left for me to say."

"I do not take your meaning."

"Think upon your words, my friend. In them is wisdom: He resists what must be."

She was much given to riddles. She left me with those words hanging in the air.

* * * * *

When we landed, the ship's support spines dug black furrows in the meadow grass. With the engine shut off, *Weatherlight* listed on the soft ground.

Gerrard assembled us on the canted deck. "Hanna, Tahngarth, and I will locate Mirri. We're here without an invitation, and the elves may not exactly welcome us. Orim, you stand watch on the bridge. If elves approach, I don't care how friendly they look. I want this ship back in the air."

Orim said, "But I—"

"I know. You're a healer, not a ship's pilot. But I'll need both Tahngarth and Hanna with me, unless you'd prefer to pick up a sword and come in Hanna's place."

Orim could defend herself if she had to, but the only blade she ever practiced with was a scalpel—and that only rarely. Her healing arts had more to do with smokes and balms and essential oils. I said to her, "I'll remind you of the controls."

"Squee," said Gerrard, and the goblin, who had been glancing nervously at the forest, jumped at the sound of his name.

"I wuz listening!"

"I didn't say you weren't. You help Orim stand watch. Tell her if elves are coming."

"Nasty elves! They don't like goblins! They wanna kill poor me!"

"We won't let them," said Orim, laying a gentle hand on the goblin's shoulder. Her touch calmed him a little.

Then to the hulking silver statue behind us, Gerrard said, "Karn, your job is to guard the ship."

"I won't fight," said the golem.

"I know. Just walk the decks and look menacing."

The silver head nodded.

And so the landing party set out, leaving *Weatherlight* in the hands of an inexperienced pilot, a cowering lookout, and a pacifist guard.

* * * * *

Gerrard walked in front. In the middle went Hanna, who watched a compass as she walked. My sense of direction was confused as soon as the trees had first closed off our view of the meadow, and we'd come quite a way since then. I said, "How do you hope to find Mirri?"

"I hope that she finds us," said Gerrard. "If not, we'll find an elven village."

I did not think this much of a plan. We walked a while longer before I said, "This is Llanowar. We could walk right into a village and not know it."

There was soft laughter ahead of us. A voice said, "One who has eyes can see."

Gerrard halted. I hefted my axe, squinting into the forest shadows. I saw no one. Hanna put away her compass and said, "We've come in peace." She repeated the sentence in the elvish tongue. Hanna is not Orim's match as a linguist, but she has a smattering of tongues. Then she said it again, "We've come in peace."

"Clearly," said the voice. "I note the peaceful way your horned friend beckons with his axe blade."

"Tahngarth," said Gerrard, "stow the axe." But even as he said this, he folded his arms in a way that was meant to be casual but let his fingers rest on a knife handle.

I lowered the axe, but had no way to "stow" it. And would he have me stand defenseless before an apparent sentinel whom none of us could see?

"We come looking for a friend of mine," Gerrard said. "Mirri by name. She and I knew one who was kindred to this forest. Rofellos, he was called."

"Many come to this forest speaking names," said the voice, "but to know a name is a poor vouchsafe."

"Then take us to her."

Laughter. "Yes. And show intruders where a village lies."

"She'll speak for us, if you summon her."

"Oh, I have issued summons already. I have raised alarm enough."

I had heard nothing and seen nothing, but I could feel the truth of his words. I peered at the forest around us, seeing nothing but trees, yet I knew. . . .

The speaker stepped forward, his face emerging from shadow. Once he was visible, I couldn't understand why I had not seen him before. He hadn't been hiding, yet somehow he'd been hidden.

Vines clung to his clothes and white hair almost as if he were made of them, and he carried a staff that sprouted flower buds and new leaves. "The forest has carried my voice," the old elf said, "and my summons has been answered. You are surrounded. Lay down your weapons."

"You're not exactly making us feel welcome," Gerrard said. He didn't move his hands.

"The druid speaks true," I said. "We are watched by many eyes. I feel it." Yet even when I had admitted this, my fingers would not uncurl and let my axe fall to the ground. In the Halls of Talruum, we would die before surrendering our arms. In this one thing, Gerrard and I were alike. Death was all around us, yet we were both frozen more by pride than by fear.

Hanna unbuckled her sword belt and laid the sheathed blade across the root of a tree.

From above, a feminine voice said, "Leave it to the lady to show some sign of manners. As for you, Gerrard, if you draw one of those knives you won't live long enough to regret it."

Looking up, Gerrard let his hands drop to his sides. "Mirri?"

Something moved in the trees. I glimpsed golden fur dappled with black spots. The cat warrior dropped to the ground almost silently to stand alongside the druid. Her tail twitched from side to side. "Tahngarth," she said, "when an elf in Llanowar tells you you're surrounded, he's probably telling the truth."

"I do not doubt it," I said, but still could not let the axe fall.

"But let us give evidence," said the druid. "Show yourselves, sons and daughters of Llanowar!"

From all sides, elves emerged in that same mysterious way that the druid had, each stepping forward into view. Every elf held a bow. Every one had an arrow nocked.

Leaves rustled. I looked up to see more elves in the branches. And still I gripped my axe.

"That one won't learn manners even as a dozen arrows point the way," Mirri said, waving her hand at me. "But I'll vouch even for him."

"Your word is your life, Mirri," said the druid.

"My life," she agreed, "that Gerrard, Hanna, and Tahngarth are no enemies to Llanowar."

The druid nodded, then stepped forward. "When you speak Mirri's name, it means nothing to us. When she speaks yours, it means all. You are welcome here."

Gerrard said, "Our thanks," then grinned at Mirri. "You do like a dramatic entrance. How long were you watching?"

The cat warrior's green eyes narrowed with pleasure. "A while."

"We weren't in any real danger then?" said Hanna as she retrieved her sword. The elves had lowered their bows. Some of the younger ones were crowding close to examine us.

"Oh, we were in danger," said Gerrard. "It wouldn't be fun if the danger weren't real. Right, Mirri?"

" *Weatherlight*," I reminded him.

"Yes, the ship," said Gerrard. "It's aground in a meadow." He waved in the general direction.

"Actually," said Mirri, "it's more that way."

Hanna frowned and brought out her compass, but Mirri clicked her tongue. "You won't have much success reckoning with that," she said. "Not in Llanowar."

Grinning, one of the young elves tapped the compass glass, then laughed to see the astonishment on Hanna's face. "He touched it, and the needle went spinning!"

To Gerrard Mirri said, " *Weatherlight* will be unmolested. I can send word to Captain Sisay if you like."

Gerrard opened his mouth, but I cut him off. "Sisay has been kidnapped. We must free her. Will you come? Yes, and we're away with you. No, and we're away without you. Answer now."

Mirri's tail flicked again. Gerrard started to speak, and this time it was Mirri who cut him off. "The minotaur asks a question, and I'll give him an answer. The village where I have lived these seasons past is close to here. An aboroth was just discovered growing nearby."

At mention of the monster, the elves grew stiff and exchanged glances.

"There is not time enough to build war machines to distract and destroy it," she continued, "so the elves must fight with their arrows and their courage. I will help them."

"We go without you, then," I said, turning away.

"When the aboroth ripens, we can destroy it together," Mirri said. "With *Weatherlight*."

I turned back to face her. "Sisay needs us now. We go without you."

"So you would have Mirri abandon her new friends, kin to Rofellos?" asked Gerrard.

"No!" I bellowed, and the elves nearest me jumped away. More softly, I said, "No. Rofellos was my friend. Mirri does right. She stays to help the kin of one who was brave. That is well chosen. But must we tarry here also? Who knows what Captain Sisay suffers?"

"Tahngarth is right," Hanna said.

Gerrard stared steadily at the cat warrior. "How long until the aboroth ripens?"

"Two days," she said.

Gerrard looked at Hanna, then at me. "We stay and help. That's my decision."

I opened my mouth, but he raised his hand and said, "I have decided."

I felt my hands clutch the handle of my axe. I thought of the words Orim wanted me to ponder. He resists what must be. Did she think those words would soften my heart?

Gerrard knew we must hasten to Sisay's aid, but he would have us dawdle here two days! He resisted what must be, indeed!

* * * * *

The next day, we flew gentle circles over the village where the aboroth was growing. The village, or so the elves who flew with us said, was in the stand of trees close beside the growing monster. I could see no signs of a village in those trees, but I lacked the elven eye.

However, it took no elven eye to see the monster. From the air, it was hard to understand how the elves, who knew their own forest so well, could have missed the mounds of swelling earth in the little clearing so close at hand, until the thing was nearly grown.

"There was a hillock there already," the tallest of the three elves said. "We knew an aboroth was sprouting only when the mound began to change its shape—mere days ago."

"And can you not dig away the earth, to kill it while it sleeps?" asked Gerrard.

I had long ago asked the question of Rofellos when he'd told me of aboroths. But to dig away the mound only drives the white threads of mycelium deeper, where the aboroth will form of stone instead of soil. The monster will take more time to form, then, but it will emerge stronger, bigger, and longer lived.

Such was the answer of the elves to Gerrard.

The plan, as Mirri hatched it, was thus: The elves would draw the waking aboroth away from the village. Without machines of war, the elves could not hope to stand against the creature for long, but ere it had born down upon them, *Weatherlight* would fly close to the aboroth. Elves upon the upper deck would harry it with arrows, drawing its attention. Then, lest it should knock us from the air, Mirri would loose some spell on it, a lightning bolt that would distract it again, drawing it close to her.

"Then the elves will attack again," said Mirri. "Then *Weatherlight*. Then I again. And so, by trading turns, we may hope to keep the wrath of the aboroth from falling square upon us. In time, it will shrink, grow weaker, and die."

"And if the aboroth turns not from one foe to the next?" I said. "What then?"

Gerrard's laughter boomed, though I could hear the strain in it. He was ill at ease, pretending. "What then? Then we stand and fight the thing as best we can. What else?"

"In aboroth season," said the tallest elf, "much of our fate goes unchosen."

I grunted. "And what season is there then, but aboroth season?"

The elf smiled. "Just so."

Another elf said, "We will plan as best we may, and take what comes. Be it for good or ill, spring follows winter."

"Perhaps Gerrard may yet hatch a better plan," said Mirri. "The artifacts in the ship's hold might produce some magical effect. What think you, Gerrard? You were always better than I in the wielding of such devices."

"Indeed?" I said. I looked at Gerrard. "He said that he must fetch you. That you would know artifacts. That you could set the Thran crystal for the world of Rath."

"Set a Thran crystal?" said the cat warrior. "Gerrard was ever the better man with artifacts. My talent is for spells."

"Gerrard," I said, "you lied."

"No," he replied coldly. "She may yet knew better than I how to calibrate the crystal."

I shook my head until my beads rattled. "You lied! Or misled us! The difference is between ice and frozen water." I pointed at Mirri. "You wanted to come for her, so you told us what you thought we must hear!" And I left him there with Mirri and the elves, who could now doubt him as I did.

I relieved Hanna at the bridge. From there, I watched Mirri and the elves continue talking. Gerrard went belowdecks. In a while, Orim came to see me.

"You go too far," she said.

"And so he goes to you and begs your intercession. He lied to us, Orim."

"No. He hoped that Mirri would know what he himself did not."

"We have lost days."

"I know."

"I would lief seek out our captain without his help, without Mirri's."

"I know."

"I do not trust him!"

Orim said, " 'He resists what must be.' Have you thought upon those words?"

"Indeed! And that is why I do not trust him!"

"You have not thought long enough or hard enough."

She left the bridge.

* * * * *

We landed in the clearing where the aboroth still slept. It would not be long in waking, the elves told us.

I went to inspect the pivot joints of the masts, to check the riggings, and, while I was about, to look for Squee. The goblin had taken to hiding whenever we had elves aboard, and he was neglecting his duties. The bridge wanted sweeping.

Gerrard paced the deck, a frown on his face. Brooding.

Did he expect an apology? I would grant him none. In truth, he did not so much as glance at me. Something else troubled his thoughts.

He sought out Hanna, walked the deck with her, talking. At last he commanded Karn, the silvery giant, to follow him belowdecks. They were gone long, doing I knew not what in *Weatherlight*'s hold. When they came onto the deck again, the golem's back was bent beneath a canvas-wrapped burden. Whatever he carried, it was as big as the hulking golem himself. At Gerrard's command, Karn took the burden forward, to the upper deck where the elvish archers were to harry the aboroth. The ships's planks creaked and bowed beneath the golem's feet.

The canvas fell away, and I saw the pyramidal shape of the Thran forge. Gerrard set to roping the pyramid into place, its surface carved with strange glyphs. I noticed that he wore an amulet—a big unwieldy thing. Even from amidships, I could see its design: a golden face with red eyes and a bejeweled mouth.

What was it? I did not then know it for the Touchstone. I understood the importance of the Legacy. I knew Sisay's determination to collect the artifacts that comprised it. But I did not know the names of all or what each of them did.

Gerrard tied another rope around the base of *Weatherlight*'s foremost lamp. He tugged hard to see that it was secure, but left the rest of that rope coiled upon the deck.

Beneath the ship, the ground shook. The aboroth was waking.

* * * * *

I had gone to the bridge to ready the ship for launch. Gerrard found me there. He was pulling on gloves.

"When we're aloft," he said, "forget our original plans. Circle in behind the aboroth. Close. Come in slow, so I can drop down onto its head. Give me to the count of ten, and then get away, fast!"

What madness was this? I could not find the words to

ask him before he had disappeared from the hatchway. He sprinted to the upper deck. The elvish archers had come aboard. With Hanna, they joined Gerrard. Orim had come on deck, and she went to the railing. Other elves were streaming into the clearing, bows at the ready. And I saw Mirri gliding swiftly through the grass to another part of the meadow.

Gerrard shouted, "Get us aloft!"

I did so. As we rose into the sky, the white-eyed aboroth raised its face from the ground and howled.

* * * * *

What happened next? How fared we in this battle with the aboroth?

I'll come to that. But first . . .

Did I not say from the beginning that the fires of judgment burned hot in me? It was so. I was born Three Beads. I still wore the red, blue, and green beads of my clan upon my head. And Three Beads of Talruum, we have ever been minotaurs who were swift to judge, to condemn.

Orim had said to me, "He resists what must be."

I had not the ears to hear what she meant. But as the aboroth rose onto its feet, as I circled *Weatherlight* behind it, I watched Gerrard. By some magical means, he had set the pyramidal Thran forge to glowing.

I approached the back of the monster's head, and Gerrard shouted something to the elves. He grinned as a ray of light flashed from the forge and showered the aboroth with sparks. Strange, pale fires flickered across the forge's surface.

The surface of the aboroth began to change from mud and vegetation to something shinier, something smooth and plated. Rivets popped up like pock marks.

Madness! I thought, for this would make the monster stronger. But I did as he'd said. I slowed the ship, and we hovered over the creature's head—Hanna, peering over the bow, guided me with hand signals. From the bridge, I could no longer see the aboroth below us. Gerrard threw his rope over the ship's side. He took the rope in his gloved hands and dropped out of sight.

I counted. The journey from one to ten seemed to take all day.

Then I pressed the engine hard, even before Hanna had signaled. *Weatherlight* bucked under the strain, then surged.

The metal-sheathed aboroth was looking up at us as we shot past its shoulder. One monstrous hand reached up as if to seize and crush the ship. But Gerrard sat upon the crown of the aboroth's head, holding on with one hand and touching the amulet with the other. He chanted.

The aboroth froze.

I circled and watched. Hanna explained it to me later. The forge had turned the aboroth into a creature of artifice, a being, like Karn, that could be switched on or off. And the amulet, the Touchstone, was a switch.

The pyramid on the foredeck continued to glow. From time to time, the aboroth began, creakily, to move. Gerrard would touch the amulet again, chant the words, and the aboroth would freeze once more.

And it shrank. As we circled and watched, the aboroth was smaller and smaller. Gerrard rode its head all the way to the ground until the aboroth had shrunk into dust, into nothingness.

Elves shook their bows and cheered. Mirri conjured a lightning bolt, just for effect. Thunder was a death knell for the aboroth.

He resists what must be.

I thought about those words. I thought about Captain Sisay, how she also might have known how to use the forge and the amulet. But would she have known how to use them together?

Gerrard was no great sorcerer, but he had a touch with the Legacy—a touch like no one else aboard *Weatherlight* would have, not even when we recovered Sisay.

He resists what must be. Gerrard had run away from the truth, from the sacrifices and pain that truth demands.

So had I.

I had judged Gerrard, as was my wont. But I had not judged myself.

He resists what must be. Orim meant me. I was resisting what must be.

Gerrard was a man of considerable flaws. But we needed him. Moreover, he needed us to help him become what he must be: a man worthy of the Legacy.

As I landed in the meadow full of celebrating elves, Orim joined me on the bridge. I said, "He resists what must be. But what will be, will be."

She smiled gently.

"That doesn't mean I have to like him," I grumbled. "Nor will I pretend to like him."

Again, she said nothing, only smiling that smile.

"We need him," I admitted with a sigh.

Orim nodded and left me alone on the bridge again. I yanked hard on the lanyard that rang the ship's bell. I rang impatiently, repeatedly, until Gerrard and Mirri said their goodbyes to the elves and got on board.

And we left Llanowar by command of Gerrard, master of *Weatherlight*.

May he yet grow to fill his boots.

Here ends the Tale of Tahngarth

A Dark Room

Ilcaster had moved from the floor to a bundle of papers, where he perched, chin on his hand, as the old man spoke. Dimly, both could hear the patter of rain beating against the windows. The wind outside whirled in an angry gale, and within its moans could sometimes be heard the hiss and clatter of hail. It was as if the heavens themselves were assaulting the library. Yet the two figures were so absorbed—one in telling, the other in listening—that they no longer paid attention to the sounds without.

"I think Gerrard must have been really clever," the boy observed. "Imagine using two artifacts together like that. And he did to the aboroth with the Touchstone what Vuel had done to Karn once before."

The librarian nodded. "Yes. Perhaps that's where Gerrard got his inspiration for that strategy. Or, perhaps, he *did* have a special way with the Legacy, some part of his mind that knew instinctively how each bit fit together to make a unified whole that was greater than the sum of its parts."

Ilcaster nodded. "Yes, I'm sure that's it. It must have been—after all, he was heir to the Legacy." He shifted his legs under him, stretched, and nestled down on the floor. The old man, looking at him, was reminded of a kitten curled at the feet of its owner.

"So now that they had Mirri on board, was *Weatherlight* ready to travel to Rath and rescue the captain?" Ilcaster asked.

"No. Mirri was ready to join the ship, but she was insufficiently skilled in magic to manipulate the crystal that would allow them to planeshift to Rath. Gerrard turned to Hanna, the ship's navigator, but she too was unable to manipulate the crystal. They would need a wizard. Hanna's father, Barrin—"

The old man broke off. "Is there something the matter with your hearing, boy?" he growled testily.

Ilcaster started and dropped the piece of parchment at which he'd been staring. "I'm sorry, Master," he said. "I was wondering . . . is this a plan of the ship?"

The old man took up the parchment and spread it out beneath the glow of the candle. "Indeed it is," he grunted. "Here, don't move that candle. You might get wax on it. There's sufficient light to see by, even with my old eyes. There."

The two heads bent in unison over the parchment: one dark and curly, the other white-haired with patches of scalp showing through the strands.

"See now," said the librarian. His fingers danced over the page, touching, indicating, almost stroking. "This is the main deck of the ship. Notice that the sails are feathered back over the stern. The bridge was located about two-thirds of the way back along the deck, while the prow of the ship was taken up with the forward cabins. Along the hull were spines for landing and support, so that when the ship put down on land it wouldn't tip over. Here's the pilot's station, and here—"his fingers hesitated for a moment"—here is where the power crystal was located."

Ilcaster nodded. "I see. And that's what they needed Hanna's father for."

The librarian shook his head. "Barrin might help them, so Hanna said. But she was reluctant to approach him, since she and her parent had been estranged for years."

"That sounds terribly sad. Why did father and daughter fight?"

"Well, Barrin was a wizard, while Hanna had devoted much of her studies to artifacts. She was convinced that artifacts were a far truer art than wizardly magic. Indeed, she held magic in some contempt. She and her father had argued on the subject for many years, but neither had persuaded the other."

Ilcaster looked thoughtful. "I don't think I've heard of Tolaria," he said. "I don't remember seeing it on any maps. Where—?"

"You won't find it on maps of Dominaria," interrupted the librarian. In fact, few people have ever been there, and the way to the island is fraught with danger. Some say that in past centuries, in years beyond count, some great disaster occurred there. Many spoke of it, but they avoided it. Hanna, though, knew the way, and Gerrard persuaded her that without a wizard, they were defeated before they even started. Reluctantly she agreed to guide *Weatherlight* to the island.

"So Barrin joined the company?"

"Well, no," said the master with a knowing frown. "Matters turned out a bit differently than Hanna and Gerrard expected."

Ertai's Tale

Hannovi Braddock

One of the things that made Barrin such an excellent teacher was his practice of bringing me into his study from time to time to evaluate my progress. I'm always delighted to hear such an expert recount my virtues, so these sessions in his tower were something I looked forward to with great anticipation.

At the last such session, seated behind his desk of blue jade, he began, as he always did, "Ertai, you are a most, ah, astonishing apprentice."

"Yes," I acknowledged. I was seated before him, but I let my gaze wander out the window, down into the Lotus Vale where the fields of flowers shifted colors in the breeze. Such a sentence was preliminary to a discussion of my recent accomplishments. It was a formula. Not that I tired of hearing it.

"Your memory of spells, your subtle sense of shifting energies, your artfulness as a young wizard all continue to amaze me. You are a credit to this island and to all who have studied the magical arts here."

"I know," I said. And I knew as well the words that always came next: You have tremendous native ability.

I was so accustomed to these words following the others that when he said, "However, there is one difficulty," I said, "Thank you."

"Ertai."

I turned to find his gray eyes studying me. "I mean . . ." I said, and stopped. I opened my mouth again, but no words came out. After a momentary struggle, I managed to utter in a strangled voice, "Difficulty?"

What about my tremendous native ability? I wanted to add.

If Barrin noticed my changed voice, he gave no sign of it. "A difficulty, yes. A shortcoming, if you will."

"A shortcoming?"

He looked as if this discussion pained him. "This isn't easy to confront you with."

Confront me. As if I had committed some crime. "Master Barrin, I stand falsely accused. I am, as you know, scrupulously honest—"

"There we touch on the matter," he said, leaning forward. "Ertai, this does have to do with your 'honesty.' Some would call it by other names."

I thought about that. "If you mean what some of the other apprentices say, they are wrong," I said tentatively. "They accuse me of boasting. However, I merely tell the truth, and it sounds like boasting to them. Can I help it that their skills are meager compared to my—"

I was going to say my tremendous native ability, but Barrin interrupted me once more. "I don't think it's a matter of your trampling on the feelings of others. The truth is, Ertai, I think the feelings of others are all but invisible to you. Brilliant though you may be with spells, in social relations you are a little . . . slow."

"Slow?" Me? Absurd.

"This is a shortcoming you must address, especially now that everything is about to change."

"Change, Master Barrin?"

"That's the first part of the change. Call me Barrin, plain and simple. You've long since earned your vestments as a wizard adept." He stood and went to an oaken wardrobe that bore the jagged sigil of lightning on its doors. With a wave of his hands, he discharged the spell into the ceiling and the clear blue sky above. The island of Tolaria crackled and boomed with the flash and thunder, and sparks of electricity still danced between the doors as he opened them.

"Your tunic and chain," he said, bringing them to me. "Put them on."

Some wizards may doubt they will earn this moment. I never had. All my previous discomfiture vanished. The only question remaining in my mind was if Barrin could bear to lose me as a student.

I slipped the tunic over my shoulders and fastened the chain about me. I would look quite elegant wearing them. No surprise. I wear most anything with elegance. It's a matter of posture, you see, and a handsome build.

"And now," Barrin said, "I must point you toward an opportunity." And he began to speak.

There were three strangers in Tolaria; strangers to me, at any rate. One was Barrin's daughter, who had returned after a long absence. Another was a Benalish master-at-arms who wore throwing knives and a swagger. Last was a cat warrior whom I'd seen in Barrin's garden, sunning herself on the stones.

"The Benalish is called Gerrard," said Barrin. "He is heir to a collection of artifacts known as the Legacy. You know, of course, what I am talking about, how important these objects are."

In truth I'd paid little attention to artifacts during my studies. There are few artifacts that can do anything a good spell can't do. Magical machines are a crutch for lesser wizards.

As these thoughts passed through my head, Barrin told me about an airship called *Weatherlight*, on which these three served as crew. For the present, Gerrard was serving as the ship's captain. The craft's previous captain, Sisay, had been abducted and spirited to another world, a plane called Rath.

By means of its Thran crystal, Barrin observed, *Weatherlight* could travel to Rath, provided a sufficiently powerful wizard could be found to calibrate the crystal. Then, as Barrin continued, I confess my mind wandered a little and I thought of travel to other planes—a fascinating prospect and one I hope to someday achieve.

"She has pleaded with me to join the crew," Barrin said.

"Who?"

"My daughter," snapped my teacher irritably. "Weren't you listening? But the Benalish has suggested that instead they take you. I agree with him. It's a chance for you to test your skills outside of Tolaria."

And to spread my reputation beyond Tolaria, I thought. "Excellent."

"No doubt you are wondering what the problem is between my daughter and myself that keeps me from going," Barrin said.

I wasn't, in fact, the least bit curious, but Barrin continued. "All the time she has been here, she has not once met my eyes—"

"Surely," I said hastily, "this is a private matter?"

He looked at me steadily. "Why, yes it is," he said. "I . . . thank you for understanding that."

I nodded.

"My daughter is an expert in magical machineries. You

might want to review what you know of artifacts before you meet her."

"Not necessary," I assured him.

"Do remember what I've said about your honesty, Ertai. Keep more of your observations to yourself. You'll do all right, I think."

"Better than all right, I'm sure."

On my way down from the tower, I stopped in the niche where a mirror was hung. To my reflection, draped becomingly in the new tunic and chain, I said, "And you have tremendous native ability."

* * * * *

When I met the crew of *Weatherlight* they were hastily wolfing a meal, refilling water pouches, and replenishing other supplies. I kept in mind what Barrin had said. It was, after all, better for them to discover my remarkable talents for themselves, and gradually so they might not be too overcome. After a first course of roasted duck, I sat in silence, only nodding now and then as Barrin introduced me and praised my skills.

The three travelers each spoke in turn of their personal histories. When Gerrard told me of his mastery of arms, I did not note how meager an accomplishment this was compared to my mastery of a more difficult subject at, frankly, a somewhat younger age. When Hanna told me of her archeological studies at the Argivian University and her interest in artifacts, I did not casually instruct her in the vast limitations of artifacts. When Mirri mentioned that she had, with difficulty, learned to cast lightning, I did not call her attention to the many Tolarian children who do so easily before the age of eight.

All three recounted their long journey to Tolaria in the storm-tossed sea. They had trouble lifting the magical veil that hides the island from most mortal eyes. Hanna had been born here, but that helped hardly at all. Merfolk attacked them, and then after they left their ship moored on the shore, they struggled through life-sapping Pendrell mists to the island's sunny heart. I thought of sympathizing with what must have been an ordeal for a party with such limited abilities. Instead, I merely observed that Gerrard had not mentioned his own magical training.

"You can feel that I've had experience in the magical arts?" Gerrard asked.

"My sense of the shifting energies around people is unusual in its subtlety."

"It's true," Barrin said. He seemed pleased. I was apparently on the right track toward correcting what he supposed to be a "shortcoming," though I still thought that honesty could hardly be counted as a flaw.

"Ertai has," Barrin continued, "tremendous native ability."

"That may be so," said his daughter, "but our needs are specialized."

"I should think your needs were general," I said. "I sense no remarkable talents in any of you."

The cat warrior clicked her teeth together. She narrowed her green eyes. "I think we've been insulted," she said softly.

"More wine?" asked Barrin, standing to take up the bottle. "Hanna? Mirri, will you have a drop more? Ertai, give me your goblet."

"Insulted?" I said. "When is the simple truth an insult? I mean only that your enemies, by snatching your captain across the planes, demonstrate significant magical power. Do you think you can match such foes with a childish lightning bolt or two?"

The cat warrior stood, and her chair rattled to the floor. She flexed her hands, unsheathing her claws.

"Easy, Mirri," said Gerrard, touching her arm. To me he said, "Perhaps you mean no offense, but you might choose your words more carefully."

"I am meticulous in my choice of words," I assured him. "I always say just what I mean."

"Then we will be as frank," Gerrard told me. "What we need is a wizard, one who can set the Thran crystal and get our ship to Rath. Can you do that?"

"It would be far more elegant to make a direct translation to Rath, to open the gate between the planes without resorting to some mere artifact."

Hanna's face grew red. "Artifacts," she said, "are the most efficient, the most reliable . . ."

"Wait," Gerrard said. "Can you do that? Can you make a direct translation to Rath?"

"Certainly."

Barrin raised his eyebrows at me.

"Not at present," I amended. "But it is within my grasp. Perhaps in another year."

"We don't have a year," said Gerrard. "Sisay needs us now. Could you set the Thran crystal aboard *Weatherlight*?"

"Sir, there is no magical obstacle that will not in the end yield to me."

"But the crystal—?"

"Take him!" Barrin shouted. He seemed surprised by his own enthusiasm and said more softly, "Ertai is quite astonishing, really. Give him a try!"

Gerrard looked from Barrin, to me, to Mirri, who still had not reclaimed her seat. But it was Hanna, staring intently at her empty plate, who spoke. She said, "We'll take him if he passes a test."

* * * * *

As a volunteer for *Weatherlight* crew, I expected nothing in return except whatever fame my exploits would inevitably bring me. And the crew expected me to submit to a test? Barrin had already declined to join them. Other adepts, even those recently promoted, would expect payment in gold, and *Weatherlight* did not offer gold to its crew. I was not only their best choice, but their only choice. Obviously.

The obvious, unfortunately, was not something they easily grasped. Gerrard and Hanna joined Mirri in insisting upon this test. So a few hours later I found myself on a hilltop, where they joined me. The cat warrior eyed me narrowly, twitching her tail. Hanna, with a sack slung over her shoulder, looked sullen. Only Gerrard wore a trace of a smile, perhaps a sign that he, at least, was aware of the irony that the likes of them should test me. Like Hanna, he carried something in a bag, something spherical and the size of a garden mirror.

In the vale below, a fog was gathering. I kept an eye on it, for Tolarian fogs can be dangerous.

"The test is simple," Hanna said, setting down her burden. She opened the bag and withdrew an ordinary looking stone. "It's an oral exam."

"You'd rather that I talked than gave a demonstration?" I said. I looked at Gerrard. "What kind of test is that?" But the master-at-arms said nothing.

Hanna handed me the stone. "Identify this."

"It's a rock," I said, looking at it. "And not even a clean one." I handed it back to her.

She frowned. "Nothing special about it?"

I had detected some spectral flow, some energetic flux in the stone, but nothing remarkable. It might be used to power an artifact, I supposed, but as artifacts were beneath my notice, I shook my head. "It doesn't interest me at all."

"It is said to have come from a lost Icatian tomb."

"From the trash heap of history," I said. "Why muck about in the past, woman, when you can invent the present or create the future?"

Hanna looked at me sternly. "The Argivian University taught me two things: always look to the past, and never dismiss what appears useless."

"My education," I replied, "has taught me considerably more than two things."

The cat warrior gave a laugh, cut off at a glare from Hanna. I smiled. If I'd made one of them laugh, it was a sign that I was winning them over.

From the bag, Hanna withdrew a helmet of some sort, but one that was unwearable. Mounted inside it was a stone similar to the one she'd just given me, though this one glowed. "What I showed you was a mind stone, unmounted," she said. "Control this, and you can power one or two smaller artifacts."

"But why would one want to control any artifacts at all? Why rely on some dead tinkerer's construction, when you can conjure by your own wits?" The fog below us, I noticed, was shifting in rather unpleasant ways, as if something were being born from within it. "Come, ask me to demonstrate something worthy."

Hanna shoved the mounted mind stone back into her bag and hastily withdrew a short rod. There was some twisty wire work at one end. "What's this?"

I handled it distastefully, though it was cleaner than the stone had been. "Another artifact," I said. I tapped the end without wires. "The effect emanates here."

"But what effect?"

"Nothing I care about, I assure you."

Gerrard laughed. "I don't believe this." That was a strange thing to say. He could rely, absolutely, on anything I said, and I told him so. Strangely, he laughed again.

"It's the Null Rod," Hanna said.

"Named appropriately," I said. "A rod of nothing."

"It's extremely useful," she insisted.

Mirri was watching the mists, which coiled and writhed, then were still. "There's something in the fog," she said.

"Not yet," I said.

"What—"

Hanna cut her off. "I have disabled the Null Rod. If it were active, then several of the other artifacts wouldn't work at all. It creates a countering field of—"

"Nothing I can't do better myself," I told her. "And as for making the other artifacts stop working, you can do the same by dropping them from a great height."

"These are great and rare inventions!" Hanna snapped. She took the bag that Gerrard had been holding and uncovered the globe within. It was a ball of metal strips. Through gaps in the metal, I saw gears and springs. "Do you know what this is?"

"How can I impress upon you the simple truth that I do not care what it is?" I said, perhaps a bit more sharply than I had intended.

"I give up," Hanna said, turning to Gerrard. "He knows the names of nothing, the history of nothing, and hasn't a clue about how things work. How is he ever going to set the Thran crystal?"

"If it's necessary, if some mechanical trick is the only way to do something," I assured her, "I'll find a way." Her arrogance irritated me. The only lesson she'd understand was an object one. Putting my hands behind my back, I cast a web that Barrin called "Abeyance."

"In truth," I said to Hanna, "I doubt that you yourself can make this ball of scrap metal do anything impressive."

"Scrap metal? You call a Chimeric Sphere scrap metal?" She set her jaw, drew the mounted Mind Stone from its bag, and tried to shift the shape of the sphere. With my spell in place, the metal warped and twisted itself, momentarily grew head and wings, but collapsed back into its unimpressive shape.

"Well?" said Gerrard.

Hanna tried again, and again her energies only partly charged the sphere, then collapsed in upon themselves. She looked at Gerrard, then eyed me with suspicion. "I can't."

"That's the difference between us," I said mildly. " 'Can't' is not a word you'll hear me say."

"You've got to like his confidence," Gerrard said, laughing.

"It's confidence well earned," I said. "Look!" I waved my hands at the sky. A Cone of Flame gyred and twisted with orange intensity. "Where's the artifact that matches that? Or this? If your enemies attack you from across the distant planes, what artifact will burn them as they cross?" As the Cone burned itself out, I cast an Aether Flash. Earth and sky flickered red. "The gateway between planes is set afire. Your enemies would sizzle before their feet touched ground."

The energies of these spells dissipated. I disenchanted my own web of Abeyance and cast a final, longer lasting spell. In a puff of smoke my familiar settled upon my shoulder, red eyes peering at my "examiners."

Mirri laughed. "That spotted blue lizard is meant to impress us?"

"He's small," I said, "but your equal in battle."

She bared her claws. "Again the insults!"

I threw up my hands. "You perplex me. I ask you again, where is the insult in a simple truth?"

"Can you summon other beings?" Gerrard asked.

"I can summon a djinn," I told him. I did not mention that the creature was almost as dangerous to me as to anyone I might turn it against. Perhaps, after all, Barrin was right that some honesty was excessive.

"You *can't* be planning to take him," Hanna cried. "He's hopeless with artifacts!"

From the corner of my eye, I saw something gray gliding through the sky. Mirri turned to face it at the same time I did. A tendril had parted from the fog in the valley, and at the end of that tendril was a ghost, a mist phantom with teeth and claws that glittered like ice. Or steel.

Hanna saw it too. "Fog elemental," she said.

"Dangerous?" Gerrard asked.

"Only when they are in a wicked mood," I observed. "But that's the only mood they ever seem to be in."

The elemental was drifting in a circle around us, perhaps selecting its prey. Mirri's sword rang as she drew it from its long scabbard.

"Not much hope in that," I said. "It's powerful. It gets in one strike before it melts into ordinary vapor, but that blow would be enough for any of us."

The elemental seemed to have decided upon its target. Silently, it swelled and opened wide its vaporous arms and began to spiral nearer.

"Ertai," Gerrard said, "this is your best chance to impress me."

I thought quickly. Perhaps he was right. Perhaps it was time to impress all of them. Hanna was reaching into her bag. I snatched it from her.

"Hey!"

Hanna had just drained the energy from the mounted Mind Stone, but the unmounted one, dirty as it was, had an untapped charge. I looked at the Chimeric Sphere, feeling for spectral lines in the Mind Stone and in the metal ball.

The fog elemental spun closer.

"What are you doing?" Hanna said. "Let me have that!"

Wings sprang into shape on the sphere. "Not the sphere!" Hanna cried. "I have a bett—"

I turned my shoulder to her, keeping the bag out of reach. "You wanted a test!" I snapped.

My control was imperfect as I set the wings to buzzing. Imperfect, but why should it be any better when, as I say, artifacts are beneath my notice? I managed. The sphere lifted into the air as the fog elemental made a sound like the long inward rush of breath. Glittering claws descended.

And closed on metal.

There was the sound of metal bands snapping, springs cracking, and rivets creaking until they popped.

The elemental melted into mist, and what was left of the Chimeric Sphere fell to the ground with a crash. I handed the stone to Hanna and brushed the dirt from my palms. "You might clean that rock," I said. "It's quite unpleasant to handle."

"My sphere!" She ran to kneel beside it.

Turning to Gerrard, I said, "I trust I have proven my ability."

"Oh, it's been quite a demonstration," said the master-at-arms.

"Thank you," I said. And I bowed.

* * * * *

"You've upset my daughter," Barrin told me in his study.

"Some people are ill equipped to encounter their own limitations," I sighed.

"Ah, yes," Barrin answered.

"I look forward to joining the ship."

"Ertai, I hope that when you meet the rest of the crew, you will be careful to make a favorable impression."

"Of course. They will quite naturally admire my abilities."

"Ah, yes," he said again. "But perhaps you might make some effort beyond, ah, just being yourself. After all, what would you do if there were a clash of styles, as it were, and they asked you to return to Tolaria?"

"You mean dismiss me?" I laughed at the idea.

"I'm serious."

Barrin was getting old, and the old sometimes have curious ideas. I humored him. "Barrin, you have been a most excellent teacher. I shall take your advice."

He looked relieved.

* * * * *

And I did as he suggested. When I followed the trio back to their ship, I made an effort to connect in the most friendly way with the other crew members. Indeed, they were the only company available to me, since Hanna spent too much of her time fiddling with that Chimeric Sphere, Gerrard was brooding in his cabin, and Mirri had, curiously, lost the ability to speak. Perhaps she was ill.

The minotaur, who busied himself with the ship's rigging, was easily drawn into conversation. I admired the construction of *Weatherlight*, a subject about which he was quite enthusiastic. I shared my suggestions for how the ship might be improved, but I changed the subject when his mind seemed to wander. I asked why he was not decorated with scars as minotaurs always are.

"You think of the Hurloon," he said. "I am Talruum. We do not scar our bodies and our horns. It is an abomination before Torahn."

"Well Torahn should reconsider," I said. "Decorations improve a minotaur."

He returned to working on the rigging, no doubt considering my advice.

Orim was the ship's healer. I overheard her fussing about the clutter of ointments and powders in her quarters, so while she was above decks, I did her the favor of sorting through her pharmacy and throwing out those things I knew to be useless. I offered to arrange what remained alphabetically, but she said I'd helped quite enough.

And finally, there was the goblin. I played a friendly joke on him, showing him the eelskin pouch I carry and asking if he did not think it was exactly the right color to be made of goblin skin. I did not, of course, actually lie to him. I am scrupulously honest.

I think my jest made an impression upon him. In fact,

and I say this with all modesty, I have made an impression upon them all. I hadn't given it much thought before, but without the slightest effort, I seem to have a knack for making first impressions.

It may prove to be another thing, besides magic, for which I have tremendous native ability.

Here ends the Tale of Ertai

"They had one more passenger to pick up: Starke." The master raised his hand. "I know, I know. But they needed his knowledge of Rath.

"But Master, surely as treacherous as Starke was—"

"Treacherous he certainly was. But Starke was equally treacherous toward Volrath."

"How do you mean that, Master? Starke was working for Volrath, wasn't he?"

"True, but people change, and Starke had been through many changes over the years. First he had been Vuel's mentor, urging him to kill his father and Gerrard, always pushing him toward the dark destiny that awaited him. Then when Vuel was transformed into Volrath Starke became the evincar's loyal servant. But one should never forget that Starke was also working for those whom Volrath served—the Phyrexians. And soon he realized that Volrath might not serve their interests as much as his own selfish ends. Starke fled from Volrath to Dominaria. It was there he learned that his daughter, Takara, had been taken hostage by the evincar."

Ilcaster nodded. "Yes, you said something about that earlier. That was why Starke maneuvered Sisay's kidnapping—so that Gerrard would go to Rath."

The old man snorted. "Starke was trying to play both sides against the middle. In fact, from his point of view he would win no matter what happened. If Volrath captured and killed Gerrard, Starke would get the credit as the one who had lured the Legacy's heir into Rath. And if Gerrard killed Volrath, well, Takara would be free and Starke, too, would be liberated from the evincar's control."

"Finding Starke wasn't easy for Gerrard and *Weatherlight*'s crew. He was a prisoner of a warlord named Maraxus, sent by Volrath to keep an eye on him. In the warlord's hands he twisted and turned, looking for a way to save his life and turn the situation to his profit. He was prepared to sell Gerrard to Maraxus, Maraxus to Volrath, and Sisay to anyone. Nonetheless, *Weatherlight*'s crew succeeded in snatching him away from Maraxus. The warlord gave chase, pursuing Gerrard, Mirri, and Tahngarth (the three who had rescued Starke) through a series of narrow, twisting canyons. At first light, they were cornered by the warlord's army. As the hulking figure of Maraxus stepped toward them, Starke pulled free of Mirri's restraining hands and threw himself facedown before Maraxus. He whined that he had personally led Gerrard and his friends into a trap just so Maraxus could destroy them, fulfilling the plans of Volrath, their mutual master."

Ilcaster's mouth was open. "What a horrible thing to do!" he cried. "What treachery! What—"

The old man nodded his head and again lifted his hand. "Well, well, such is the nature of those who betray. Once they begin, they find it difficult to stop. Such, perhaps, was the case with Starke. He saw the world through a series of twisted, tortured angles, all converging upon himself. That, after all, was always his primary goal: to preserve his own miserable skin."

The librarian chuckled. "Fortunately, just at this point, as Maraxus's soldiers were advancing on Gerrard and his companions, and as they drew their swords, prepared to sell their lives as dearly as possible, there was a great shadow from above. *Weatherlight* dropped from the sky upon the soldiers of the warlord, crushing some, frightening others. Like all bullies, they fled in disorder, leaving behind only Maraxus himself. Knowing that if he failed he would have to face Volrath's anger, Maraxus rushed upon Gerrard, sword drawn, and the two thrust and hacked at each other, the noise of their battle echoing through the surrounding canyon.

"As Gerrard battled the warlord, seeking only to defend himself, Starke had one last bit of treachery up his sleeve: appearing suddenly from behind a boulder, he buried his dagger in his captor's back."

II

TEMPEST

A Dark Room

An enormous crash of thunder resounded, and a flash of lightning split the sky. There was a splintering from beyond the library windows. That will be the oak tree in the courtyard, the old man thought sadly. For how many years has it stood? He sighed and turned back to the room's interior, where the boy perused a leather-bound volume, his finger following along the lines.

" ' The hum of *Weatherlight's* engines dropped an octave as the flying ship emerged from the aether between worlds. Dominaria slipped past its hull like water running down glass . . . .' "

Ilcaster broke off his recitation from the book and looked up at his master. "So they *did* manage to get to Rath. And did they rescue Sisay?"

From beyond the window came the faint echo of cries,

as if others had seen the destruction wrought by the lightning bolt. The white-haired librarian sighed.

"Bar the door, boy, so we won't be disturbed!" he said. "I don't feel like rushing about outside on a night such as this."

Ilcaster lifted the solid wooden bar with some difficulty and slipped it into the large metal staples on the iron-studded doors. He stared at them for a moment, then turned abruptly to the librarian. "Well, what happened?"

The man looked at the boy with the first signs of tenderness. "Very well. As the ship entered Rath, the crew came upon a strange and violent world. Clouds stretched from the heavens to the earth in swirling columns of black and violet. Far below the very ground seemed to sway and flow below the ship, as her sails flapped in a raging storm."

The Master fumbled for a moment through the pile of documents through which the boy had sorted, then finally plunged his hand into the middle and drew forth a slender volume, bound in black leather. On its cover was the faded title, *The Book of Rath*. The librarian ran his hand lovingly over the spine. "Here," he remarked, "is the most complete account of Rath." He held it out to the boy with both pride and trepidation. "Be careful now."

Ilcaster took the book cautiously and looked somewhat suspiciously at the dense columns of writing. The librarian leaned over his shoulder, flipping expertly through the fragile pages.

"Ah, yes. Here."

Ilcaster squinted at the heading on the page. "Flowstone." He traced the faded letters with a slender finger as he read aloud.

"The entire realm of Rath is comprised of this artificial substance, an aggregation of cell-sized Phyrexian devices. These nano-machines collectively form a material that is malleable, ultra-tough, and responds to mental commands, usually given by the current Rathian governor.

Phyrexia constructed a titanic mechanism to produce this substance in vast amounts. This factory created the vast mountain in which the Stronghold, seat of the evincar of Rath, is located. Waves of newly created flowstone are constantly spewed from the top of the peak and hurtle down the mountainside, creating enormous flowstone plains."

The boy finished the passage and looked rather helplessly at his mentor, who sighed and took the book from him. "Flowstone," he said severely, "is—or rather, was—produced on Rath by a factory located within Volrath's stronghold."

"But what did it mean, Master, about responding to mental commands?"

"Just what it said. The flowstone *moved*, flowing from one place to another, even engulfing unwary intruders, at the psionic orders of the evincars of Rath. That made it one of the most dangerous hazards with which Gerrard and *Weatherlight* had to contend.

"As the crew gazed over the side of the vessel, they saw the seacoast below gradually give way to forest. Trees clung to one another so closely that the ground was hidden. Starke told Gerrard that this was the very edge of the great Skyshroud, a vast canopy of trees that hid a swamp beneath. But, he warned the new commander of *Weatherlight*, the true dangers of Rath often came suddenly upon the unwary from those things *not* seen.

"As if to confirm his words, Tahngarth the minotaur, first mate of the ship, cried aloud in warning. And from out of the clouds above the ship, plunged a dark and menacing vessel. It was *Predator*, and on its bridge *Weatherlight*'s crew, if they looked closely, might have been able to see its captain: Greven *il*-Vec."

Greven's Tale

Philip Athans

Vhati il-Dal knew that he was about to die. The rough, sickly purple hands of his captain, Greven il-Vec, held Vhati's coiled locks in a grip like a steel trap, and the first mate didn't bother to struggle. He knew he was going to die, but that didn't make the prospect any less terrifying. He tried to scream but only opened his quivering lips to his furious master's face in a tormented rictus of desperation.

"Ambition, Vhati il-Dal," Greven hissed at him, the evincar's face so close to Vhati's own that their breaths mingled even in the sharp warm wind of the skies of Rath, "is a meal that oft times bites back."

"Damn you," Vhati managed through his tight chest.

Greven laughed, and Vhati imagined that hideous sound ripping into his chest to freeze his exploding heart.

"Damn me," Greven growled through the shrieking hiss of his own laughter. "That's a good one!"

Vhati felt his feet leave *Predator*'s deck, felt the frigid Phyrexian metal of the rail slide down his back. His master, his captain, his murderer was a huge man, twisted and distorted—a horrid parody of the human he had once been. Greven wore black Phyrexian armour, all graceful spikes and flowing metal that gave him the appearance of a monstrous crab. His bare arms were corded muscle and twisting veins of purple against pale flesh. The commander was drenched in the mingled blood of scores of mogg goblins and humans. A thin trail of red trickled from a corner of Greven's small, tight-lipped mouth. The evincar's face seemed grafted onto a steel-hard skull. His glaring eyes sloped in sharply to meet a flat nose.

The blood was beading on Greven's face, the skin—if it could be called skin—shining whitely beneath the scarlet. The fingers that held Vhati's hair were long, powerful, and tipped in pointed caps of the same black metal as his armor. Vhati wanted to scream, almost cried, but still he managed, as his leather clad rump slid over and off the rail, to say: "I die for my failure, Greven, not for my treachery."

"The fall," Greven told him, smiling as he always did when he was about to kill, "will give you time to think on your failure."

Vhati had time for a scream and four last, gasping breaths as he fell through the roiling gray skies of Rath. Tumbling end over end he saw but couldn't understand the bulking horned form clinging to *Predator*'s black keel. If he thought at all it was to wonder what Greven would do now that the fight with *Weatherlight* was over and his first mate had been tossed over like the morning's chamber pots. The Legacy, the pieces of which they had sought, was safely stowed in *Predator* 's hold, along with Karn, the strange silver creature whom Greven's goblins had captured in the course of the fight, and whom Greven had ordered hauled aboard with every appearance of glee. Now the commander's ship would make for Volrath's Stronghold, and no one would ever speak the name Vhati *il*-Dal again.

Vhati felt the wind whistle through his ears, and saw his long braids streaming by his face. Lightning flashed around him, and he screamed again and again, his cries lost in the sound of the storm. Then, against the dark background of Rath's sky, he caught a glimpse of a figure of infinite grace and beauty: the fallen angel Selenia, wings outstretched. Her hands seemed to gesture toward him, and for a brief, eternal moment Vhati imagined he was saved. Then he realized her face was smiling, that she was mocking him, rejoicing in his downfall and impending death. Her wings beat, and she was gone.

He felt the top of the tree puncture leather then skin, and he knew it came out his back. Blood exploded before him in a red haze. Sliding down the penetrating branch hurt him the worst, but it was a pain that lasted only the space of a single grunt.

Vhati *il*-Dal was dead.

* * * * *

Greven didn't bother watching his former second-in-command fall. One more death, one more tiny, hollow victory, and it was back to the task at hand.

"Bring us about," he shouted into the confusion still winding down on *Predator*'s wide deck. He didn't bother waiting for a response and didn't look to see that his order was carried out. His crew knew how high they were. "Back to the Stronghold. We have a package to deliver."

A package indeed, Greven mused. Most of the Legacy had been brought aboard and as the commander moved amidst a flurry of scurrying moggs to the stairs that would take him to *Predator*'s vaults, he smiled at Vhati's obvious timing. The second-in-command had waitied until *Weatherlight's* exquisite booty had been brought aboard to begin his feeble grab for power.

Greven had been aboard the enemy vessel, crossing swords with its captain: Gerrard, whom they had been warned of and told to sieze the moment he entered Rath. Vhati, who had stayed behind to look after *Predator*—look after her, not sieze her, Greven thought angrily—had spun the mogg cannon around on its mount himself.

* * * * *

On board *Weatherlight*, Greven hacked and slashed at Gerrard, watching his opponent's sword carefully as it parried the thrusts of his polearm. For a moment he got past the man's guard, and Gerrard staggered back. Greven moved in for the kill. Around him he heard the war cries of the moggs and the shouts and screams of *Weatherlight's* crew as they battled the invaders. Greven gave a shout of triumph. Victory was before him, and he closed his fist around it.

Then, from the corner of his eye, he saw Vhati shove the slavering mogg into the cannon with hands Greven thought must have trembled. Vhati was a coward, but he was an ambitious one. With shaking hands, he lit the cannon, and the mogg came at Greven with a speed no natural thing had ever achieved before the invention of this cruel and effective weapon. The mogg overshot Greven, and Vhati screamed a command to the other gunners aboard *Predator*, a command that Greven had not time to countermand.

The human's sword rang out again on the Phyrexian steel shaft of Greven's black polearm, less than an inch from the commander's temple. Greven saw his triumph dissolve in a flurry of flashing steel, and now it was Gerrard who was laughing.

The human had fought well, Greven remembered. The sword shrieked off Greven's polearm with a shower of blue-white sparks, and a mogg behind Greven screamed at the sound. The commander swung the pole around, letting it roll through his long fingers. Another mogg raider came out of *Predator's* cannon, then another in the eyeblink it took for Greven to bring his blade to bear. There was a blast of heat and that lovely sound from the weapon that had first brought to heel. Vhati was using everything *Predator* had, and that was a lot. *Weatherlight's* deck shook again from a mogg cannon barrage, and for the first time Gerrard, the stupid, courageous human, faltered. Greven's night-black blade traced a razor line across Gerrard's pink, sweating face, and the human let out a sharp hiss.

Greven's polearm spun around again, and Gerrard took a step backward, his sword coming to the ready, to defend or attack as openings presented themselves. None did.

Neither Greven nor his enemy had time or opportunity to strike again before a mogg goblin fired from Vhati's own cannon ripped one of *Weatherlight's* fragile stabilizers and the ship slumped into a sharp starboard list. Greven held his feet in a wide stance, and *Weatherlight* began to spin. It was going down by the bow. Crewmen—silly, screaming humans in shirts the color of their own spilling blood—staggered across the deck like autumn leaves before a storm. Some of Greven's moggs continued to grapple with the humans and were slain.

Now two of *Weatherlight's* crew members lost their footing. Together with one of the moggs, they toppled over the narrow railing that ran around the ship's decks. Their screams faded, as they fell toward the Skyshroud forest far below.

Gerrard's foot slipped. He'd already backed away from Greven who had slid a bit himself on the deck, now awash in human and mogg blood. The human put a hand up to his slashed face, trailing tendrils of hot blood into the whipping wind. "Too high, Commander," Gerrard snarled. "You won't kill me today after all."

Gerrard came at Greven then, all at once, his blade raised high and his face twisted in anger. Greven growled, bringing his polearm up across his chest to meet the human's downward arching blade. The deck bounced from another mogg cannon barrage and Gerrard, his face a comical mask of surprise, went over the side.

The moment came and went so quickly that Greven's shock, delight, and disappointment at being deprived of his foe manifested as an absurd squeal. He advanced in three quick strides down the listing deck and clutched the rail as he stared over it, searching for the falling body. Blood from Gerrard's wound streamed from the blade of Greven's polearm to splatter against Greven's face, and the commander grinned at the iron taste of it.

He pulled himself back to the present. There was no time to savor the moment; Volrath would want to know as soon as possible of the death of Gerrard and the capture of the Legacy. Greven shouted the order to withdraw and turned back for *Predator*.

His spine tingled then blazed to life. Greven let out a grunt. Volrath was displeased. The spine that Volrath had grafted into Greven's back was an alien, torturous thing. It couldn't move Greven, but it could nudge him with pain. It could hurt him, punish him, and most of all remind him. Captain and master he was, but only at the whim of Volrath.

Greven, accompanied by those mogg raiders who survived, poised on the rail, balanced above the void. Then he leapt. As he did so, he felt *Weatherlight* fall away beneath him. His hands reached out for his own ship, scrabbled vainly for a moment, then found something to grasp, to help him haul himself aboard *Predator* . A few of the moggs were not so lucky, and he heard their shrieks die out of earshot below. Greven told himself that when he'd come aboard his enemy's vessel, he'd had only a bit less trouble.

* * * * *

The difference between tactics and cowardice is decided by the victor. If he'd lost the Legacy and failed to kill Gerrard, Greven's following a horde of slavering, rampaging, inept little moggs onto *Weatherlight*'s deck would have been described as cowardice. Instead, Greven told himself, the moggs had been there to soften the human defenders and cut a wedge into *Weatherlight*'s desperate, fearful crew, a wedge that Greven could walk through, straight to Gerrard.

The tactic worked almost according to plan. The wedge was thinner than Greven had wanted, and he found himself having to push many of his goblins back into the fray. A human's spear came nearly close enough to take the commander's nose off, but for his superior reflexes. Greven had to trip the mogg to his left to get his polearm up in time to kill the not-lucky-enough human. Hitting the deck on its rump led to a slightly faster death for the mogg he'd tripped. The human who beheaded the mogg couldn't get his battle-axe free of the deck planks in time to deflect the three simultaneous blows from mogg swords that ripped him to shreds.

Mogg goblins, by anyone's estimation, were pathetic creatures at best, monsters at worst. Only the tallest of them were eye-level with Greven's chest, but they were solidly constructed beasts. Green skin was stretched tight over their rippling muscles. They wore no clothes—probably couldn't work a button or clasp to save their lives—or armor, but all of them were armed. Uncharacteristically delicate picks set atop black metal poles were favorite weapons, as were the wide, curved cutlasses or simple short, straight swords. Their heads were dominated by huge, red, saliva-soaked mouths lined with rows of teeth meant for rending flesh from bone. To say that a mogg goblin has a sloping forehead is an understatement, thought Greven dryly. A ridge of bone capped their neckless heads. Greven had always wondered what that bone was meant to protect until he saw a mogg goblin kill a mountain goat by butting it head to head.

The moggs had ears more like an elephant's than anything else's, and they could hear as well as they could fight. Greven had so many at his disposal he'd lost count of them weeks ago. Volrath's stronghold held no limit of them. They bred, or were produced, like maggots.

* * * * *

From his position in the center of the fray Greven saw waves of howling moggs mobbing, overtaking *Weatherlight*. The smaller ship was awash in goblins faster than Greven had dared hope, but the humans were fighting back. He could see the moggs now flooding into *Weatherlight*'s hold like water draining. The smell of the moggs—sweat, anger, fear, and urine—was as nauseating as it was exhilirating.

Greven killed only a few humans in the next few moments and shouted fewer orders. The moggs had made it to the holds and were now starting to emerge, beaten, bloody, some even missing an arm, an eye, or an ear. Two of them emerged clutching a stick with a tangle of wire at one end. The Null Rod. Greven allowed himself a smile to accompany the grudgingly appreciative tingle in his alien spine.

"To *Predator* with it," he screamed over the din of battle. The order was unnecessary. The goblins knew what to do and were too stupid to change theirr minds.

Just then Greven caught sight of Gerrard's sweating, angry face and spared only a glance at the mogg who emerged from *Weatherlight*'s hold, bearing a small sphere shining like sunlight in a dark place. The mogg carried the delicate artifact in its right arm and its severed left arm in its teeth. Greven advanced on Gerrard, smiling.

The human captain cut down two moggs, but soon found himself hard pressed by three more; now Greven was only a few paces from his enemy.   Something wet, hot, and soft hit him across the side of the head and nearly caused him to misstep. It was a dead mogg, its head crushed. A sailor wielding a cutlass had cut down the goblin and flung it through the air.

Instinctively protecting his flank, Greven looked toward the source of this grim projectile. The sailor moved away, slashing at a crowd of attacking creatures, and Greven could easily see the surreal form of the silver golem Karn towering over a cloud of moggs. It almost appeared to Greven that the golem was intentionally allowing itself to be overwhelmed by dozens of fear-soaked goblins. One more part of the Legacy to be added to *Predator*'s haul.

Greven didn't have time to rejoice, even if he would have considered such behavior. Gerrard was now free of his moggs, who had begun to part to allow their captain his prize. The captain of *Weatherlight* advanced on Greven, his sword at the ready and his fear pushed back enough to be dangerous. Gerrard was only angry now, Greven could see it. The human knew he was losing, but he must have know all along that he would. Gerrard must have known that the moment *Weatherlight* appeared in Rath, the second that its presence was detected. *Predator* had come at *Weatherlight* like a hawk—from above.

* * * * *

As *Weatherlight* steadied in the roiling violet-gray clouds of Rath and began to lose altitude, shying away from the sky's destructive, lightning-laced fury, *Predator* dropped upon it. Greven himself fired the first shot from *Predator*'s main gun. A blinding, blue-hot flash of energy exploded outward and slammed hard into the smaller ship. Even from a distance, and even amid the whirling, thundering winds of Rath, Greven could hear *Weatherlight* tremble at the weapon's touch. Greven knew then that his victory was at hand. The shouts of *Weatherlight*'s human crew finally bridged the violent span of the sky, and Volrath's commander ordered his moggs to gather.

Weatherlight was damaged and confused, and *Predator* came in fast. The distance between the two ships closed; Greven didn't have to bother giving the order to cast the grappling hooks. Vhati *il*-Dal snapped a command and the ropes shot through the gray sky to their target. Greven laughed, and Vhati looked up sharply. Greven stared at his first mate, estimating just how far Vhati might go to destroy him.

"Stay behind," snarled Greven to the mate. "Leave the fighting to those who have the courage for it." And with those words, he leaped through the air toward the enemy ship. His moggs followed him.

A few of the goblins in the front ranks either overestimated their ability to jump or underestimated the distance still separating the two ships. Fully a dozen of them fell to their deaths. Greven snorted irritably at the waste and the stupidity. It was a good thing he'd brought so many of them.

Crews of slavering moggs pulled hard on the ropes and dragged *Weatherlight*, resisting feebly, closer still. Now a wave of moggs were able to jump the distance easily.

The battle was joined by *Weatherlight*'s crew, who immediately started falling back, pushed at the front of an advancing tide of creatures that had no qualms about standing astride their fallen comrades to press the attack. *Weatherlight* was soon awash in blood and moggs.

A thin human with a shock of blond hair and some

ridiculous tabard lofted a gnarled staff into the air. Greven's skin crawled with the magic that suddenly coursed through him. The spine that Volrath had grafted to his body bristled with static and made Greven itch. The sensation drove the commander forward.

Weatherlight twisted violently on its ropes like a gaffed fish, and a few moggs, no more than a half dozen, were bucked to their deaths. The wizard's feeble magic couldn't pull his ship away. It couldn't stop the tide of red-dripping green flesh that was having its way with *Weatherlight*'s crew. Only in retrospect, as *Predator* got under way with a full cargo hold did Greven remember that glimpse of the flowing silver figure that in some bizarre form of honor or misplaced pity, refused to kill the drooling moggs that swarmed it like mosquitoes with steel blades.

Through all this initial assault *Predator*'s guns had kept up a constant barrage. When Greven was satisfied that the moggs had things as well in hand as a mob of moggs was ever likely to, he shouted the cease-fire order across the gulf. Vhati il-Dal echoed the order, as he was trained to do, but it sounded hollow, as if he were mimicking his captain. Greven knew then that, one way or another, Vhati il-Dal would never see Volrath's Stronghold again.

* * * * *

For the rest of that battle's events Greven put Vhati il-Dal out of his mind. He knew part of his strength as Volrath's commander was his single-mindedness, fueled by his master's torturing spine. But by the time he'd regained *Predator*, swept back to his ship in the receding tide of moggs, he knew it was time to kill his first mate.

Below his craft, *Weatherlight* was losing altitude fast, and Greven resisted the urge to watch it fall. He went fast and straight to Vhati il-Dal. The mate, in an unexpected show of courage, stood waiting for him.

A Dark Room

"Gerrard died." Ilcaster put his head in his hands and groaned. "Why

do heroes always have to die?"

"Did I *say* he died?" snapped the master.

"Well, no, but—"

"But me no buts. You have made a deduction unsupported by evidence, a sign of ill-thinking and careless logic. Does Tramian Spaldath not say in the forty-third book of *The Foundations of Concise Thought, as Expounded by the Sages of Lat-Nam from the Second Millenium*—"

"Master!" interjected the boy.

"What? Don't interrupt me. I never saw such a boy for interrupting. What is it now?"

"Your robe is on fire!"

In the energy of his perjoration, the master had brushed

against the candle, and the flame had run up the seam of his tattered gown. The librarian leaped up with a shriek, beating himself with his gnarled hands. Swiftly Ilcaster smothered the flames and gently led the old man to his seat again.

"Won't you sit quietly, Master, and tell me more of the story? I promise I won't interrupt again."

The librarian glared at him but relented and continued the tale. "Very well. Where did I leave off?"

"Well, Master, Greven had just hurled Vhati il-Dal over the side of *Predator*."

"Ah, yes. Now I remember. We have several accounts of what happened next, and some of what we know can be reasonably deduced from the careful correlation of these stories. If we compare these different versions—"

"Yes, Master, but what *happened*?"

Ilcaster clapped his hand across his mouth as the words left it. The old man, one finger lifted in a hortatory position froze, glaring at the boy. There was a painful silence, during which a high, damp wind whirled and shrieked outside, rattling the windows, and bringing with it a rich smell of running water.

"*As I was saying*," growled the librarian finally, "if we compare these different versions, we learn that the fallen angel Selenia, floating in the air far below *Predator*, saw Vhati fall to his death. She did nothing to aid him, having business of her own to report to Greven.

"What neither she, nor Greven, nor indeed many of the members of *Weatherlight* crew had observed was that as *Predator* pulled away from the smaller ship, Tahngarth the minotaur, with a shout of rage, clasped a trailing rope and hauled himself hand over hand up to the hull of Greven's ship. Hanna caught a glimpse of his figure as *Predator* hove out of sight, and she breathed a silent prayer for his safety."

"So," observed the boy, "now both Tahngarth and Karn were aboard *Predator*."

"That's right. But at least at this point, Greven knew only about Karn, taken prisoner by the moggs. Tahngarth intended to rescue his friend the golem, though how he expected to get them away from the ship is more than anyone can guess.

"Now meanwhile, as Greven *il*-Vec thinned the ranks of his own crew and Tahngarth searched the lower decks of *Predator* for Karn, Hanna and Mirri were eagerly seeking some sign of what had become of Gerrard. *Predator*, of course, had gotten clean away, carrying with it Karn and those parts of the Legacy *Weatherlight*'s crew had stored in its hull after so many years of painstakingly collecting them. Badly damaged, the ship spiraled down into the thickly shadowed forest, crashing through the canopy and coming to rest amid the muck and swamp water beneath the Skyshroud."

"Could they relaunch the ship?"

The scholar shook his head. "Not without considerable work. Hanna set the crew to their tasks, repairing the hull and tallying their losses. Meanwhile Orim was busy tending to those wounded in the fight. But amidst all this activity the navigator's thoughts were constantly on the ship's missing captain."

Hanna's Tale

Miranda Horner

"Any sign of him?" Hanna asked Mirri and Crovax. She felt sure that she had kept her voice steady, but Crovax turned from his position at the railing and gave her an appraising look.

"No. But then I don't see how he could have survived that fall, Hanna. Even if he did, we wouldn't be able to . . ."

"I agree with Hanna," Mirri cut in without turning from the railing. "We must land to fix the ship. I would like to give him a decent burial if we can find him down there."

Hanna joined Mirri at the railing, looking at the dense treetops poking through the ever-increasing mist. "Visibility is low, and *Weatherlight* isn't in very good shape. Not only are we descending quickly, but I've checked the

Thran crystal. Those moggs cracked it extensively when they tried to pry it loose. Without the crystal, we won't be able to shift off of this plane once we've found Sisay. We have no choice but to land here and attempt to repair the ship."

"Do you see what I mean about the superiority of sorcery over artifacts, Hanna?" came a voice from behind. The wizard adept Ertai moved into position next to her, his expression even smugger than his words. "Because we are dependent on that crystal to move between planes, we find ourselves stuck in an untenable position," he observed. "If you had had the patience to allow me to develop my magic so that we could make a direct translation to Rath we would not be marooned here now."

Flashes of past lectures that her father Barrin had given her while she was growing up passed through the navigator's head. Grief for the loss of Gerrard mixed with the anger that her father's arguments—now put forward by his pupil—always brought to the fore.

To prevent Ertai from seeing that his words flustered her, Hanna mentally counted to three before replying, "When you come up with a sorcerous way to shift between planes, come talk to me. Until then, please continue helping Orim with the wounded as Mirri asked you to earlier. We have very little time before we land."

"Be assured that I will," Ertai said, sauntering back toward the healer. "No doubt I can show her a more efficient way of healing . . ." His voice passed out of hearing.

"That one must always have the last word," Mirri commented while scanning the forest below. "For him and for your father, sorcery is the final answer to everything. Yet this ship and the Legacy clearly indicates otherwise." Mirri turned to Hanna with a grim expression. "How soon before we land?"

Orim's voice momentarily cut through their conversation. "No, no!" she exclaimed. "You two should carry him by the shoulders and feet! And watch out for that wound on his arm!"

Hanna, Mirri, and Crovax looked over to where the healer was directing Ertai and other crew members in moving the wounded belowdecks. Ertai's smirk was gone now, replaced with concentration as he levitated a wounded crewman just after the mishandled one. "Mind his head," Orim warned the young wizard. Ertai frowned briefly and then adjusted the crewman's position in the air.

Both Hanna and Mirri turned away from the spectacle at the same time. Although Hanna was startled at Mirri's support of her just now, she decided to answer the cat warrior's question before she commented on the reference to her father. "Within two minutes or so, *Weatherlight* should be able to handle a decent landing." She turned to Crovax. "I'll need you and Mirri to help me ready the ship for landing. Without Tahngarth or Gerrard here, we're a bit light on command crew."

"Two minutes?" the nobleman exclaimed. "So soon? How are we going to break through those trees? They'll break us, most likely!"

"If we don't choose to land in two minutes, the ship will breach those trees not long after that anyway. I should be able to maneuver the ship into a better landing position—with your help." She hoped that the ship could withstand some amount of rough travel through the dense treetops. "I'll need you and Terrance to stand lookout and tell me what adjustments, if any, I need to make while I'm steering."

"Well, I hope you know what you're doing," Crovax muttered before walking off.

Hanna turned back to Mirri. "Thank you for your support, Mirri. It couldn't have come at a better time."

The cat warrior shrugged. "It was necessary. Besides, I've watched you long enough to have faith in your judgment and abilities. Now, what can I do to help?"

Once again, Hanna was startled at Mirri's uncondi-
tional support. She must have changed during the time
she and Gerrard were absent from the ship. Before the
moment could leave, though, Hanna seized control of it.
"Mirri, can you help gather the rest of the crew that isn't
wounded and have them stand ready to hack at tree
limbs on the way down? That forest canopy is so thick
that even my best efforts will still leave us with a lot of
branches to deal with. Can you also send someone up to
me to help in the bridge?"

"I shall do so."

Hanna ran up to the command center of the ship,
pushing aside thoughts of Gerrard. Concentrate, she told
herself. Think about how to approach this landing. She
narrowly avoided walking into Squee, who was running
past her from below decks.

"Squee! Where have you been? We thought you were
dead!"

The goblin paused but still looked around as if searching for something. "They're gone? No more moggs?"

"No more moggs, Squee," Hanna reassured him. "Why
don't you go help Mirri or Starke? We have to land
soon."

The goblin nodded and then scampered off toward the
cat warrior. As she continued toward the bridge, she
heard Squee ask Mirri about Gerrard's whereabouts. For
a moment, sorrow almost overwhelmed her, and she felt
tears coursing down her cheeks. Then, with a heavy sigh
she brushed them away. There would be time for grieving
later.

The navigator opened the door to the area that held
all of the steering and navigating equipment that guided
Weatherlight through her journeys.

"You need my assistance?" came Ertai's voice from
behind her.

Hanna turned toward him and noticed that he seemed very preoccupied. She was startled for a moment at his presence; then she realized Mirri must have sent him to the bridge to help with the landing. Despite his arrogance, the young wizard could be useful to her.

"Yes. I need to set up our descent. If you could aid me, it would go much more smoothly."

Ertai nodded briefly, still distracted. "Yes, I am sure it would. Though I should think your limited abilities as a navigator would be sufficient to crash-land a ship."

Hanna ignored the comment. "First of all, keep an eye on Terrance and tell me if he directs us to make any adjustments." She gestured at the windows that looked out over the foredeck of the ship. "Watch him closely: This is going to be tricky, if we're to avoid puncturing the hull. Then, when I tell you to do so, adjust those knobs over there." She pointed to a bank of controls to the left of the wheel.

"Have you ever had to do something like this before?" Ertai asked as he stared out the windows.

Hanna changed a few of the settings, turning knobs and punching buttons before answering. "Not really," she admitted, as she set the approach vector. "With any luck I'll finally find out exactly how the controls on this panel work. . . ."

Ertai was sufficiently startled to half turn toward the blonde navigator. "Find out?" he exclaimed. "Do you mean to say you don't know what all these things"—he gestured to the array of protuberances around them—"all these devices *do?*"

". . . Making my knowledge of this particular station almost complete," the navigator finished calmly. She stared out the window, nudging the wheel this way and that. "My training in artifact studies at the Argivian University, along with some good instincts in matters dealing with artifacts, has been of great help in learning about this ship, but the fact is *no one* on board *Weatherlight*, not even Sisay, knows all about this ship. Sometimes it seems as if it's changing beneath our feet, finding new ways of doing things."

Hanna turned toward Ertai, who was staring at her, looking as astonished as it was in his nature to be. "My experience has led me to believe that the purple lever with the iridescent markings allows the ship to make controlled falls. In past tests with this knob," she continued, "the ship seemed to fall for a limited distance. Over time, I changed the setting and pushed in the knob to see what happened. Depending on the setting of the lever controlling the 'wings' and the marking on the purple knob, the ship drops straight down at a certain speed for a certain distance."

Ertai's eyes never left the window. His hands moved this way and that, relaying signals from Terrance, who stood on the far forward deck, leaning over the rail, watching the tree tops as they drew ever closer.

"So *Weatherlight* still holds some mysteries for you?" the young wizard asked.

"Quite a few, actually. I've discovered a lot of them, but just when I think that I completely understand something, I find out that some other knobs, levers, or buttons have more of an impact on the one I'm testing than I originally thought." Hanna shrugged. "I think I've got enough of an understanding of this particular knob to use it to bring the ship through the canopy of trees to the land below with minimal damage. Hold onto something, just in case," she added with a half smile.

Now that she had set the ship for a straight course instead of the spiraling one that they had been on, the navigator moved over to stand by Ertai at the control station.

"During my time on board *Weatherlight*," she told the young man, "I've discovered what most of the controls on the navigation and command stations do. However, my understanding of the station that deals with plane-shifting is not as complete." She pointed to a panel to the right of the central command area. "Since the Thran crystal is damaged, this is dark." The command panel, however, seemed to be in good working order. Hanna lifted a long tube and blew into it, preparing to make an all-hands announcement. "Is the crew ready?" she asked Ertai.

"I believe so."

Looking out over the foredeck, she noted at a glance that Orim had finished taking all of the wounded belowdecks. Starke and Terrance were stationed at the front of the ship where she and Ertai could see them. Mirri, Squee, and the unwounded portion of the crew waited with machetes and other weapons to help the ship's progress through the trees. They looked as ready as they would ever be.

"Prepare for descent!" Hanna announced into the speaking tube. "I'm taking the ship down now." She feathered back the ship's long wings delicately. "Starke, Terrance, we should be heading for that dip hidden by the fog. In about five minutes, we should be over it. Wave to me just before we reach it."

She moved over to the navigation station to prepare the controlled fall that would be necessary to sink through the trees. When they had first passed over the fog-filled dip in the trees, she had noticed that it seemed to be one of the few areas with less trees clustered togeth-er. She hoped they would be able to sink to earth with-out causing too much damage to the ship.

"Ertai, please stand over here and be ready to push the green lever all the way down," she told him after setting the wings into a flat position. "I'll take over the com-mand station now."

Ertai nodded and moved over. Now she had a few minutes

to think before she needed to implement the navigation changes on the command panel.

In the past Sisay had stood at this panel, ready to translate her navigation commands into reality. Even further back in time, she remembered, it was Gerrard who had stood there. Now, both he and Sisay were gone to fates unknown. Although she missed them both intensely, Gerrard's questionable fate caused her more pain than Sisay's absence had.

She remembered her first meeting with Gerrard. Sisay had brought him on board, accompanied by Mirri and Rofellos. He was sulky, almost like a child. Yet she somehow knew that he would be important to her. Past battles taught her to rely on his steadiness, while causing her to worry over his well-being.

Most clearly, though, Hanna remembered the moment when she realized the true depth of her feelings for Gerrard. Those feelings had given her the most joy in her life as well as the most pain. The joy came from the knowledge that he was someone she could love without reservation and that he seemed to have warm feelings for her. Her pain had come in a sudden jolt when, just as she and Gerrard were on the brink of full understanding, he deserted both her and the ship.

At first, she'd thought that she was somehow responsible for Gerrard's decision to leave the ship. In time, her usual good judgment and wisdom prevailed. She was not, she thought wryly, the center of the multiverse—even if she wanted to be for him. Gerrard's decision had been reached out of his own agony of self-doubt; she was no more than one of many factors in his calculations.

Once she got through the phase of self-blame and self-doubt, however, Hanna had to deal with the pain of his absence. As in the past, when she had to confront the pain of anger that her father dealt her, Hanna fell into her old solution: work.

Since childhood Hanna had been intrigued by puzzles. This was one of the reasons she had pursued the study of artifacts so avidly. Because *Weatherlight* was part of a collection of artifacts, it sparked her interest. After Gerrard's departure, Hanna, with Sisay's enthusiastic support, threw all of her spare time into trying to understand how the Thran crystal worked. The time that she spent on this puzzle brought her even closer to the ship.

Occasionally she found herself thinking of the ship—a part of the Legacy, after all, and thus possessing some deeper destiny—as having some type of base intelligence, perhaps a very low-level self-awareness. She would suddenly understand what function a certain control performed, and the leap of understanding felt like more than just an instinctual guess; somehow it seemed guided. Of course, Hanna never shared these thoughts with anyone else. Telling people that a ship, even an artifact ship, had an intelligence might cause them to doubt her sanity.

Once again, Hanna's brow furrowed. She had tried to grab for Gerrard as he fell over the ship, but he'd been out of her reach as he battled the monstrous commander of that other ship that had fallen upon them so suddenly from above. Images of him falling to his death caused a renewal of that familiar yet sharper pain. If he were dead, as Crovax had suggested, what would she do? What would they all do? He was the key to the Legacy.

"Hanna, Starke is waving his arms," Ertai announced. "Is there something I should be doing?"

"Not yet." She immediately implemented the new navigation instructions and set the control station to manual control. During the early years on *Weatherlight*, Sisay had flown it completely by manual control. However, as Hanna discovered more about the navigation and control stations, she learned that it was possible to set long-range courses so that the ship could automatically move on course without someone guiding it at all times. With the situation they were in now, though, Hanna needed all the control she could muster over its movements.

Outside, Mirri, Starke, and the others were already cutting or knocking away branches as they reached for the ship. Hanna moved the ship slightly to starboard just before Starke waved her in that direction. As they passed further down, tree limbs bounced back into place above them, sometimes rocking the ship violently. Hanna found herself tossed from side to side, clinging to the wheel as she tried to steer a course.

"Hold on, Ertai," she warned. She gritted her teeth against the nerve-wracking sound of scraping branches and continued their descent. After Starke waved his hands in an effort to direct her to the right, and Hanna quickly adjusted her course. The trees continued their protest at the ship's descent, but not quite as vehemently. Broken branches from above fell onto the decks, knocking crew members hard into the railing, but thankfully not over it. After a few more moments, Hanna moved the ship to port and then hard aft again at Terrance's behest. With a last bit of protest, the lower limbs of the trees gave way with much yawing and scratching. A shuffling of leaves and flurry of branch was Terrance's only warning before a particularly large damaged branch fell from above, hitting the crewman and flinging him against the railing. Hanna saw that his head had been knocked against the ship's wood before she turned her attention back to what she needed to do. I hope Orim can get to him in time, she prayed.

Hanna adjusted the speed of the ship's descent. Like some damaged bird, its wings broken, it floated down to the ground. Hanna let go of the levers and stood back from the panels with a sigh. She felt drained. "Go ahead and pull that lever down, Ertai."

The door to the command center slammed open as

Squee rushed in. "You did it, Hanna!" He slammed against her legs and held them in a tight embrace. "We're down. But not inna good place," he warned in a somber voice. "Mirri is gettin' ready to find Gerrard. I'll stay on da ship with ya."

"Yes, you'll stay on the ship," Hanna announced as she walked quickly out of the room, "but I'll be going with Mirri to find Gerrard."

* * * * *

Outside, the crew were already collecting the broken tree branches that had fallen onto the ship to throw them overboard. Mirri was poised on the railing and looked as if she were about to jump to a nearby tree and shinny down it. "Wait!" Hanna cried out. "I want to go with you!"

Mirri turned around. "It is not necessary. You should stay with the ship and direct repairs on it."

Hanna leaped over a limb and ran to stand beside the cat warrior. "The others can handle the ship's repairs. Once they get the decks cleared, the crew can start working on repairing any hull damage while Orim, Crovax, and the others bury the dead."

Orim, who was standing nearby, turned when she heard her name. "Of course we can take care of this. Go find Gerrard," she said brusquely, immediately turning back to direct the crew in the removal of a large tree branch covering Terrance. The crewman was apparently unhurt, but his body was pinned against the deck. Several of the crew strained as they pulled at the heavy branch. Suddenly, with an impatient grunt, Crovax brushed them aside and with little apparent effort lifted the branch and tossed it high over the side. Orim stared at him and started to say something to Hanna, who was, however, too absorbed in her argument with Mirri to hear the healer.

"Well?" Hanna asked. "The crew knows what they're doing; Sisay trained them well." Mirri stared at her, her green eyes large and unblinking. "I need to see him— dead or alive," the navigator added softly.

Mirri shook her head. "With Tahngarth gone, I am ranking mate of the ship. You must have my permission to leave *Weatherlight*,."

Not that I wouldn't leave anyway, Hanna thought.

Mirri, as if she read the navigator's mind, gave a slow nod. "Yes, we are sisters in this concern of ours," she said. Then she turned and with a fluid movement leaped from the ship onto a nearby tree.

Before Hanna could follow, Orim came up behind her and placed a water skin into her hands. "You'll need this. If you need food, you've been gone too long."

Hanna nodded her thanks, threw the strap of the canteen over her shoulder, and gathered herself for the jump. Fortunately, the tree consisted of two main trunks, forming a V that allowed her to get a foothold. Once she made the leap, scraping her hands on the rough bark in the process, she cautiously made her way down to the ground. The "ground," however, she discovered consisted of the twisted roots of the trees and murky water. Looking around, she saw that Mirri had already moved several trees away from the ship. Carefully jumping from root to root, Hanna moved to Mirri's side.

"This place is strange. I don't see any dirt—just roots and water," Hanna declared, a hint of wonder in her voice.

Now that Hanna could look around, she noticed many more details about the forest in which they found themselves. Thanks to the hole knocked into the forest's canopy by *Weatherlight*, she could see several yards out from her current position. After that, the tall, thick trees allowed little light to filter down. If the whole area consists of tree roots growing from water, Hanna thought, the lack of light could prove to be a problem. She bent down to look more closely at the water pooled between the roots. Startled at what she saw, she glanced up at Mirri for confirmation.

"Yes, the trees grow out of deep water," Mirri stated. "Don't fall in. Things probably live down there."

Hanna straightened up and nodded a little fearfully. In the murky depths of the water, she had seen something staring up at her—and it wasn't her reflection. "Let's keep moving," she suggested. Inwardly, she was grateful that she always carried a small dagger. Mirri's sword might not be the only weapon needed if they met something hostile.

Once they left the lighter area of the watery forest, Hanna found the going tougher still. Mirri, with her cat eyes, could see in darker conditions. Hanna, on the other hand, found herself stumbling. Fortunately, the trees grew so thick in this forest that she was able to regain her lost balance by grabbing onto their trunks before she fell into the water. Scraped palms, she thought, were an easy price to pay for not plunging into the depths of the swamp and encountering whatever lurked down there, whatever was still watching them with unseen eyes.

Mirri continued to move ahead of her silently, her cat's grace allowing her to keep well hidden in the shadows. Hanna attempted to move the same way, but gave up when it made her even more clumsy than before. Mirri glanced back occasionally with her normal inscrutable expression. Hanna imagined that the cat warrior was regretting her decision to allow the clumsy human along. Or, Hanna thought to herself, she has the same sense of being watched that I do.

As they moved farther away from the ship, Mirri pointed out some characteristics of the forest that Hanna missed in her efforts to maintain her footing. "Those trees you keep hugging form part of the canopy," she said. "Since they need the light to live, I would think they sprout up quickly and don't form branches until they approach the height of their older relatives."

Hanna noticed that these infant trees were a strange, mottled gray color with pulsating roots. She theorized that the trees must have a source deep below the water for their nutrition for the first year of growth. After that, their roots probably solidified into the huge, gnarled walkways that the two of them were currently traversing.

Other trees grew in strange tangles. "This type of tree might grab part of Gerrard's clothing—if he were still alive and walking," Mirri pointed out.

Hanna stopped for a moment, staring at the dappled figure of the cat warrior. Was it possible she believed Gerrard still lived? Hanna had seen him fall. No one could survive a fall like that.

The limbs of these trees held many sets of branches, causing them to spread out instead of grow up. Since they tended to grow in clusters that acted as obstacles to forward progress, Mirri led Hanna around these trees instead of into them. The leaves on these tangled trees ranged from light gray to ebon black in shade, causing occasional whitish blurs in the distance to Hanna's eyes.

"Mirri, he's dead," Hanna said, a deep ache resonating within her. "He fell a long way."

"Do not make assumptions," Mirri declared. "I'm looking for signs of his passage without judging what might have occurred." Hanna shrugged her shoulders and doggedly followed.

Mirri stopped abruptly. Hanna froze, following the cat woman's gaze. Moments passed, and Hanna could see nothing. Suddenly, Mirri started forward again at their normal pace.

"What's wrong?" Hanna whispered to the cat warrior.

Mirri turned back and said merely, "Watch for watchers."

* * * * *

Mirri and Gerrard had joined the crew of *Weatherlight* at the same time, but Hanna knew little of Mirri's past. Gerrard had once mentioned that Mirri had been abandoned when she was young, but that was the most that she had been able to discover about the cat warrior. Since Gerrard and Mirri had returned to the ship, Hanna sometimes felt that Mirri disapproved of her. She couldn't pinpoint exactly what made her think this, but Mirri clearly trusted no one but Gerrard. Indeed the cat warrior had once said as much to Gerrard within earshot of Hanna.

Ahead of her, Mirri paused again. This time, as they waited, something winged in front of them and continued on into the darkness of the forest. A mournful cry echoed off the trees and water for a few moments, and then the forest swallowed it up. Once again, silence took over. Mirri turned back to Hanna.

"Something besides us startled that creature," she whispered. "That is strange if our watchers are as skilled as I think they might be. Keep an eye out."

Hanna nodded shakily and followed Mirri.

They walked for some time before Mirri stopped them again, putting out a hand in warning. "Something is following us closely," she whispered back to Hanna. "Remain still."

They stood still long enough for the navigator's muscles to start cramping. Around them, the forest remained silent. Then there came again that mournful cry, echoing through the vastness of the swamp. Hanna noticed that now and again bubbles rose to the water's surface at their feet. Before she could bring this to Mirri's attention, the cat warrior motioned them forward again. As Hanna stood up, she noticed that the bubbles beneath them were growing larger. Something white glimmered below the surface of the water, slowly growing in size. She saw a humanoid form with light-colored hair moving upwards. "Hanna!" Mirri whispered.

She looked up for a moment and then back down. The form was gone. Shaking her head, she moved over to Mirri.

"We're still being followed, Hanna. Please stay close by. I don't wish to lose another comrade so soon." The cat warrior gave her companion a look of startlingly intensity.

Hanna was surprised to hear this sentiment. "I wasn't sure you'd care that much," she whispered in return without thinking.

Mirri turned away for a moment and then looked back at her. "I didn't like you when we first met, I admit that. But I changed my mind about you a long time ago."

Then, with an abrupt change of subject, the cat warrior said, "Now that you've figured out how to walk in this forest, watch our backs for us. Something strange is happening."

Hanna did her best to look behind while moving forward, but it took every ounce of her concentration. They traversed several hundred yards of the forest, with no sound but the steady drip of moisture from the leaves overhead.

There was a whirling blur of motion from before them, and a wave of water that swept against the tree trunks with a sound that beat back the silence. The two companions staggered back, as a feral snarl filled the thick, damp, heat-laden air.

Mirri's sword was out in an instant. Hanna watched as the cat warrior nimbly moved over the roots of the tree, taking her first strike at their foe. A clang sounded throughout the forest as the enemy flourished a sword, refuting Mirri's blow. Mirri danced away to avoid the counterstrike, allowing Hanna to get her first glimpse of the creature.

It was Mirri! And now Hanna! And now it looked like a nightmarish combination of them both. Hanna's mind refused to acknowledge it at first, but the foe that they were facing seemed to be a mixture of both her and Mirri. Mirri was also evidently taken by surprise at the shifting form of their foe. Her momentary hesitation allowed the creature's sword to slip past the cat woman's guard and cut her left arm. With a hissed exclamation, Mirri stepped back, barely managing to retain her footing on the gnarled roots.

Hanna pulled out her small dagger and made as if to move forward, but Mirri hissed angrily, "Stay back. I can't worry about you."

The shapeshifter—for that was what it was, Hanna decided—mirrored Mirri's form exclusively now as Hanna stepped out of its range of vision. When Mirri pressed another attack, it seemed as if she battled against herself. Each fighter launched a flurry of attacks and counterattacks. Finally, parrying a low, wicked thrust, Mirri—the *real* Mirri, Hanna reminded herself—lost her footing and staggered. The shapeshifter's sword bit into the cat warrior's left leg.

Mirri stumbled, trying to catch her balance again. Hanna lunged at the pair of fighters. The shapeshifter hadn't seemed as fast when it tried to take on both her form and Mirri's. Some part of her mind told her that she didn't have the same grace or quickness possessed by Mirri, so when the shapeshifter took on part of her own form, it lost some of the agility and speed that the cat warrior had.

Mirri regained her balance and pressed another attack. Hanna, with her dagger ready, circled around behind

Mirri, attempting to position herself within view of the shapeshifter while maintaining a good distance from the fight.

The shapeshifter saw her, and its body twisted and melted. It began to take on some characteristics of Hanna, while losing some of Mirri's. This abrupt shift caused it to lose some balance and allowed Mirri to strike a good blow to its sword arm. As an equilibrium was reached within its form, however, it attacked again. Sword clanged on sword. The shapeshifter used some of its new strength to push Mirri back. She tripped over the tree root again, and before she could regain her balance, the creature sliced her other leg.

Mirri's warrior training and experiences stood her in good stead. She fell across the gnarled roots but held onto her sword, using the momentum of the fall to roll away down a wider tree root and end up back on her feet. Bouncing off of a nearby tree trunk gave her even more speed and set her up for an excellent strike at her astonished foe.

Hanna watched Mirri's comeback with amazement. The cat warrior hacked a blow through the shapeshifter's chest, at the same time shoving her foe back into a small pool.

Hanna breathed a small sigh of relief at the victorious outcome. "How did you—?" she started to ask, then broke off as the shapeshifter, now in Mirri's form, burst from the pond in a spray of water, mud, and algae.

The creature, apparently undamaged by Mirri's stroke, sprang at the surprised cat, knocking her against a tree trunk. Mirri's sword went flying and would have fallen into a pool of water but for Hanna's quick grab for it. Undeterred, the shapeshifter slammed the cat warrior's head against the tree and let her limp body slide to the ground unconscious.

Hanna cried out incoherently to get the shapeshifter's

attention and rushed it. The creature looked away from Mirri and up at Hanna. Its form shifted with startling speed, but before it could take her form completely, Hanna bowled it over against another tree.

The navigator slipped on the rebound and found herself on her back, precariously balanced on a gnarled root. Fortunately, she retained her grip on Mirri's sword and on her dagger. As the shapeshifter and Hanna rose, they both moved onto the wider root. Hanna raised Mirri's sword as the shapeshifter moved nearer and feinted an attack. She knowingly left her left side open, expecting the shapeshifter to take advantage of the opportunity. The creature stared back at her with her own blue eyes, but dead and empty of any expression. They narrowed slightly, and Hanna braced to move out of the way of the attack.

The creature leaped, and Hanna leaped as well, managing to move out of the sword's path while making a move she had seen Mirri execute a few times in past years. Admiring it, Hanna had practiced it on her own in her cabin aboard *Weatherlight:*. Now she twisted, kicking one foot high, aimed directly at her opponent's sword. She ended up on the ground again, as she knew she would, but a swift roll put her in a position that allowed her to come up beneath her opponent with her sword ready to eviscerate it.

The blade sliced through her opponent's lower torso. Blood poured out on the ground, splashing the navigator's face and hands. With a violent heave she pushed herself out of the way. As she watched, the thing slowly shifted into a larger, buglike form. Hanna's astonishment lapsed into resolve. Before it could shift fully into its new, chitinous form, she ran her sword through the fleshy abdomen as high as her arms would reach and then brought it down. She jerked the sword out, ready to do the same again. The weird amalgam of bug and human tottered backward and fell into the pool of water, disappearing beneath the black, oily surface.

The navigator turned back to Mirri's still form. Laying the ichor-coated sword beside the cat warrior, Hanna checked her pulse. She breathed a quick prayer of thanks when she found one.

"Mirri, wake up," she whispered. "Come on, Mirri. Can you move? We need to leave this area."

Mirri stirred a little and then opened her eyes. "What happened?" the cat warrior asked.

"The thing knocked you out, and then I killed it." She shuddered, remembering how much it had looked like the navigator before it changed into that hideous bug-thing.

The cat warrior was staring at her with unblinking green eyes. "Forgive me," Mirri whispered. "I thought you a burden, and you saved my life."

Hanna nodded, quietly accepting the apology. Inwardly, she still couldn't quite believe that she had succeeded in killing the creature. "Let's bind you up before you lose more blood," she whispered.

She cleaned the cat warrior's wounds with the water from the skin and then bandaged them with the fabric that Mirri carried in a small pouch. Hanna's own aches set in. "You know that move you do where you kick the sword out of your opponent's hands and then slice him open?" she observed to her companion. "How do you do that without bruising every muscle in your body?"

Hanna stood up stiffly, her muscles protesting every move. With Hanna's help, Mirri slowly stood up as well. "It takes practice," replied the cat warrior in a quiet voice as she leaned on Hanna's shoulder. "Even then, some bruises still result. If you do it right, you don't dislocate your shoulder and tear your leg muscles."

"Oh. I must have done it right then."

Mirri patted her gently on the shoulder supporting

her. "Yes, you did it right. I wish I could have seen you."

Hanna helped Mirri over one root and onto another. "I used to watch when you practiced against Gerrard," she said. "Then I would practice the moves you two did in my cabin. I don't want to be a burden on others."

Mirri nodded wearily. "We should practice together sometime."

"I'd like that. Now, let's see if we can find what we came for."

* * * * *

Mirri pulled them to a stop. "Look!" she urged. With Hanna's help, Mirri bent over. "Gerrard has been here," she whispered. "And since he is not here now, he has either been carried off or he moved away on his own."

Hanna's heart skipped a beat. "Are you sure?" she whispered back. "He's alive? How is that possible?"

Mirri looked up and pointed. "See those branches? It looks as if he fell here. This scrap of clothing proves it," the cat warrior handed her a bit of brown cloth.

Although she couldn't see the branches that Mirri spoke of, Hanna knew that the shred of fabric came from Gerrard's clothing. She remembered seeing him in the brown trousers and leather jerkin that morning. "I would have missed these signs myself," Hanna admitted in a soft voice. "Where do we go next?" she asked quietly.

Mirri pointed to their left. "We should be able to track him despite the water everywhere."

Mirri and Hanna moved forward a few more paces. "It looks as if there was a fight over here," she stated. Mirri supported herself on a tree trunk. The roots of the trees in that area were scuffed. The water pool between the roots looked larger than most. It appeared as if something huge had blasted its way out of the water, breaking roots along the way. "That way," Mirri pointed straight ahead.

Once again, they moved forward several more paces before stopping. "Gerrard is running from something at this point," Mirri declared, holding up another swatch of cloth. "He *is* alive."

Hanna felt a quiet joy spread over her. But, he might have yet died at the hands of whatever was chasing him, her inner voice warned her.

"My guess is that something came out of that larger pool back there and attacked Gerrard," continued Mirri. He broke free from the attack and ran this way. Since he is running, we should be able to track him fairly easily. Keep an eye out for waterfolk, though."

Hanna nodded and once again helped Mirri move forward. "The light is changing," the cat warrior announced in a whisper. "It is brighter ahead."

"Do you think it's another hole in the trees?"

"Perhaps," came Mirri's response. "We should be careful, though. Gerrard's trail takes us in that direction."

Together, they made their way along Gerrard's path. As they got closer to the lighter area, they discovered that it was indeed caused by a break in the canopy of trees above them. The light from the break centered over a lightly bubbling spring. Around the spring, the trees seemed somehow healthier. "They stand taller, straighter, and thicker," Mirri noted after Hanna remarked on this.

"Perhaps the spring has healing water flowing from it," Hanna suggested.

"Water would be good right about now," Mirri agreed. "You used the water in the canteen to clean my wounds. Now would be a good time to refill it."

Mirri and Hanna settled down next to the spring. "Is the water okay?" Hanna asked.

Mirri hunched over and smelled it. Then, she dipped her fingers into it and touched it to her lips. "Yes, it seems better than okay," the cat noted.

Hanna dipped her canteen into the water and handed it over to Mirri to drink. As she took another sip of the water, Hanna noticed that Mirri straightened a little and seemed to lose her expression of weariness. "Is it healing water?"

Mirri nodded. Then, as if apprehensive, she looked around at the dark tree trunks, marching in endless ranks down the aisles of the wood. "When we first set out from the ship, we passed several unusual life forms," she observed. "When these disappeared, I knew that something was wrong. Then, that strange black creature went by. I haven't seen any life besides trees and the shapeshifter since then. It's as if something has warned all the local animals to stay away."

Hanna stared about them. She had the itchy feeling that they were being watched again, and she whispered her fear to Mirri.

"I've had the same feeling for quite a while now," Mirri admitted. "Just keep an eye out once we start moving."

Hanna nodded her assent, and Mirri got up and took a step forward. Suddenly, she went completely still. Hanna looked around wildly for the thing that had caused this reaction but could see nothing.

"Don't panic, Hanna. Stay still. We are surrounded," Mirri whispered.

"Surrounded? By what?" Hanna's hand crept down to her dagger.

"No! Leave it be. We must not resist," Mirri declared in hissed tones. Then she straightened up and called out, "You may come out now. We will not resist."

"What?" Hanna cried. "Who is it?"

Before Mirri could respond, several lithe forms stepped forward. Their pale skin told of lives spent beneath the shroud of trees.

Mirri stared at them. "These elves will do us no harm

as long as we do not resist their will," she informed the navigator.

Hanna wished she had the cat warrior's confidence. The elves were clad in snakeskin and wielded swords, staves, and polearms. As Hanna watched, about twenty elves revealed themselves. "Have they been following us for long?" she whispered to Mirri.

"We know of your ship and are readying to move on it," answered one of the elves. He stepped forward with two sets of vines.

Hanna looked at Mirri questioningly. Surely the cat warrior didn't mean for them to be captured like this? she thought. Mirri gave her one of her inscrutable looks and then held out her arms so that the approaching elf could bind her with the vines. Shrugging, Hanna did the same. After having lived with the Llanowar elves for as long as she did, the navigator concluded, Mirri must have some insight into the behavior of these elves that was denied her.

"Where are you taking us?" she asked the elf as he bound her wrists behind her back. Another elf took her dagger and Mirri's sword and flatly ignored her question.

They walked for another eternity before reaching the elves' goal. During their journey they saw no other creatures, though once they heard the same unearthly howl that had disturbed them early in their search.

A massive entanglement of roots supported the many huts of the elves' village. To Hanna's surprise, no water was visible once they entered the village. Their escort immediately surrounded the two prisoners, blocking their view of the villagers, although Hanna did see a few younger elves drilling together. Evidently, these elves were always ready for battle.

They were taken to one of the larger huts. Hanna noted before being shoved through the door that the building itself consisted of an intermeshing of living roots shaped to form the walls and ceiling of the hut. A light feathering of dark leaves covered the roof, no doubt preventing any rain from dripping into the building. Their escort gestured for them to sit down, untied their hands, and then left the room with all but two elves, who stayed behind to guard them. The guards withdrew to stand on either side of the exit.

Minutes passed before Hanna dared ask a question of Mirri. "What is going on?"

Mirri shook her head. "May I have some water?" she asked instead.

Hanna handed the cat warrior the canteen and watched as she took several swigs. "Now, you must have some," Mirri ordered.

Hanna looked over at the guards, but they stared impassively back at her. She took the canteen from Mirri. The water was a bit sweet to the taste, Hanna thought as she took a sip. The water quickly spread its healing effects throughout her body. The pain of her various bruises eased. Hanna watched her scraped palms heal. "Would you like some more?" she asked Mirri.

Mirri shook her head and leaned over to Hanna. "My wounds are gone," she noted in a low voice.

Hanna nodded. She took comfort in the fact that the cat warrior could once again defend herself should matters turn worse. They remained silent for several more minutes before Hanna asked another question. "When did you change your mind about me? And why?" she began.

Characteristically, Mirri thought about the question for a few moments before answering. "I would have to say when Gerrard and I left the ship," she replied at last. "At times, I can be stubborn about how I see things. It took leaving the ship for me to realize that you were a positive, steadying influence in all of our lives. You remain calm and collected in the face of adversity, which is a soothing thing to have near you when adversity abounds. Even when faced with the prospect of returning to a problematic family relationship, you remained calm and admitted that the action was necessary."

Hanna thought this over for a few moments. She wondered exactly how much Mirri knew about her relationship with her father. "Why didn't you like me in the beginning?" she asked finally.

Mirri's answer was brief. "I did not know you. Later, when I learned you had bad relations with your father, I did not understand you."

"Why?"

"Because I do not have a family and would like to think that I would cherish them if I did," Mirri admitted. "You have a family and don't. While I still do not understand, I know you well enough now to realize that you must have your reasons."

Hanna thought about this for a moment. She didn't want to tell the whole story, but she did want to help Mirri understand her position. "He wanted me to follow in his footsteps so that we could learn more sorceries and make even greater magic spells," she said finally. I was a tool to be used, not a family member to be loved and cherished." She thought a moment, then continued with a sigh, "When I started showing an interest in studying artifacts in Argive, he expressly forbade me to think about it."

"But you went there anyway."

"Although Tolaria's library didn't have much material on artifacts, some of the students had studied the subject," Hanna replied. "As students came and went while I was growing up, I found the ones who knew about artifacts and learned from them what I could. Then, to complete my studies, I decided to go to the Argivian University with a student who left the island to study there. Father had already refused to let me study artifacts."

Hanna paused in her tale, and Mirri asked, "Did you tell your father you were leaving?"

Hanna hesitated before answering. Remembering this made her both angry and sad at the same time. "Before I left with the Argivian student, I tried to tell my father how much studying there meant to me. He didn't understand. Instead, he set a few wards around my room and the island that would have prevented me from leaving. He was very angry when I foiled them—he underestimated my sorcery abilities."

"It seems as if a lot of people underestimate you, Hanna," Mirri said wryly. "What happened then?"

"I received a letter from him telling me that I must return. 'Your duty is to sorcery, not artifacts,' he wrote." Hanna shook her head. "Not once did he say that he missed me or loved me." She sighed again. "I didn't see him or talk to him again until you and Gerrard joined us to help find Sisay."

Several minutes passed before Mirri said in a soft voice, "Still, having a father whom you dislike and who misunderstands you must be better than having a family that disowns you completely. Right now, I consider Gerrard my only family, but he is not of the blood, and he was not always there."

Hanna heard the guards snap to attention suddenly. Another elf entered the room, followed by the one who had lead their captors. "Ah, the ones who left the ship," he noted as he passed them. "Good, Dreanilis." He turned to his captives. "We shall soon attack your ship," he observed with a cool smile.

The one called Dreanilis smirked. "I'll attend to that gladly, my lord." He motioned for the two guards to stand behind Mirri and Hanna. "In the meantime, we have other guests."

The sound of voices came from outside the hut. For a moment, Hanna thought that one of the voices sounded heart-rendingly familiar. Then the hut door opened, admitting several people.

"There you are," the man Dreanilis had called "lord" noted. "I would like to warn you that I haven't much time to waste on foolishness, Oracle."

Hanna's guard knocked her head forward before she could see the people, but the person she had thought she'd heard earlier spoke again. "We don't have time to waste on foolishness, either, Eladamri. Please listen to the Oracle."

"Gerrard!" Hanna cried. She jumped up from her kneeling position and nearly fell over when the guard shoved her again. "You're alive!"

Another shove from the guard brought her to her senses. Her heart pounded with relief and the cessation of worry and fear for him. "We feared you had perished," she managed to say in a more even tone.

The elf whom Gerrard had addressed as Eladamri interrupted her. "They came from that ship you mentioned. We found them in the forest, no doubt looking for you."

Gerrard was looking at Hanna with a strange expression on his face. "Yes," he said finally, "these are two shipmates of mine. The cat warrior is Mirri, and the woman is our ship's navigator, Hanna."

Eladamri gave a short, mocking bow. "So pleased to meet you," he said in a lilting voice. "Now, onto business. What's this you say about joining forces to challenge Volrath?"

An old woman stood beside Gerrard. She was pale and clad in white, a turban bound around her head. Gerrard bent his head as she spoke in a gesture of respect. The woman stared straight at Eladamri and stated, "This man is the *Korvecdal*, the Uniter."

"Yes, yes, you've said that already." the elf said impatiently, leaning forward. He addressed Gerrard. "Your shipmate mentioned something about rescuing someone. Is this someone under Volrath's control? Do you plan to face the evincar?" The elf seemed bent on egging Gerrard on, as if seeking some definite reaction from him.

"We of *Weatherlight* have a primary goal. We must find our ship's captain, Sisay, and rescue her from Volrath. If Volrath chooses to fight, we will most certainly oblige him. Does that satisfy you?" Gerrard growled. Clearly, Hanna thought, the elf had gotten under his skin.

"Yes." Eladamri turned to the woman. "Oracle, explain to me why this man is the *Korvecdal*," the elf demanded.

"Very well, Lord of Leaves," she answered with a firm, yet quiet tone. "As prophesied, the *Korvecdal*, or Uniter, will come to rally the humanoid tribes against the evincar. He," here she pointed to Gerrard, "is the *Korvecdal*. I found him at the appointed spot at the appointed time, as the prophecy tells us. With his help, we can bring together a force of arms that will surely bring down the evincar."

The old woman stopped, and a troubled expression crossed her face. She reached out a trembling hand and touched Gerrard's face. Her fingers traced a long gash on his cheek where Greven's sword had cut him during the fight on *Weatherlight*. "There is something else," she said. "Something even I do not fully understand. The *Korvecdal* means so much more to those opposing the evincar than even I know." She let her hand drop back to her side and returned her gaze to Eladamri, her voice growing in power and fervor. "Surely you can see that by coming together our forces will be stronger! We *must* do this, for the sake of the prophecy and for an end to the evincar!"

"Stronger, yes, but will it be enough to defeat Volrath? It has always been our duty to endure, not prevail," Eladamri said.

"I've had enough of this," Gerrard snapped suddenly. Hanna almost jumped at the force in his voice. "If you don't wish to join forces, please let my shipmates go. We need to return to the ship. If you could assist us in finding it, we will leave you to endure or prevail, whichever you choose. We can fight with you or against you. After the day I've had, I'd prefer the former."

Eladamri moved around the low table, deep in thought. "We have already surrounded your ship," he stated in a detached tone. "But with a fire such as yours on our side ready to attack the evincar, I think it is time that the Skyshroud elves do more than just endure. Very well, I will tell our people to stand down from their offensive against your ship. Your shipmates are free. Oracle *en*-Vec, we must discuss a few things." The elf looked up sharply at Gerrard. "We will return in a few moments. Be prepared to leave for your ship, *Korvecdal*. We must stop the attack by our presence, though I'll send word ahead."

Once the elves and the old woman left the room, Hanna flung her arms around Gerrard, reassuring herself by touch that he was indeed alive. "We were so worried," she murmured. She could feel their hearts beating together. So many torn feelings and so much heartbreak remains between us, Hanna thought. I have no idea what he feels.

"*You* were worried," he muttered darkly. Hanna looked up at him with a smile on her lips, about to comment, when his eyes caught hers. Slowly, hesitantly, he dipped his head down and pressed his lips to hers in a long, drawn-out kiss. This is the way it should be, Hanna thought, as warmth spread through her limbs.

"Ahem," Mirri cleared her throat in a kind of half-growl that brought them back to the real world. Gerrard reluctantly released Hanna, and they moved apart.

"We have much to discuss before they come back,

Gerrard," observed the cat warrior. "During the fight on the ship, the invaders stole the Legacy, including Karn. Tahngarth leaped to *Predator*, probably to try to save the golem. But we don't know what happened to him, and the ship needs repairs. Tell him, Hanna," Mirri urged.

Throughout Mirri's brief report, Hanna stared into Gerrard's brown eyes. There is a warmth in them that I have not seen before, she thought. At Mirri's behest, she continued the report.

"After you fell, I discovered that the damage to the ship was causing it to slowly sink. We had to crash through the trees and land so that repairs could be made. I wasn't able to get an idea of the full extent of damage to the hull before I left, but I know that our descent through the trees did some damage. The crew is effecting repairs to the ship's interior. The worst of it is that when the creatures jumped aboard from the other ship and tried to take the Thran crystal, they cracked it pretty badly." She looked full at Gerrard. "We can't planeshift anymore. Unless we can find some way to repair the damage, we're trapped here."

Gerrard's brow furrowed. "We'll have to find a way off this plane. Perhaps the Oracle can help us. She seems to place a lot of importance on my being this *Korvecdal* person."

Hanna shook her head in puzzlement. "Who is the Oracle, Gerrard? And what happened to you after you fell from the ship?" Hanna knew that she would be haunted by images of Gerrard's fall for weeks to come.

Gerrard sighed. "A lot happened after I tumbled off *Weatherlight*. more from my own stupidity than anything else. I think I used up all my good luck and all my bad luck in the same fall," he admitted with a wry grin. "Since we don't have a lot of time, though, I'll give you the short version. On my way down, Crovax's dark angel Selenia snagged me with the intention of taking me to

Volrath. I fought my way out of her grasp and crashed through the trees to the forest below. Since she'd broken my fall, I wasn't injured nearly as badly as I might have been, and I had the good fortune to fall into water. Selenia tried to find me, but I hid until she left."

He shuddered slightly and continued. "Then, the merfolk who evidently live in the water attacked me. I broke free and fled from them, but they were gaining on me. Just as I thought my luck had completely given out, I stumbled into a procession of humans who call themselves the Vec. I gather they're natives of Rath—making some sort of pilgrimage through the Skyshroud. I met the Oracle after that. She was looking for me, somehow knowing what would befall me."

"How did she know that you were there?" Mirri asked curiously.

"She has the gift of prophecy, so she just knew where to look, evidently," Gerrard explained. "Somehow, she knows that I am the *Korvecdal*, or the one who will unite the human tribes to fight Volrath. This prophecy holds great importance to these people. In fact, the Oracle told me that she doesn't know the full ramifications of the arrival of the *Korvecdal*. My thinking is that I'll work with this situation and turn it to our own ends; I don't really care if I am their Uniter or not!"

"So, what is our next step?" Hanna asked.

"We must get back to the ship and ensure the elves don't attack it," Gerrard declared. "Then, we must find a way to repair the ship and the Thran crystal. After that, we find Sisay—and now also, evidently, Tahngarth, and Karn. The ship that attacked us would have taken the Legacy back to Volrath. So we'll continue on to the Stronghold, just as we would have done in any case."

As Gerrard finished speaking, the door to the hut opened and admitted Eladamri. Hanna wondered for a moment if he had been outside the door, listening to

Gerrard's tale. If so, he showed no signs of it. "We must leave for your ship," said the elf lord. "Are you ready?"

Gerrard stepped forward, with Hanna and Mirri close behind. "Let's go!"

Here ends the Tale of Hanna

A Dark Room

"I'm so happy Gerrard survived," Ilcaster sighed. "I love a happy ending."

The master snorted. "Happy! Who said anything about happy or the end? Had they found Sisay yet?"

"Well, no, but—"

"Had they entered the Stronghold yet?"

"Well, not yet, but—"

"Had Gerrard confronted Volrath yet?"

"Not exactly, but—"

"In fact, at this point in the story they had not accomplished anything of their quest."

"But surely getting the elves to agree to help them fight Volrath was important!" Ilcaster pushed back a lock of blond hair that had fallen over his flushed face. Neither he nor the master seemed any longer to hear the wind that filtered faintly through the high glass windows and stirred the thick curtains.. Both knelt over the chest, its papers spilling about them, the candle casting long shadows that streamed away across the flagstones. The master drew packets from the chest, pointing to where the boy should place them on the shelves. As he did so, he continued speaking.

"Of course it was important! But *Weatherlight* had a long way to go yet."

"Well, I thought—"

"You thought! You thought! That's your trouble, boy: you're always thinking and never listening.

"While Gerrard was consulting with Eladamri and the elves, Crovax, Ertai, and Orim were burying their fallen crewmates in the forest. Just as they finished, though, they were surrounded by the elves' patrols, swords drawn. Under the control of elvish magic, the very shrubbery of the Skyshroud grew around *Weatherlight*, pinning the ship to the forest floor.

"Fortunately Gerrard chose just this moment to return to his crew. While he put the fears of the elves to rest, Eladamri invited them to return to his village for counsel.

"Gerrard informed Eladamri that the attack that brought down *Weatherlight*, damaged the Thran crystal that enabled them to planeshift. Unless it could be repaired, they would be condemned to forever remain in Rath."

"Forever," softly repeated Ilcaster, with a shiver.

"Eladamri knew the elves had not the magic to repair the crystal," continued the master. "But he suggested to Gerrard that there might be another way out: a portal, though none knew where it led.

"The elf lord also promised that his forces would besiege the Stronghold. If nothing else, their attack might serve to distract Volrath's attention long enough for Gerrard and his friends to enter the fortress and steal away Sisay, Tahngarth, and Karn.

"Through all this talk, Starke sat silent, listening. A thousand thoughts and a thousand schemes flitted through his mind. Most he feared the Oracle. She was *en*-Vec, while he was *il*-Vec—"

"Just a minute," interrupted the boy. "I don't think I understand. What's the difference between *il* and *en?*"

"I explained that earlier?"

"No, Master, you didn't. Though you said Greven's name was *il*-Vec. But I thought that was just part of his name."

"No, no, you're confused, boy. I'm not surprised." The librarian looked at Ilcaster's eager face, and his tone softened. "Well, it's a bit confusing at that, I suppose. No, the Vec were a people, long ago accidentally trapped in Rath. They came originally from the plains of Dominaria, and in Rath they lived a semi-nomadic existence, trying desperately to survive. Some members of the tribe, however, turned their coats and joined with the forces of Volrath. Their own people renounced them, and they became *il*-Vec, while the others were *en*-Vec."

"I think I see now," said Ilcaster happily. "So Greven actually used to be an *en*- Vec."

"That's a bit simplistic, but yes. And in fact, though none of *Weatherlight*'s crew knew it, Starke was also *il*-Vec. This was what he feared the Oracle might discover. And so he watched and plotted."

Starke's Tale

Jennifer Clarke Wilkes

"It's only going to get more difficult." Starke sweated and looked meaningfully at Gerrard across the elven council table. "From here on in, the way to Volrath is full of danger even worse than what we've just escaped."

"Still, we have no choice." Gerrard's dark eyes no longer held their twinkle. "Volrath not only has Sisay, he has the Legacy. And if he thinks I'm dead, perhaps he'll let his guard down."

"His guard is never down," Starke muttered. Then, more audibly: "And how are we to leave once you've accomplished your mission—assuming you do? Your navigator has already told us *Weatherlight*'s Thran crystal is damaged, destroying any hope of shifting from this plane."

"There is . . . another way." Eladamri, the glowering elf lord, spoke now for the first time since the Oracle *en-Vec* had proposed this joint campaign against Volrath.

Eladamri continued, "Within a deep canyon, a long way from here, there lies an ancient gateway. Legend says it is a portal to some other world, though none know if it is a better place than this. At least it does go elsewhere.

"As for defeating Volrath, do not forget the many allies who will fight at your side. At last we can realize our dream of escaping this evil. And while we take the war to the evincar's gate, you can enter forgotten passages to find your comrades and your treasure."

"What passages?" Gerrard asked. "Nobody told me about these before. And don't be so eager to rush into battle when you're unlikely to win the war."

"We can win. We will win. We *must* win." Eladamri folded his arms. "There will be no discussion on this point."

"He's right about a back way . . . sort of," Starke chimed in. "It's unbelievably dangerous, but we probably would be able to slip in unnoticed."

"A convenient piece of information," said Gerrard suspiciously. "Were you planning to tell me of this at any point on our way? Or did you simply intend to lead us to the slaughter?"

Has he heard something? Starke sweated a bit more. "Your mistrust wounds me. Do you think I'm in a hurry to die? I barely had the opportunity to get our bearings when *Predator* attacked us. Now I have a better sense of where we are, and can more effectively guide you to the heart of Volrath's realm."

"Go on."

"With you apparently dead, Volrath will turn his attention to the artifacts he stole. That gives us a chance to move without being noticed. The mountain that covers his Stronghold is pierced by furnace vents and tunnels. These passages are narrow and perilous, but they offer access to the fortress if we can navigate them."

"Let me see if I've got the plan straight. You"—Gerrard pointed to Eladamri—"throw yourselves at the front gate by the thousands, while we squeeze through some crack in a mountain, with a good chance of burning up or being eaten alive. And then, assuming we make it out of there again, we run to a magic portal that could take us somewhere *worse?*"

He grinned wryly. "So tell me: what's the downside?"

* * * * *

The war council wore on long into the night—not that it was easy to distinguish from Rath's dreary day, especially under the overhang of Skyshroud forest. Starke's mind wandered, and he thought again of Takara caught somewhere in Volrath's dungeons. She was so beautiful, so like her mother. He could not let her end the same way. His wife's death still tore at the heart, and he winced with the pain of it.

His thoughts were interrupted as he realized the Oracle was looking at him. Starke had a sense that she was trying to recall something. About him? He felt a trill of disquiet.

She and her foolish Vec hoped to bring down Volrath. They really didn't understand what they were dealing with. Surely the only sensible response was to side with the winner. But they didn't see that. Only a few like him had the sense to offer their service to this world's masters. If these fools knew who really stood behind Volrath. . . . Starke shuddered, but quickly caught himself as he remembered the Oracle's stare.

More than twelve years had passed since Starke had traveled to Jamuraa on his insidious mission. He'd had his orders, and disobedience was out of the question. *Their* displeasure was too horrible to imagine.

* * * * *

Rath shall be his Legacy. The prophetic words suffused Starke's thoughts in sleep and in wakefulness, a spreading stain. They were the last things he'd been aware of before he was cast between worlds as heedlessly as a bit of rubbish.

Now he lay face down in the dust, parched and aching and close to death. *They* had left him here for the local tribesmen to find. But no one had come. Starke knew he had little time left.

He lifted his head and again began to crawl toward the distant line of hills where surely he would find water. Each spurt of effort brought him a few more short paces, but each time it took him a little longer to get up again. The air swam with heat, filling his eyes with illusion. That couldn't be Aniyeh stooping over him, unless she had come to witness his death.

Starke awoke with nostrils wrinkling at the fetor of beasts and unwashed clothing. He rested on something soft, and his mouth no longer cracked with thirst. Opening his eyes the merest slit, he saw that he lay within a rough tent whose hide panels dimmed the sun's glare to a soothing twilight. Nearby, a figure sat with crossed legs on a mound of skins and worked at something unseen in his hands. Now Starke could hear bleating outside, and he guessed that this was the home of a goatherd.

The man looked up and set aside whatever he had been working on. He came over and laid a hand on Starke's brow, muttering softly in words Starke could not understand. He reached aside and then brought a damp cloth to Starke's mouth.

Starke drew at the water greedily, even though the fabric was not the cleanest. He tried to speak, but his dehydrated throat wouldn't allow much more than a croak. "Where . . . ?"

The other shook his head and motioned silence. Again he spoke in alien words, but Starke understood well enough that he was being ordered to lie still. That was fine with him. He closed his eyes again.

* * * * *

Weeks passed in the company of the goatherd, who Starke learned was named Jumok of the Cheetah warclan. Slowly Starke attained a halting grasp of the Zhalfirin tongue as the two traveled along the goatherd's circuit, moving the flock from one vanishing water hole to the next. Once the rains came, Jumok returned to the clan's central village to celebrate the annual harvest festival and, later, to observe the rites of passage.

During those conversations, Starke learned about Sidar Kondo of the Triangle, supreme leader of the warclans, whose son Vuel was to undergo the rite of passage this year. He learned also of Kondo's adopted son, Gerrard, a pale-skinned youth from some northern clime, who was Vuel's closest companion and widely seen as a rival for the old man's affection.

Starke knew the name of Vuel. *They* had impressed it on him before sending him here. *This one has potential*, the voices hissed, *a great gift for destruction. He is an excellent candidate*.

And who better qualified than you to seek him out? Aniyeh's voice snarled in his mind.

* * * * *

Starke's memories yielded to the present when the council finally broke up with a general agreement to take the war to Volrath. It seemed that Gerrard had been persuaded by this talk of a portal and was planning to take *Weatherlight* there now to investigate. Starke stirred himself, trying to argue against this action. "It will delay our arrival at Volrath's stronghold," he said. "Every moment that you take away from this goal means that much more torment for your comrades and less opportunity to infiltrate unnoticed."

"The portal is the only way we can leave this world," replied Gerrard. "That's assuming it works. We need to know that first."

"If it doesn't work, will that change your plans?" Starke countered. "Will you abandon your search then?"

Gerrard's face darkened. The fresh scar stood out just above the narrow line of his beard. "We will save our people and recover the Legacy. But if we can do so and get out of here safely, then that's our best course of action. We're going to the portal, and that's final."

Starke sighed, but he knew he couldn't overpower Gerrard's will any more than he could his masters'.

He felt the touch of eyes, and looked up to see that accursed Oracle appraising him again across the table. Clearly she knew him, though they had never met in the flesh. How much did she know, was the question. And what would she do with that knowledge? Starke again felt himself at a disadvantage.

Well, he'd get the better of *this* bargain, he thought.

Later Starke paced the courtyard outside Eladamri's council hall as the delegates drifted from the meeting. Scattered lanterns dimly lit the elven village. No other light broke Skyshroud's close night. There were no stars, no moon in this sky of leaves. Not many steps away, Gerrard and the Oracle were conversing quietly. What was she telling him? Starke fingered the edge of his dagger, hidden in the folds of his cloak.

Gerrard made a slight bow to the Oracle, then departed for the night with his companions. The Oracle, too, retreated to her billet. Starke, seeing an opportunity, casually approached the door.

A quiet welcome from within responded to his gentle knock. The Oracle looked up from her prayer mat as

Starke entered.

"Good evening, Revered One." Starke painted an appropriately respectful look on his features.

"Good evening to you as well, child." The Oracle's eyes crinkled in a concerned smile. "I see how fear sharpens you."

So perceptive, thought Starke with an inner sneer. I guess that's why you're the Oracle. But outwardly he only nodded. "Yes. This attack on Volrath is dangerous. And I don't like wasting time." He edged a little closer.

"We all shrink from the evincar, yet we also thirst to destroy him. We must have patience. Rash moves play into our enemy's hands."

Starke was confused. The Oracle appeared genuinely interested in him. She seemed not to recognize him at all now. Again, she smiled warmly. "We will overcome, child. You must have faith."

Then she closed her eyes, just for a moment. Her eyes opened again and, glinting, fixed Starke. "Trading in hearts earns poor profit."

He recoiled as though from a blow. "What's that supposed to mean?"

"I say what I see. The listener understands."

Starke covered his apprehension with a mocking chuckle. "I guess that message was meant for some other listener, then. It certainly didn't make any sense to me."

"It seems bad business takes a toll."

"Stop that!" Had she really heard his thoughts? "You might call yourself an oracle, but you don't know anything about me. Maybe I'm just annoyed by presumptuous old women."

"Or perhaps you are troubled by bad bargains. When the market is soft, is it not wise to consider a change in commodity?"

"What do you know of business? Leave me alone!"

"If you insist. But think about this: disaster may drive up

a price in the short term, but success means continuing prosperity."

Starke was close enough. His knife blade could end it all now, still that croaking voice so it would never call him out, never taunt him again. A quick cut, the body into the swamps—perhaps they'd think the merfolk did it.

Yet he hesitated. Those words had struck close to home. He shaped his mouth to make an answer, but nothing would come.

"Wise one!" A man's voice penetrated the doorway from the darkness, followed by the tall form of one of the Oracle's guard. "You should not be alone, Mistress."

"My guard," sighed the Oracle, with a tired smile toward Starke. "I choose not their duty, but duty chooses me."

Starke mumbled something, bowed, and backed away awkwardly from her quarters while the guardsman took up his post. The opportunity was gone. Had he lost his touch entirely? He'd been very good, once. After all, that was how he got into this.

* * * * *

Cloud-dark skies and sultry air heralded the onset of the rains. Jumok turned his charges to the east and the distant hills where the village lay. By now Starke had convinced the man of his friendship, and on their arrival he was welcomed into the home of Jumok's family. But they were far from his thoughts as the time of Vuel's passage approached.

How to trap the destiny of the sidar's son? He hadn't much time to find a way to open Rath's dark doorway for Vuel.

In pidgin Zhalfirin, Starke asked all he met about the rite of passage and what it entailed. The villagers were remarkably patient and willing to offer any information—

the trusting simpletons. They told him that the child must survive alone a dangerous test of both physical and spiritual strength.

Everyone knew that Vuel's successful passage would ensure his leadership of the warclans. So, reasoned Starke, interfering with that inheritance might be just the thing to direct Vuel's thoughts toward a different destiny. There must be some way to turn the encounter to his fearsome masters' purposes.

Weakening the candidate so that he would fail, without destroying that valuable property, would be best. Perhaps a drug would do, in quantities sufficient to disorient but not to seriously harm. Introducing the drug would be a problem, though, since Starke had found out that candidates underwent purification and fasting in the week preceding the rite. However, the opening ceremonies of every such rite were identical and included songs, prayers, dances, and ritual body painting.

This last presented a possibility. Getting someone to consume poison wasn't as easy as the storytellers would have you believe, but paint—who would suspect that medium? And who would notice, in the midst of the general merrymaking?

Starke had some familiarity with drugs and poisons. He'd learned not to be too fussy in accepting commissions, or to ask too many questions about the destination. A couple of simple herbal preparations could serve his purpose, if such things existed in this world.

Conveniently, the clan's *mundungu*, its healer and chief shaman, had been one of those most eager to teach the newcomer of their ways. The fool would never think twice about an innocent request to learn more of how the paint was made. Even a conversation about treating the sick would give Starke the opportunity to peruse some of the shaman's materials.

It was just that easy. While the old hedge wizard

prattled on about his healing herbs, Starke took careful note of the less salubrious ingredients within the workspace. Yes, there was bitterleaf, and thoughtsease too. Both could be prepared for absorption through the skin. It remained only to obtain a quantity of the herbs, and to somehow introduce them into the paints.

But that, too, was simple, for no one here thought to lock their doors against thieves. They wouldn't last five minutes on Rath, thought Starke, where even the dirt is an enemy. It was child's play to sneak into the workshop in the dying hour, that time of night when souls' ties were weakest, and gather a few of the precious leaves and roots. And another "tutorial" while the *mundungu* mixed his paints offered Starke the opportunity he needed.

This wasn't so different from his commission for the *il-Kor* client. A pinch of powder, never seen again, and a tidy profit—if only Aniyeh hadn't interfered. Why had she reacted that way? She wasn't involved. She could have kept quiet.

Starke cursed and shook his head violently. Old thoughts. Useless clutter. He had to keep his mind on the task. The rite of passage would take place in two days' time.

* * * * *

Two days had passed since the war council's conclusion. *Weatherlight* sailed over the eyeless Rootwater depths and into the empty lands beyond. Day and night passed in equal drear, until at last the ground began to crack like raw skin. Small hills, gullies, and boulder fields broke up the flat terrain. Before them, one extinct riverbed opened into a deeper cleft that twisted between walls of scabby stone.

"This must be the place," murmured Gerrard absently as he stood at the ship's bow.

"I must protest again this delay," said Starke. "Volrath is

strengthening his forces and growing more ambitious. Every minute makes us that much more vulnerable."

"I know." Gerrard's voice held a tired edge. "But we have no other choice. We're not turning back now."

Rage flared in Starke. The arrogance of the man! His voice grew more insistent. "Have you even thought about how to operate this portal? It's ancient, foreign magic. Can we afford to take the time to figure out its workings?"

"I'll just have to worry about that when we get there. Complaining won't make things any easier. We do have a wizard with us—Ertai." Gerrard winced faintly as he indicated the fair-haired youth. "Maybe he can find the way to activate it."

Ertai didn't notice Gerrard's expression; he stood straighter at the mention of his name. His eyes gleamed and he spoke up confidently. "Gerrard respects my talents. There is no device whose mysteries can elude me for long."

"Bold words. We'll see," grumbled Starke.

"Meanwhile," said Gerrard pointedly, "you might think of ways for us to approach the Stronghold safely. You are the expert, after all."

Starke wondered if Gerrard knew just where his expertise lay.

* * * * *

Each year when the rains tapered, bringing a sort of springtime to the Jamuraan plains, the warclans repeated their timeless acknowledgment of life's wheel. The harvest was past, and the young had come of age.

Dawn came early now, and there was a promise of warm weather as the ceremonial day began. The village was a-bustle even before the sun cracked the clouds; the smell of bread and roasting meats and sweet brew crept among the houses. There would be great feasting this day, after the trial of the sidar's son, who would share in the celebration once he was a man.

Starke traveled about the public spaces, greeting friends with an open smile but searching every unknown face for the one he sought. When he spotted the tall, dark youth with the haughty bearing, he did not need to ask the stranger's name. Vuel caught Starke's gaze and regarded him for a cold second before turning away, leaving Starke to feel like a grubby child wandering about a banquet. Indignation burned behind the *il*-Vec's outward smile.

The chieftain's son continued toward the sacred enclosure. At his side strode his pale half-brother. The two youths conversed in whispers, smiling and sometimes laughing quietly, sharing an easy intimacy. Starke noted an old scar across the back of Gerrard's hand and another, its mate, on Vuel's.

The time of the ritual had come. Vuel stepped into the circle of the clansfolk and presented himself to the war chiefs and the *mundungu*. He stood proudly before the ceremonial fire, naked but for a knife bound at his waist. The ritual words were spoken and the sacred symbols painted across his body.

A drum began a slow pulse. The crowd began to sway and chant in unison with the *mundungu*'s recitation. A ram's horn blatted, a stone-filled reed rattled. Flutes ululated while the drum's throb grew more insistent. The people danced and shouted. Vuel turned in their midst, arms upraised, singing the ancient words so many had uttered before him. His eyes closed and he swayed with the ecstasy of the rite.

The *mundungu* spoke one sharp syllable.

Sudden silence. All eyes were on the youth, whose bright eyes met those of the shaman pronouncing the form of the trial. Starke could not make out all the words, but the gestures conveyed the message. The *mundungu* turned and pointed to a jagged spire of stone perhaps a mile distant. He returned his gaze to Vuel and spoke words of closing.

The sidar's son made the ritual response, then held his arms out with steel hooks bound tightly to his wrists, Vuel thrust his hands into the fire. After a second of anguish, he pulled them back and raised them briefly over his head. Then he set forth resolutely toward the spire. Behind the youth came the *mundungu*, then the chieftains, then Gerrard. The rest of the clansfolk followed at a distance, maintaining a silence at once reverential and tense.

Vuel came to the tumbled rocks at the crag's foot and without hesitation drove a climbing hook into the rock face. He pulled himself up and clawed with the other. The pale scar on his dark hand gleamed in the afternoon sun, and Starke saw Gerrard glance at the matching mark on his own hand before turning his eyes upward.

Vuel was climbing quickly now, eager in his quest to seek the holy vision. His paint-limned skin was slick with sweat. He reached again. . . .

Something was wrong. The hand hung in midair, and Vuel shook his head like a goat plagued by flies. Kondo's hands clenched helplessly, and worried glances flashed between the other chiefs. The crowd drew a collective gasp, but Starke smiled inwardly. The drug was taking effect.

Vuel's head drooped for a moment, then lifted weakly. The hook flailed weakly at the cliff face and missed. His footing gave. Vuel fell.

Kondo turned away his eyes. Someone sobbed audibly. The youth tumbled, hundreds of feet up, death certain. Starke's stomach gaped with terror. No! I need you alive!

One hook somehow caught an outcropping, bringing Vuel's headlong plunge to a momentary halt. But it was precarious indeed—the dazed youth dangled two hundred feet above the ground.

Kondo looked up again, anguish on his face. He could

not do a thing. The youth had to survive the passage on his own or die in the process. Tears tracked his cheeks, but he kept his eyes on his son. Many others turned away.

Starke too could not take his eyes off the drama. He wasn't about to risk his own hide, but this was going all wrong. Come on, he urged silently, you've got to make it. He was sweating almost as much as the sidar's son.

Suddenly a figure appeared on a ledge, just above Vuel's flailing arm. Gerrard stretched out his scarred hand to his imperiled half-brother. How had he got there without help? But there was no time to wonder. Starke watched anxiously as Vuel shouted something to Gerrard and drew back his free hand. He rocked dangerously, and the hook slipped from the outcropping. Gerrard cried out and grabbed at Vuel's wrist, pulling him onto the rock.

The crowd gasped again, but this time in sorrow rather than fear. Sidar Kondo's face fell. He hung his head, turned, and slowly walked away. The others followed suit.

Meanwhile, Gerrard had slung the fainting youth over his shoulder and carried him with difficulty to the foot of the crag. He bent over his half-brother with concern as Vuel raised himself groggily. But there was no gratitude in that one's eyes. He screamed at his rescuer, hurling him backward with his words.

"You have stolen my legacy! It was my right to win my destiny or die in the attempt!"

Gerrard, stung, shouted back, "What did you want me to do, just let you die?"

"Yes, damn you! It is my life. My choice how it shall end. Far better to die than to be disgraced like this!"

Vuel pushed away his half-brother. He drew his knife and cut the hooks from his arms with furious strokes. Then he slashed viciously at the back of his own scarred hand. He spat at Gerrard's feet and stalked away.

No one said a word.

* * * * *

The stony face stared wordlessly into Starke. Below the sculpture surmounting the portal's arch and the tethered *Weatherlight*, two figures studied the gateway's carvings. Starke could see them waving their arms, the young wizard's excitement obvious. The Samite healer, Orim, was nodding her head thoughtfully and seemed to be asking questions. At one point there was a flash, and Ertai actually sprang into the air. Finally Orim made a gesture of approval and returned to the ship, while Ertai continued to run his fingers over the walls.

"Ertai believes he has the ability to open this portal," the healer reported. "However, it will take some time. The symbols are very ancient and, as Ertai has discovered, do not react well to random meddling," She stifled a chuckle. "So Ertai suggests that he remain here to study the runes and learn how to properly activate the device."

"We may be gone quite a while, and we don't know how safe it is here," pointed out Starke. "Wouldn't we be better served by having a wizard with us when we enter the Stronghold?"

"If we can't get the portal open, it won't make much difference what happens there," said Gerrard. "I agree, though, that we don't know how safe it is here."

"Well, you know Ertai." Orim smiled. The rest rolled their eyes. "He is very confident of his ability, and assures me that he can take care of himself."

"How will we know if he succeeds?" Starke pressed.

"We'll know if he's done it when we come back. There'll be good cause to worry if we bounce off the door." Gerrard's lips twitched in a faint smile. "Meanwhile, I think this is the best option we have. We'll spend the rest of today here getting Ertai set up with the supplies he needs and cast off in the morning. Make sure to post a guard with him overnight."

He turned to face Starke. "This is where we need your help the most. From here on, you're the only information we have about the Stronghold and the approach to it."

"It's very dangerous, as I said before," Starke replied, "and things are going to be even trickier since we took this side trip. However, the 'rear entrance' is unlikely to be guarded, especially with the elves and Vec providing a distraction.

"But the peril is great. To be honest, I don't know if the ship will fit through all of the openings. And we could lose some of the crew. But attempting the main gate is certain death for everyone."

"I need to know everything you can tell me. But first I need to know what heading we should take."

Starke considered. Destiny lay before him, and behind.

* * * * *

The stunned clansfolk were making their way back to the village in mumbling groups. But at the moment of Vuel's disgrace, Starke had felt what he'd been sent to retrieve—a powerful presence, potential advantage. He chose a different route, tracing the young Jamuraan's angry path away from cliff and clan.

The tall figure was no longer visible, but he had left tracks in the drying mud of the plains. Starke followed the trail eastward into the foothills of the Teremko mountains. At that point the rocky ground obscured the footprints. Starke was compelled to trust his instincts.

Dusk was approaching rapidly. Starke reasoned that Vuel would seek shelter for the night, probably not too far from where he had entered this rugged country. All the while, he kept an inward ear cocked for the rage that had been almost tangible.

It was nearly full dark when he came upon the youth, crouched in a hollow near a trickling stream. Vuel looked up sharply at Starke's approach and leapt to his feet, knife in hand. "Who is there?"

Drawing near, Starke became even more aware of the power behind that burning gaze. He ran a hand across his balding pate as he smiled and spoke gently. "I mean you no harm, son of Kondo. I am a friend. Perhaps I can help you."

"I am son of no one," growled Vuel. "I need no help." He waved the knife in punctuation. "Leave me!"

Starke stopped and spread his hands. His well-oiled voice slid into the evening. "Then you do not wish to claim your legacy?"

"I have no legacy." Vuel's eyes were flat and hard as they focused on his interlocutor. "As you well know. I remember you. Have you come just to mock me?"

"It would hardly be worth my while to follow you all this way for such a petty thing. No—I've come to offer you destiny."

"My destiny was with the warclan. That is gone forever."

"A road has many bends, and fate can find the way no matter how twisted. You *do* have a destiny, Vuel—far greater than the one you've lost."

"The only destiny I wanted I cannot have." Vuel turned away. "I am outcast now. I will die here, naked and filthy, like a wild beast."

"Is that what you really want? How can you let yourself be thrown away like this?" Starke's voice took on a wheedling tone. "What if you could take what was stolen from you? I have influential friends. With their help, you can have power far beyond anything you've imagined."

"Taking the clans by force won't restore my inheritance. It is worse than destroyed—the ancestral talismans will fall to the hands of another. It would be better if nothing remained."

"That can be arranged," Starke said quietly.

Vuel stared.

"I come from another place, somewhere most people have never heard named. Its masters call it Rath."

An unidentifiable expression washed over Vuel's face. "I have heard that name before." He seemed to be speaking to himself. "When I was a boy, a wise woman passed through our village, seeking alms in exchange for her visions. She stopped before me and said, 'Wrath will be your legacy.' I thought she meant some conflict in my future. Now I see."

He glared at Starke again. "And these masters—your 'friends,' I take it—who are they?"

"For the moment, it's enough to say that they are beyond anything you've known. But they cannot yet enter this world. They need a mighty leader for their campaign. In you they see that leader."

"And why should I serve their will?"

"With them, you can avenge your shame. If your father hadn't taken in that northerner, none of this would have happened. You would be rightful chief of all the clans. Kondo is as much to blame as Gerrard. Make them pay!

"And once you've punished them, you can seize the sidar's talismans for yourself—the ones that Gerrard stole from you along with your title. You'll have taken the first step toward your true legacy: ruling a world!"

Starke produced a fist-sized amulet from his pouch and dangled it before the youth. "This is the Touchstone. It is the first piece in claiming your true legacy." Its jeweled silver face reflected the moonlight onto Vuel's. "You may have death and disgrace, or revenge and power. How will you choose?"

* * * * *

Gerrard had considered Starke's advice, then given his orders to the helmsman. *Weatherlight* headed south, then west toward the dreadful heart of Rath.

The fuming mountain rose to starboard, perhaps thirty leagues away from *Weatherlight*. Even at this distance it seemed to claw the wounded sky. A weird glow lit its peak and cast wriggling shadows on the tortured land about its feet.

As they looked at it, Starke spoke to Gerrard. "That is the Hub, the center of Rath, where Volrath's Stronghold lies. The world flows out of that mountain."

"You say the passage is on the south face?"

"Yes. We should drop down as far as we can. There are usually sentries about, though they mainly watch the front entrance.

"To approach we will have to pass through the area where the Stronghold's furnaces exhaust, a nasty mix of sludge and ash called the Cinder Marsh. Some things live there, but they're crawling beasts. They aren't dangerous as long as we keep off the ground." At least, Starke hoped so.

"Once past there, the going's much stickier. We'll have to get into one of the exhaust vents. A few of them are wide enough to admit the ship, though the inner passages can get very narrow.

"I'm also less sure about what we'll meet there. Some things I know of; others I've only heard about. One peril I do know of is the 'slivers.' There is a great nest of the things. I've seen them before, but I don't know much about them other than the more there are, the stronger each becomes."

Gerrard was thoughtful. "The same is true of the Legacy. Perhaps we can use the same tactics as Volrath. What else?"

"As I said before, this is where the Stronghold dumps its wastes. There are slag heaps, furnaces, and other things whose nature I can't even guess at. I spent some time here, but I was not privy to every secret. We'll have to be on the lookout for anything."

Gerrard ordered the change in course. He looked grim. "If that's the back door, then I hope for their sake that the elves and Vec have changed their minds about attacking the front gate."

* * * * *

Vuel chose.

He came to manhood in a ritual of slaughter. The next two years were painted with the blood of the warclans as the vengeful son of Kondo waged war on all who had dishonored him. And behind him crept Starke, his mentor, instructing him in how best to use the dreadful powers with which he had allied himself.

First fell the Legacy, torn from the belly of a silver golem who was left to stand forgotten in a distant village. Starke knew the function of many of those artifacts and spent long days disclosing their abilities to Vuel, whose thirst for knowledge and for revenge grew with every act of destruction. The items with no immediate use were sold for funds to raise troops.

Next came the warclans. One by one Vuel crushed their villages and ground their bones into the Mtenda's dust. They resisted heroically, but the end was inevitable. When Vuel learned that Gerrard had been sheltered in the caves of a maro-sorcerer, not even that one's power could withstand the forces ranked against him. Vuel's armies ripped through the caves and killed all they found, but Gerrard was not among them.

And finally Vuel confronted Kondo himself. Kinship was empty to Vuel now, and nothing the sidar said would sway him. At the last they faced each other, and one on one amid the corpses of the final battle, Vuel blasted the life from his grim-faced father's body.

Still it was not enough. Vuel bayed for the blood of

Gerrard, but he was nowhere to be found. The plains were empty and Vuel's heritage meaningless.

"Is this my destiny then, fat man?" Inside his command tent, Vuel snarled at Starke. "I am the leader of no one now. Where is the power you promised me?"

"You wanted revenge. You got it. That was just the first stage. Now that you've proven your worth, you're ready for your true role."

Starke produced an object. It resembled a lantern but was shaped in ways quite foreign. He set it down on the general's desk. "The gate key," he explained. "It's time for your audience. Are you ready?"

Vuel drew himself up coldly. "There is no reason to remain here. Do whatever you must."

Starke's brow glistened as he wordlessly bent over the device. A foul green light sprang from the central globe and bathed the floor in its gangrenous glow. Starke motioned toward the livid pool, eyes averted. "There is the doorway. After you."

Vuel sneered at the cowering Starke and stepped without hesitation into the circle of light. As he did so, his body swirled into a black spire of smoke that was drawn into the lamp like brew through a straw. When the last trace of smoke had vanished, Starke quickly snapped off the beam, shuddered, and pocketed the device. He strolled with forced casualness out of the general's tent.

* * * * *

Weatherlight glided slowly over the Cinder Marsh. The ground below seemed indistinct: it heaved like something alive, and from time to time a sparkling shower sprayed across its surface. The sludge was punctuated by chimney-like growths that occasionally spouted ash and gobbets of molten metal.

"This whole place could use a good coating of sand,"

muttered Mirri. The cat warrior looked disgustedly over the ship's side.

"We should pass through here safely enough unless we get forced down to surface level," Starke said, sounding more confident than he felt. "We should make for that inactive chimney ahead. It's a good-sized one, and we'll need that to get inside."

The ship moved to the lip of the fearsome vent, but unlike the others its maw was cold and dark. The helmsman's face was white as paper, but he obeyed Gerrard's command to steer *Weatherlight* into the gaping pit.

Slowly the ship dropped into the shaft. Sailors swarmed over the deck, lighting lamps fore and aft to lessen the gloom somewhat. Starke, Gerrard, and Mirri watched in silence as the blackened chimney walls slid past.

The passage narrowed to a tight tunnel, sometimes so strait that the ship's masts nearly scraped its walls, yet it admitted them. The mountain's mass seemed to be aware of their presence but for the moment was indifferent. The tunnel became a winding duct uncomfortably reminiscent of intestines. Navigation now became an intricate process of climbing, sinking, banking, and yawing. Hanna stared ahead, straining her eyes against the darkness.

"How far is it to these slivers?" Gerrard asked in a whisper. The closeness of the place seemed to demand quiet.

"They live in the ventilation ducts of the fortress, which branch off the passages we're traveling through. We should be especially watchful from now on."

Gerrard spoke to Mirri. "Put the crew on battle alert. We could be attacked at any time." She nodded and went aft, tail twitching and bristling in anticipation of combat.

As *Weatherlight* painfully rounded another bend, the walls spread into a cavern. At the same time, an insistent pounding filled the air like the rush of blood in the ears before sleep.

Gerrard looked about. "What's that sound?"

"It must be—" but Starke didn't get a chance to finish. From all sides of *Weatherlight* burst clusters of reddish creatures. They looked like needles, but sported birdlike beaks and insectoid build. They flung themselves from the cave walls and shot toward the ship. The slashing beasts were among the crew almost before swords could be lifted. Gerrard shouted frantic orders and hacked at the nearest one.

Barely had the crew engaged the first wave when the ship shuddered under an assault by bulky, toothed versions of the creatures. They smashed into and clambered up the timbers. The whiplike slivers already on deck became more muscular and powerful, while the lumbering ones sleekened and sped.

Another cluster of the things dropped from the ceiling, bristling with spines and tearing at flesh. Instantly the others also began to sprout spikes. Interspersed among the fleshy creatures were others that glinted with a metallic sheen. They too became more powerful, spiny, and swift along with the others.

Starke, with only his useless dagger at hand, fled. He shrieked as something gouged his back. He slipped in something—gods, was it his *own* blood?—and fell forward. The dagger skittered from his grip. He scrambled after it, crying out again in pain. A shadow fell over him. He sobbed in panic.

The sliver fell in two pieces by his face. Starke looked up in terror at Crovax's dark and tragic features. But the Urborg noble barely glanced at him before he spun again into the fight.

Starke stared at the metallic corpse. He touched it and recoiled from the sense of evil that almost screamed from the metal. His eyes grew wide. He began to back away, then turned and ran for the nearest hatch.

The slivers overran *Weatherlight*.

Hanna shouted, "They're all sharing the others' characteristics! We've got to break that link somehow!"

Gerrard gasped, "Starke said these things get stronger the more there are. We have to find a way to cut their numbers."

"Some are artificial," called back Hanna. "Maybe they control the others. If I can destroy enough of those, that might weaken the swarm."

Without waiting for a response, she turned toward one of the metallic creatures lunging at her. Shouting a few harsh words, she slapped an armband and gestured at the attacker. It crumbled instantly. She whirled toward another bearing down on Mirri, who was screeching with bloodlust. That sliver, too, vanished into flecks of rust.

But their destruction had no visible effect on the rest of the things.

Hannah cursed loudly—an unaccustomed sound. "That didn't work at all." She aimed her sword at another creature. "I don't understand the purpose of the metal ones. Obviously they aren't the leaders, though. If only we had a chance to study them. . . ."

"Couldn't you wait till they stop trying to kill us?" panted Mirri.

"Get our backs together!" Gerrard shouted. "We can take them, as long as we can see them coming."

Another group of slivers swooped in to attack, this time from above. Immediately, others around them began to take to the air.

Gerrard growled angrily to himself. Dimly, above the noise of battle, the others heard him admit, "Maybe that wasn't the best idea."

"We are doomed." Crovax's tone was fatalistic, even as he cleft another attacker. "We cannot hope to overcome this many."

"Wait!" cried Hanna. She pointed. "Look at that. The ones nearest us are flying—but those farther away are not. Maybe their influence is limited."

"If that's true," Gerrard grunted, "then the worst thing

we can do is bunch up together like this. Scatter!"

Knots of combatants moved out across *Weatherlight's* decks, pushing fore and aft. Like iron filings to a lodestone's poles, clumps of slivers followed each group.

It was working. Fighters concentrated their attacks on the flying slivers, and the others dropped. They flailed at the brutish ones, and the rest grew less bulky. More and more insectoid bodies littered the decks. Suddenly the remaining swarm pulled away and vanished into pits in the walls. The crew of *Weatherlight* stood knee-deep in corpses.

Orim immediately busied herself with tending to the wounded—and they were many—while Gerrard and Hanna inspected the slaughtered creatures. In death, each had reverted to its basic form and lost the shared characteristics of its hivemates.

A hatch opened. A disheveled Starke peered about at the mounds of dead slivers, then hauled himself from the hatch. Behind him, a small goblin's head popped up briefly, goggled, and ducked below decks again. The hatch door clanged shut.

Starke went up to Gerrard with a grin of relief. "Remarkable! Truly remarkable! You've somehow learned the secret of the slivers' destruction. I'd never been able to figure that out."

Gerrard whirled angrily, his hand striking at Starke's cheek. "Where were you, our trusted guide? We needed your help."

Does he expect me to die for him? Starke snarled inwardly. Aloud he said, "That's right—I'm your guide, not a bodyguard. Would you fare better if I'd fallen defending you with my mighty dagger? I gave you the best advice I could. Now that you've figured out how to defeat the swarm, they won't be a problem again."

Hanna spoke up. "What about the artificial ones? I thought they must be something special, but destroying them had no effect."

The blood drained from Starke's features. It was a moment before he answered. "Volrath's power is greater than I ever suspected. We must be even more careful from here on in." He walked away without another word, leaving Hanna and Gerrard to look at each other with puzzled concern.

* * * * *

His duty discharged, Starke hurried away from Vuel's encampment. The otherworldly lamp he smashed with a rock, burying its remains. Never would *they* use it to drag him back.

He crossed the devastated plains as quickly as he could, following the great Femeref trade road to the sea. Get as far from here as he could, that was the idea. Maybe *they* would lose track of him and leave him alone at last.

He felt a guilty pang for leaving Takara behind. She'd raged and wept and pounded his chest with helpless fists. The look of abandonment on her face was almost more than Starke could stand. But she did listen, eventually, and went reluctantly to stay with the family of Aniyeh's brother in the Dal village of Khorin.

At least she'd be safe there. The gods alone knew it would never do to have *them* know of Takara's existence. Bad enough *they* had learned of her mother's end—and how Starke had "demonstrated useful abilities."

His usefulness was at an end now, and he didn't need to ask what his fate would be. He could afford to leave no trace.

A month later, he paced the streets of another in an endless string of wretched dockside towns. Starke headed for the dingy inn he'd seen from the docks. It would do until he had a chance to scout out the land and perhaps this time locate a wealthy patron. Too exhausted to consider a meal in that dreary hall, he went straight to his room and bed.

He started from sleep at a scratching sound. Listening again, he realized that the scrabbling was intended to be a knock at his door. It was the most timid example he'd ever heard.

Dagger in hand, Starke wrapped his nightshirt about him and moved to the door. "Who's there?"

"Please, sir. I've a message for you, sir." The voice seemed to be that of a child. Boy or girl, Starke could not tell.

"What is it?"

"I don't know, sir. It's all wrapped up."

"Fine, then. Just slip it under the door."

"I can't, sir. It won't fit."

"Then open it up and tell me what it says."

After a long silence: "Well?"

"I wouldn't know what it says, sir." The tiny voice was even smaller. "Never learned my letters."

Grunting in exasperation, Starke swung open the door. He kept his blade at the ready. A tattered waif was standing there with a grubby package, a slip of paper protruding from it.

"Well then," he forced a smile. "Let's see what we have here, hmmm?" Starke pulled out the slip of paper and raised it to his eyes—

—and screamed as his gaze was drawn across the mystic script and the room swirled away behind him and the stench of tortured metal filled his senses.

Starke was lying on his back in a vast hall. Above him, sprawling across a cruel throne crafted of unearthly metal, loomed a hideous figure. Once, perhaps, it had been human but now it was twisted beyond recognition. Fleshy, hornlike flaps framed the pallid face, and plates of weird metal cased its body like armor.

"Old friend. It is so good to see you again. I have missed

you." The figure smiled, and Starke wished he'd been looking somewhere else. But he recognized the voice, altered though it was.

"V-v-v-v—" Starke sputtered as he struggled to his knees. "Vuel? Is that you?"

The horror chuckled. "There is no Vuel. That name died with a stolen destiny. Remember? The one you helped to steal?"

Starke cringed.

"Oh yes," said the other, and there was no smile now. "I have learned a lot since we parted ways. Your *friends* had much to tell me. I wish you could have been there."

"I really did mean to come! Something went wrong. I—"

"Be silent!" The ground beneath Starke heaved like a beast stirring from sleep, knocking him to his belly. "I am not interested in your story, fine though I am sure it is. You *will* pay proper respect.

"Do you think it was an easy thing to win an entire world? I suffered for eternities. I abandoned my flesh as well as my soul. To wrest the throne I had to challenge my predecessor. I prevailed, though at great cost. How do you like my insignia of office?

"Vuel is dead. I am Volrath. This world answers to me."

Starke trembled and pressed his face against the squirming floor. He dared not speak.

"Still, you have done me a favor, little man. Here is power beyond my dreaming. In that, at least, you did not lie.

"My destiny, however, is not *quite* complete. It seems your associates have need of certain ingredients, and they have charged me with obtaining them. I know that my loyal friend and mentor Starke will be eager to help me in this quest."

Starke raised eyes trembling from the floor. "Me?"

"Who else is so well qualified?" The words crushed Starke's face to the floor once more. Again he saw

Aniyeh's face, her eyes even more terrible than Volrath's. "You have proven yourself capable of anything."

So began a new cycle of servitude, discovery, and terror. Starke was at once the evincar's chamberlain and his whipping boy, and there was no way to tell which role he would fulfill at any given moment.

Volrath often sent Starke on trivial errands within the Stronghold, a place much like the memory of Aniyeh's death—at once frightening and horribly fascinating. Around every corner was something even more ugly than the last. Oversized insects prowled the vents. Clots of moggs and their taskmasters blocked most corridors. Sometimes a stronghold guard swept past, animate shadow in ornate armor. The oozing flowstone constantly altered the pathways, so that no landmarks remained for long.

But these expeditions, unnerving though they were, caused Starke far less terror than the external tasks the evincar charged him with. Too often he was compelled to walk the stinking deck of *Predator* with its glowering commander and barbarian crew, raiding for treasure and experimental subjects, or pressing villagers into Volrath's service. He prayed Takara hadn't seen him when the ship lowered over Khorin's sky.

Worse yet, sometimes he was sent out of Rath again in search of Gerrard or clues to the Legacy. There was no satisfying Volrath; he was suspicious and impatient, and even when Starke brought him the commanded prizes, they were never quite what he wanted. Volrath found fault in everything Starke did.

There was no chance to escape this time. Despite Starke's efforts, Volrath had found his dear Takara. Now she was trapped in the evincar's dungeons—the final indignity, the end of every bargain.

* * * * *

In his cabin, Starke began to shake, quietly at first and then with increasing force. He clutched his head as the painful memories swooped about him.

Starke had always considered himself a pragmatist. All he'd ever wanted was to make the best deal, pocket his profit, and stay out of untidy moral issues. He'd had a commission, and he'd fulfilled it.

And when the situation changed, Starke had offered another deal: Sisay as bait to bring Volrath's enemy to him, in exchange for Takara. Starke had kept his side of the bargain, though with every moment on board ship he dreaded the truth's escape.

And still Volrath kept Takara in his dungeons, forcing Starke to perform yet another task for him, and another, and another. Clearly he would never release her. One bad bargain deserves another, Starke mused darkly, then started as he remembered the Oracle's cryptic words.

New horror woke at the throbbing pain in Starke's shoulder where that beast had bitten. He knew there had been no metal ones among the slivers when he had encountered them, but now these constructs were part of the hive. It was unnerving how quickly and easily Volrath had infiltrated their population to exert his own influence over them. By doing so, he was privy to their shared thoughts.

And now the hive knew Starke was here with Gerrard.

Volrath was becoming something much bigger than Starke had expected, perhaps bigger even than his dark masters had planned. Starke trembled at the thought of their reaction. No doubt he would be blamed for Volrath's designs.

Perhaps, if Gerrard retrieved this Legacy, he could defeat Volrath and his overlords. At least with him Starke stood a chance of getting out of this in one piece, and maybe even rescuing Takara, too.

But now Volrath knew he was coming. His daughter

might be the price for escape. Could Starke pay it? Turning against him meant turning against *them*, and their fury at betrayal would be immense. He moaned at the impossible choice, but he knew which way he would decide in the end.

Starke chose.

Here ends the Tale of Starke

A Dark Room

"So what happened to Ertai at the portal while the others were traveling to the Stronghold? Did he just wait there for them?"

"No, not precisely." The librarian gave a knowing smile. "Waiting patiently for anything was not really Ertai's strong point.

"As you've heard, Orim the healer was able to read the ancient script that was carved on the archway above the portal. It explained how the portal might be opened, but Orim pointed out to Gerrard and Ertai, who crowded close behind her, that activating it would take some time, and, once open, it would not stay so for long.

"Ertai volunteered to stay at the portal and work the necessary magic, and Gerrard hastily agreed. He and Orim reboarded *Weatherlight*, and the ship disappeared into the blackness of the canyon."

The master stroked his chin absently. "It's hard to say precisely what happened next at the portal. It seems clear that while Ertai was there, someone appeared to him."

"Who, master? Who else was in such a barren place? Surely not the elves."

"No. A humanoid named Lyna. She evidently told him she was a Soltari, a race of people pulled through the portal into Rath years before, together with their enemies the Dauthi and another group caught in the conflict, the Thalakos. These peoples, she told the young wizard, were unable to react with the real world. Rather, they existed in it as shadows. In this form, they continued their war on one another as ghosts upon the Field of Souls."

Ilcaster tapped his chin thoughtfully, unconciously imitating the librarian. "An eternal war of ghosts. It sounds like a fairy tale."

"It does a bit," agreed his master. "But for the Soltari it was all too real—a neverending torment. In the presence of *Weatherlight* and her crew, she saw the salvation of her people.

"It would seem she and Ertai struck a bargain: she and the Soltari would help him to open the portal if he would agree to let them pass through it. She told him other things about Rath, but her words were cryptic and riddling, and when Ertai impatiently asked her to explain herself so that a normal person could understand, she was evidently unable to do so."

Ilcaster paused in his sorting through the papers. They were neatly stacked in heaps before him, and he picked up a roll of twine to begin bundling them. "Master . . ."

"What is it, boy?"

"Why do you say, 'evidently' and 'seemed'? Don't we know what happened from Ertai's account?"

"Ertai didn't leave an account of this part of the voyage."

"Why not?"

"All in good time, boy. Not so impatient! Hurry, hurry, that's all you young folk do. Just take my word for it, that while Ertai was at the portal talking to Lyna, *Weatherlight* had entered a long tunnel leading to the Stronghold, Volrath's fortress, set in the middle of a hollow mountain."

Ilcaster shuddered. "The Stronghold sounds like a horrible place."

The master grunted. "Yes, it was. You can imagine any place that held such a being as Volrath would be."

"I don't completely understand, Master. What exactly did the Stronghold look like?"

The librarian fumbled among the papers remaining in the chest and finally pulled forth a crumpled and grubby parchment. "Here's a drawing that Orim made of the Stronghold. It might not be entirely accurate, though. Remember, the crew only saw parts of the whole thing."

Ilcaster bent eagerly over the document, his eyes straining in the faint candlelight.

"I think I see. Here's the mountain, and here's the Stronghold, right inside it. What's that below it, though?"

"A city."

Ilcaster's mouth formed a small O. "The mountain was big enough to fit a whole city inside it?"

"That it was indeed, boy. The mountain of Volrath's Stronghold was three miles high. The Stronghold itself was a mile and a half in height. The cone of the mountain touched the sky."

Ilcaster was plainly more impressed with this detail than with anything thus far in his master's story. "Who would build such a thing?" he finally asked. "Was it Volrath?"

The librarian shook his head. "No, in fact not even Volrath had the power to create such a vast construct. Where it came from none have ever said. It was mighty beyond human conception—that much is sure."

"And now *Weatherlight* was on its way to that place?"

The master nodded. Yes. You see they had to approach it down this long passageway to avoid being seen.

"But master, what's this mean: Furnace of Rath."

The white-haired man took the document from the boy and caressed the paper thoughtfully, his eyes far away.

"Orim's account is not entirely clear. She writes of traveling through twisting tunnels of rock, barely large enough for the ship to edge its way along. She says they emerged above a place where geysers of flame spewed into the sky, and lightning flashed from above and below, filling the cavern with fire and light. Then she mentions traveling near a place of blackened oil, where skeletal hands clawed at *Weatherlight*'s hull." The old man worked his lips in and out in thought. "Perhaps that place of flames was the Furnace of Rath. This second place . . . I'm not sure. Maybe . . ."

There was a pause, and then Ilcaster said gently, "Go on, master?"

"There's a reference in another document . . . ." The librarian shuffled among the papers next to the chest. "Yes, here it is. The Death Pits. That must have been the place with the skeletons."

"But they got through," the boy said solemnly.

"Oh, yes. They got through. But their trials were not at an end."

III

STRONGHOLD

Hanna to get them out of that horrible place before the healer was fried to a crisp. Then the crew saw that she had wrenched a thin metal rod from the ship's rails. Hanna placed it on the bow of *Weatherlight*, where it drew the electrical bolts, sparing the crew—and her—from the threat of sparking death.

"The ship struggled up out of the Furnace through another maze of passages until at last it emerged over a dark, oily mass that swayed and bubbled."

"Was that the place you called the Death Pits?" Ilcaster shivered.

"Yes. There Volrath's servants brought those experiments of their master that had failed to meet his exacting requirements. The black ooze swayed and surged beneath the ship and then rose in a great wave, threatening to overwhelm *Weatherlight*. On the crest of the wave rode skeletons who leaped aboard the ship, grappling with the crew."

Ilcaster shook his head. "Out of the frying pan, into the fire," he said solemnly. "It just seems like every creature they met was worse than the last." "It seemed that way to the crew, I'm sure," agreed the librarian. "In any event, they panicked, rushing this way and that, tumbling down the hatches belowdecks. Squee, the goblin cabin boy, however, climbed up one of the masts."

"Don't tell me," said Ilcaster, "that's the end of Squee."

"Don't get ahead of me," cautioned the old man.

"Squee, as I say, climbed the mast. Gerrard, seeing the little goblin in danger, went after him. The skeletons swiped at the captain, but Squee, who clutched the Salvation Sphere, an artifact for which he'd developed a peculiar attachment, accidentally activated it. Its gentle glow suffused both Squee and Gerrard, and the skeleton attacking them hesitated and turned away. Evidently the Sphere could stop the skeletons. The other creatures gave way before Gerrard as he carried Squee, who carried the Sphere, and the ship moved quickly away from this dangerous place."

Ilcaster breathed a sigh of relief and settled once more at the librarian's feet. From beyond the walls, came a new wave of rain and hail. It shrieked and groaned, as if the heavens themselves were being tortured. But neither the boy nor the man paid any heed to it.

"With the Death Pits behind them, the crew brought *Weatherlight* to the Stronghold itself. For long minutes that seemed to stretch into hours, Hanna, standing at the wheel, searched for a sheltered spot on the lower part of the hulking menace in which to dock the ship. At last she drew up alongside a tiny balcony. Beyond it, a dark entryway gaped in shadow.

"Just as the ship drew up to the balcony, a guard emerged from the door. His mouth opened to cry a warning, and instinctively he stepped back."

"What happened?" The boy was open-mouthed.

"Mirri the cat warrior leapt from the ship's side and smothered the guard in a sudden flash of claws and fur. The guard was dead before he knew what had struck him."

"I'd love to have seen Mirri," the boy murmured. "Are there any pictures of her?"

"One. Here." The librarian opened a raggedly bound manuscript.

The boy stared thoughtfully. "Somehow I thought she'd look fiercer, more warlike."

"Don't underestimate her. From all accounts, she was a superb fighter. Gerrard make it very clear in his notes that Mirri was more than able to take care of herself."

The boy nodded. "So she killed the guard. What did they do next?"

"Gerrard, Starke, and Crovax joined her on the balcony. Turning, Gerrard told Hanna that if anything happened, they'd rendevous at the Gardens."

"Gardens? You mean the Stronghold actually had Gardens?"

"Yes, but far above the place where *Weatherlight* was docked. Starke gave hasty directions to Hanna on how to find them, and then the rescue party stole into the Stronghold."

Ilcaster shivered. "I'm glad I wasn't there. I'd have been too scared to go with them."

"Don't be too sure of that, my boy." The librarian looked at him. "Heroes can come from the most unlikely material and in the most unlikely places.

"No sooner had they entered the fortress than they encountered a beast, its limbs twisted and misshapen. Crovax pursued it, sword drawn, and the others followed the passage as it twisted and turned deeper and deeper into the Stronghold. After what must have seemed hours to them, Gerrard, Starke, and Mirri burst into an open space, just in time to see Crovax standing over the fallen body of the creature. He was hacking at it, slashing its body to pieces, though it was already dead. When Gerrard remonstrated him the noble replied, 'The Legacy may be your destiny, Gerrard, but Selenia is mine.' "

Ilcaster shook his head as if trying to clear it. "That's an odd thing to say. What did he mean?"

"You'll see.

"Gerrard and the others looked about the room in which they found themselves. It was a massive chamber ringed with seats around a central command table. On top of the table was a three-dimensional map that Gerrard, with his years of traveling, recognized immediately as Dominaria."

"Dominaria? Really?" the boy asked. "But why was Volrath interested in Dominaria? Did he have some plan to . . . ?" The lad's voice faded slowly as the implication of what he was about to blurt hit home.

The old man looked at him soberly and then continued. "Gerrard, of course, didn't know anything about it, but from the map he realized something of what Volrath was intending. He manipulated the figures of it, including a tiny model of *Predator*. He saw a dark blanket spread across Benalia in the wake of Greven's ship. And in that moment he wondered if he and the Legacy were all that stood between Dominaria and an eternal darkness."

The librarian walked to the window and looked out at the storm, then resumed his tale.

"Gerrard and the others left the map room and climbed through the maze of passages winding through the Stronghold. Higher and higher they ascended, until *Weatherlight* must have been far below them. Still they remained undetected, and still they searched for their companions. And then, at last, they found them."

Karn's Tale

J. Robert King

Karn stood in a dark, hot cell. His massive arms hung dejectedly at his sides. His silver bulk was statue-still. Voluntary deactivation. It was his last refuge when the chaos around him or within him grew overwhelming. In such times of trouble, he would not act, but simply stand and wait.

The chaos around him now was terrible. *Weatherlight* had been crippled by *Predator*, Gerrard had fallen overboard during the fighting, Karn had accidentally slain a mogg goblin before surrendering, and Tahngarth had boarded Greven *il*-Vec's ship to save Karn, only to become a fellow prisoner within the Stronghold. He was even now shackled to the wall of an adjacent cell. The sound of his struggles stabbed beneath Karn's stout cell door.

And Tahngarth would die. There would be torture, of

course—Phyrexians thrived on torture—and after that, death. Flesh and blood captives did not last long among the Phyrexians. They were either executed or transformed—filled with metal studs, trussed up with spinal implants, warped into monstrosities. Phyrexians believed in the perfection of flesh through pain, turning muscle into metal, and when they were finished with Tahngarth, he would be dead or so changed he would wish he were dead.

But the chaos within Karn was even worse. He knew he was responsible for his friend's plight. Guilt. Shame. Regret. Rage. Hatred. Though outwardly Karn was motionless, inwardly, he boiled. Despair. Desperation. Bloodlust. Emotions churned chaotically through him, fighting to emerge. Every threat Tahngarth shouted at their captors, every sound of minotaur limbs thrashing against implacable shackles, fanned the firestorm in Karn.

But none of it boiled forth. Despite the tempest raging in him, Karn stood, inward chaos masked by outward calm. It was his final refuge. No matter how terrible the tempest within or without, he could always stand and wait.

Meanwhile, shackled in flowstone, Tahngarth still fought. That was the real difference between Karn and Tahngarth. Both were massive, powerful, physical creatures, unswervingly loyal to their masters, ravaged by inner storms of emotion. Karn's rage ended in paralysis, and Tahngarth's in—

"I'll kill you, Greven il-Vec!" seethed the minotaur between gasps of exertion. "I'll break loose and hunt you down and kill—" The threat ended in another roar of fury.

Karn's massive jaw ground slowly, and his fists clenched. Guilt. Shame. Regret. The chaos of emotion threatened to topple him. Twice before, violent passion had unbalanced him, and death had resulted. Now, honor and moral resolution bound him, held him firm—stronger shackles than any other. And he stood. It was his last refuge.

To stand.

* * * * *

He had been standing that way the night it all began, the night he had slain an innocent. It had been dark then, too, but it was a verdant darkness, a darkness filled with the sibilance of insects and growing things.

Karn did not breathe, but he wished he could. He wished to feel the vibrant heat of the foothills sliding into him, the warm balm of life. Instead, he stood, still and listening, among fat green stalks of bamboo that grew near the water hole. A gentle breeze stirred fronds and leaves. Vines buzzed with rows of cicadas. Beyond the lush greenery of the oasis, the desert brooded: arid, implacable, and deadly. But here was water, and life.

Overhead, Sidar Kondo's arboreal village glowed, bamboo windowsills warmed with oil lamps. Here and there, human voices sung lullabies or spoke quiet assurances to fretful children. Hushed laughter circled amid cycles of stories and platters of food. Bare feet padded quietly along bamboo walkways. Guards peered out into the lush night that surrounded Karn, watchful and contented.

Karn was a village guardian, too, though unlike the others, he remained on the oasis floor . . . and remained discontented. While sounds and smells of life breezed over and around him, a gale of emotions moved through him. Strange, wild, ever-changing, this storm of passions was as troubling as it was wonderful. One moment, his spirit would exult in the majestic symphony of tree frogs and songbirds all around, and the next, he would tremble with the thought that a snake might somehow slither past him and climb the bamboo stalks to the loft above, where Gerrard slept.

Karn thought then of the boy, sixteen years old, brown-haired, keen-eyed. His skin was as light and fragile as porcelain, unable to bear very long the direct sunlight that had so handsomely burnished the other villagers. The orphan Gerrard was out of place in other ways, too: a year younger than his stepbrother, Vuel; a bit too young to navigate the lofted courts of his stepfather; cut off from Sidar Kondo's succession; instrumental in Vuel's estrangement from the sidar; heir to a much-coveted magical treasure that Vuel had even now pillaged Gerrard was caught squarely between the peaceful grandeur of his stepfather's lands and the violent revolution his stepbrother was fomenting. The effect of Vuel's betrayal of the tribe had been to make Gerrard seem younger than he was, as if he sought to bury the memory of his once blood brother by reverting to the simpler days of childhood. Karn told himself that this stage couldn't last, but it had already lasted longer than he expected.

At every turn, danger awaited the boy, and that fact stirred a storm of worry in Karn. He felt a sudden stab of guilt that he was too heavy to ascend to the bamboo platform where Gerrard slept, beneath the green canopy of the frond roof and the spangled black vault of night. Guilt gave place next to pride, for Gerrard was among the smartest and strongest boys his age in the village, treated by the sidar as his own son. Next came regret as Karn thought again of the sidar's true son, Vuel, embittered and rebellious, declared foe of Kondo and Gerrard, alike. Then anger about the stolen pieces of Gerrard's Legacy. Into the midst of these emotions came sorrow. It took some moment before Karn recognized the source of this feeling—a soft sobbing sound from the sleeping platform above.

Craning backward, Karn looked up at the magically suspended loft and called out quietly, his voice rumbling in the verdant air, "Gerrard, what troubles you?"

A head appeared at the edge of the platform. Though shadowed and sleepy, the boy's eyes seemed to glow silver in the night. "Nothing," he said sullenly. His sleepy voice made him seem younger, almost a child. "I'll go back to sleep."

Karn stared, watching impassively until the face disappeared. "Goodnight, Gerrard."

The boy's voice came over the pallet's edge, "Nothing you would care about."

Karn gave a slow nod. "All right, then. Sleep well, Ger—"

"I mean," interrupted the boy, "you don't even care that already Vuel stole my Touchstone and some of the other stuff that's supposed to be mine. We were blood brothers, but he wasn't to touch those things unless I say so and you don't even care about that—"

Something lay behind the boy's words, something Karn did not quite understand, something from that dark land of emotion where Karn was only a fearful sojourner. "Your stepfather has sent warriors to bring back those pieces of your Legacy. I believe the warriors will succeed. I don't understand what you mean by saying I don't care."

Gerrard's head reappeared, and he was still talking, "They're part of you, after all, the pieces of my Legacy. You'd think maybe you'd miss them just a little bit since they're part of you like my lungs and liver are part of me, but I don't hear any complaining from you about it, let alone anything like if you cared what was happening."

The lung-liver comparison boggled Karn. "I do not respire air or metabolize lipids—"

"You didn't even notice when we were by the lake and the other boys were making fun of me and saying that my brother was off in Albiuto selling my Legacy to buy an army. One of them even said his brother had signed up, said he got a new lizard-skin vest and a knife. That was part of my Legacy, what that boy got—my Legacy and parts of your body is what he got, like it wasn't lizard skin but your own skin—or my own skin, since you don't even have skin. Doesn't that make you mad?"

It did. Anger set Karn's jaw on edge and made his joints stiff. Still, what use would such feelings serve? "Gerrard, you are sixteen years old, on the verge of manhood, so this complaining ill-beseems you. The warriors have gone to get your Legacy back—"

"In fact, the boy even said that his brother said that Vuel said that you'd be too scared to do anything about it. Vuel said you wouldn't even care, and even if you did care you wouldn't do anything about it because you wouldn't want to scratch your polish, that you were no more dangerous than a silver spoon that I was born with, and I'm starting to think maybe he was right. I mean, wasn't he right, after all?"

Wasn't he right after all? The words grated like a saw blade through Karn. His insides began to boil, and his vision narrowed to red tunnels. What good would such feelings of anger serve? None here, beneath a well-guarded arboreal village, but in Albiuto? In Albiuto, rage could do some real good.

Gerrard sighed gustily. "I should have known you wouldn't go. Serves me right for thinking you were more than a guardian, for thinking you were actually my friend."

That last comment hurt worst of all. Karn lowered his gaze from the sleeping platform and peered out through the dense black night. His metallic head ratcheted slowly about until his direction-sense homed in upon the exact position of Albiuto. It was higher in the mountains, some eight leagues distant. A shallow river, now dry until the desert rains came, a deep chasm, and the higher foothills lay between Karn and the town, which itself floated upon the surface of a shallow black mountain lake. But these obstacles were nothing. Karn's anger could sear away rivers and melt mountains. If he strode out steadily, he would reach the town a few hours before daylight. The red rage growing in him at last blossomed in the first step he took toward Albiuto.

A furtive shuffling sound announced Gerrard's surprise. "You're going? You're doing something about my Legacy?"

"I'm going," Karn said simply.

The boy's voice was excited now. "Don't worry about me. I'm safe here. Father has five guards working tonight."

Karn had, truth be told, quite forgotten his pledge to forever guard Gerrard, and that fact alone gave him a moment's hesitation. Never before had he abandoned his charge. Emotion was a strong thing, indeed, if it could blind him so fully to his duty. Still, the pause was only momentary; Karn had already given himself over to fury, and it was intoxicating. Besides, there were five other guards. The boy would be fine when the silver golem saw him again.

Karn's long strides carried him quickly from the village. The glowing windows retreated behind him in the trees until they seemed only distant fireflies. Beyond, the desert was darker, denser. Once the golem passed the boundaries of the oasis, the sounds of night animals faded, and he could hear nothing but the moan of the desert wind and the faint hissing of the sands. None of this mattered to Karn. His eyes could see in utter darkness, his silver skin was proof against rocks and snake bites, and he heard nothing but the loud buzz of anger in his head. He thought of Gerrard—fragile, besieged Gerrard—and the anger grew.

"He treats me as a friend," Karn muttered darkly to himself, "but what kind of friend am I?" Stoic, unimaginative, unimpassioned, slow, immense, and now uncaring. Perhaps this one night, this one decision, would change all of that, would prove something at least to Gerrard, and perhaps even to Karn as well. "I must earn his trust."

The forest fell away quickly to his relentless steps. The

riverbed was cool and stony after the heat of the sands. It crunched beneath his feet. The chasm beyond took one mighty leap to cross. Then, slowly, patiently, he rose higher into the mountains, where Vuel, his mercenary army, and pieces of Gerrard's Legacy awaited.

In time, ancient, rock-bound Lake Albiuto appeared ahead. At its center, arrayed in a glowing circle, was the town itself. Held atop the water by means of magic and pontoon alike, the town was anchored to shore by day, and to the center of the lake by night. Around the lake stretched a thin strip of greenery, leaves swaying gently in the wind. On one side of the city, numerous gangplanks of bamboo and reed were drawn up, and on the other, jutting docks were full of boats. Between the two were a collection of tall, improbable buildings, jumbled together on the vast floating quay. Leaning on each other, connected by a series of wood bridges and rope walkways, the houses and shops of Albiuto were tall, ornamented with bay windows, turrets, arches, and towers, all in wood and bamboo, thatch and reed. That night, the town glowed with festival fires, its walkways crowded with revelers in warriors' armor.

So, Vuel was mustering an army, and he had chosen a most defensible spot to do so. On that floating settlement, Vuel could safely gather thousands of warriors before marching. The town was safe from invasion by any but aquatic creatures or armies with boats . . . or silver golems that did not breathe.

Emerging from a brake of cane, Karn waded down into the black water of the placid lake. Cool silt rose around him, caking his legs and grinding in ankles and knees, but still he continued. Soon, water poured into the deep silver collar around his neck, and lapped at his jaw. He sensed, too, the empty inner cavities of his torso filling, the spaces that were supposed to hold the items of Gerrard's Legacy. Though cool liquid coursed into his innards and water closed over his head, Karn's anger felt hotter than ever. The ropes of seaweed that dragged past him as he descended into the murk only stoked the flames of fury. Vuel would pay not only for the injustice of taking his stepbrother's possessions and using them to buy an army, but also for the indignities suffered in recovering that Legacy.

The bed of the lake dropped away in lightless steppes to a bottom perhaps fifteen fathoms deep. The cold, muddy depths did not deter Karn. He could see past the blackness to the spot below where five gigantic anchors clutched the bottom. Tireless, Karn strode to the central one, grabbed hold of the massive chain that rose from it, and climbed.

Above, the festival lights in the center of the town made a gold and fervid glow in the water. Through the undulating surface, Karn caught glimpses of drumming hands and leering faces, lizard-skin vests and feather-festooned spears. There were cups of ale there, too, and roasting haunches of pork. It was quite a feast that Vuel threw for his men, the kind that precedes a great battle, and all of it bought by ransoming Gerrard's future.

Hand over hand, Karn pulled himself up through the turgid flood. He reached the bright-shining surface and hauled his streaming metal frame onto the wooden superstructure above. He found himself in the slanted hold where the anchor was kept when it was raised, and from that concealment, he peered over the capstan to survey the center square of Albiuto.

After the cold, muffled murk of the lake bed, the center of town was loud, hot, crowded, and bright. The settlement was the center of many caravan routes and was rich in commodities brought from faroff parts of Jamuraa. Soldiers milled about in laughing, arrogant clusters, their cups of ale so full they foamed down upon the planks at their feet. Torchlight glimmered from their dark faces and the irridescent scales of their lizard-skin coats. Here and there, jesters cavorted, entertaining the crowd by juggling torches and knives, singing songs, and exchanging items from their own many pockets with those of others'. Long, low benches—fat logs split down the center and laid out upon the deck—held steaming platters of pork and grilled leeks. Wagons laden with raw haunches of boar and bags of onions stood here and there about the square.

At the far end of the open space, a more orderly group of warriors clustered around a broad table where a map lay spread. Above it stood a lean, young figure, bare to the waist, his powerful physique glistening like carved onyx in the torchlight. He was poised on an upturned barrel, a cane of bamboo in one hand, with which he gestured imperiously at the map.

Despite the distance between them, Karn immediately knew this to be Vuel, rebel son of Sidar Kondo, and knew the map to be a schematic of his father's arboreal village. Karn tuned his ears to the exact timbre of Vuel's voice and heard the plans of war.

"There will be three main bridges from the ground to the treetops. Once they are cut, the villagers will be trapped. Then we set fires here, here, and here. The largest will be beneath the warriors' lodge. We'll roast them in there like grub worms"—harsh laughter interrupted this comment—"but I also plan a particularly fiery end for Father, here. There will be plenty of plunder, of course. Larders and strong-boxes, jewels . . . and our famed women. Bamboo-dwellers have strong hands and long legs, you'll find." More laughter. "While the rest of you are finding sport elsewhere, I'll be conducting a boar hunt of my own—chasing down a squealing little piglet that has the pretense of calling himself my brother. He'll be stuck more than once before the hunt is done."

Still streaming algid water and slimy muck, Karn rose from the anchor hold and strode wetly onto the deck, into the midst of the revelers. His mere presence ended the laughing and drinking. Warriors fell back, dropping cups of ale and lifting swords and spears. Karn pushed past them with no more interest or concern than he had shown in pushing past brakes of cane and bamboo. Those few with nerve enough to take a swing at the massive man of silver found their swords jangling in nerveless hands, their spear hafts crunched in the golem's grip.

Ahead, Vuel stopped his battle planning and raised his eyes. A broad smile broke out upon his face, and he gestured widely with his arms. He shouted over the muttering soldiers, "Ah, if it's not my stepbrother's silver spoon, come to join in the fun. We could use a silver golem—if you'll fight. So, you want to kill the bastard as much as I do, eh?"

Karn's metallic face was incapable of scowling, but he suspected the fire in his belly shone bright in his eyes. "I am not here to join you. I am here to warn you. Anyone intent on harming Gerrard will have to deal with me, first."

Catching the flippant spirit of their leader, the warriors around Vuel let out a moan of feigned dread.

Vuel jumped from the barrel head and, swaggering, approached the silver golem. "A terrible threat, indeed. These warriors have battled goblin armies and giant serpents, but an encounter with you? All that sermonizing and angst—every last fighter would be bored to death!" The hilarity that followed this comment was exaggerated, perhaps as much from fear as from derision.

But Karn could not discern such subtle differences, and his fury mounted. Gigantic hands moved with sudden, fierce speed. Karn grabbed Vuel by the torso and hoisted him into the air. The ring of soldiers around the two widened, and those in front lifted weapons high.

Vuel gasped, true dread blossoming in his eyes, and his face reddened with the pressure of blood filling it.

Karn hissed at him, "Your stepbrother is destined for greatness. He is the heir to the Legacy. He is the one child born to defend this world. He was forged of flesh as I was forged of silver, and each of us bear within the hope of generations."

Mastering his terror, the young rebel spat on the silver golem's face. "What good is my brother's Legacy?" he cried. "Greatness cannot be handed to a man. He will denigrate and despise it. Nor can greatness be stolen from a man who truly possesses it. I am the one destined for greatness, not that little piglet. I have taken Gerrard's precious Legacy, what was never truly his, and with it, I have raised this army. And now, I will take what belongs to my Father, and soon what belongs to all the world."

Karn growled. "I have come to take back the Legacy."

"No," replied Vuel, his vicious smile returning, "you have come to fall into the trap I set for you. You have come because I wanted another piece of the Legacy—you."

A wave of dread moved through Karn, but his hold on the rebel only grew stronger. "I will kill you if I must."

Vuel shook his head, eyes creased in pain. "You wouldn't kill the sidar's son. You couldn't bear to see the look in Kondo's eyes."

"I will kill you unless I get the Legacy."

"I am not afraid of death."

With slow deliberation, Karn squeezed his hands together. "So be it."

Vuel let out a blast of breath, lungs emptied by the massive pressure. Karn curiously felt the man's flesh slithering away beneath his touch. Humans were such fragile things, soft as soap bubbles. He gazed into the man's bulging eyes. Vuel's face clenched in a knot of pain, and his mouth opened to shriek, but there was no air to bear the sound. In the sudden silence came the ominous pop of ribs.

The warriors around rushed forward en mass, pummeling the silver giant with swords, clubs, spears, whatever came to hand. Karn's own frame rang with the assaults, mournful bell-tones from the empty chambers where the Legacy once resided. But none of the pummeling weapons left even the slightest scar on him.

"Tell me where the rest of the pieces are, or die," Karn said, and he marveled at the cruel glee in his own voice.

Vuel resisted for one more moment before his hands waved frantically about him. Karn released the pressure, and the warriors fell back. Weak as a kitten, Vuel hung in the silver golem's slackened grip. He panted brokenly, and his sides trembled in pain.

"Where are they?" Karn demanded.

Head drooping in surrender, Vuel gasped out, "Bring out . . . the man."

The crowd of warriors parted, some moving purposefully toward a locked, bolted, and guarded doorway. The building was perhaps the most solid one in the town, constructed of vast timbers and reinforced with iron. A prison. As the guards worked at unlocking and opening the front double doors, a murmur of dissatisfaction and incredulity moved among the gathered warriors.

"You won't be able to . . . to get them that easily, though," rasped Vuel. "I hid them . . . well."

A manacled man emerged from the prison, flanked by four guards. The man was huge, a head taller and twice as wide as the rest of the crowd. His figure was enormous and muscled, his eyes proud as he shuffled forward in rags and chains, steadying himself on the running board of a laden wagon.

"The Legacy is a valuable treasure. . . . Not something to be left . . . lying about," Vuel continued. "I was so impressed by your personal guardianship that . . . I came up with another guardian. I found . . . the biggest villager in Albiuto—turned out to be the blacksmith—and cut him open . . . stashed your treasures inside."

Only then did Karn notice the long, crude vertical slice up the blacksmith's distended belly. The skin had been stretched to accommodate the stolen pieces of the Legacy, and then thick leather thongs had laced the man's muscles back together.

"I don't know his real name," Vuel continued. The smile had returned to his wicked features. "I'm not interested in such trifles. To me, he is simply Karn—my vessel for the Legacy. Of course, now that I have captured you, I don't need him anymore. One Karn will have to die."

Stunned, Karn dropped the grinning rebel to the planks and waded through the crowd toward the man with the butchered belly. Reaching the wagon beside which the blacksmith stood, Karn extended a silver hand and said in a voice choked with pity, "Come with me."

Vuel staggered after. "Oh, he can't come with you. To make room for all that stuff, we had to pull out his own innards. He is kept alive only by the workings of my archmage, to whom a number of the Legacy artifacts are promised when I am through with them. If you take my Karn away from me, he'll die."

Overcome, the silver golem dropped to his knees before the man, and gazed into his eyes. Unblinking, the blacksmith returned this look, courage and sorrow written across his tormented features.

"So, you see," came the harping voice of Vuel, "the only way you and your precious Gerrard can have the Legacy back is if you kill this man to get it. And, if you wouldn't kill me, the patricidal son of the sidar, how would you ever kill an innocent man?"

Shame, dread, and fury warred within Karn. He had been a fool. He had fallen into Vuel's trap. His emotions had not been his own to command, but marionette strings pulled by Vuel. He was nothing more than a silver spoon, as Vuel had said, nothing but a pretty tool to be traded and used. Now, to all the other emotions Karn felt, there was also self-loathing, utter despair.

And Vuel was laughing. The rebel clutched his aching

chest as he laughed, but he laughed all the same. The warriors around him added their guffaws, and merriment spread mockingly through the crowd. Soon, the whole square broke forth in peals of laughter, the whole square except the two figures at its center. Karn and his namesake regarded each other.

Holding his sewn-up belly, the blacksmith spoke, softly and evenly. "I am dead one way or another. I cannot blame you if you reach within me and draw forth what is yours. Vuel has killed me, not you."

Over the roaring crowd, Vuel shouted, "Behold, the helpless guardian! Behold, the silver golem with a heart of glass and a gut of paper. Fear him. Tremble before him!"

The blacksmith was still speaking, "One way or another, you must act, Karn. Listen to your fear and flee, or listen to your fury and take what is yours. Return to Gerrard and guard him from Vuel, or strike me down and, with the treasures once again in your grasp, strike down Vuel once and for all."

"—Creatures like this one, hulking powerful creatures that are too fearful of their own might to use it, are the creatures that will roll over before us and grant us the world—"

"You must act, Karn. You must act."

Karn crumpled slightly forward. Vuel was right. He couldn't kill this man. He couldn't kill even these hyenas. In rage, Karn reared his head back, howled, and flung out a massive arm. His fist struck the food-laden wagon. It lurched up into the air. Raw haunches of pork tumbled up. Onions pelted down. Wheels turned in languid suspension above the ground. Soldiers scattered, and with a great crunching boom, the wagon smashed onto the quay. Its profound impact was followed by shocked silence from the warriors.

"Behold—" crowed Vuel viciously, "the guardian has slain someone at last!"

Karn looked. There, jutting from beneath the wagon's ruined bulk, were the lifeless legs of a small village boy.

"Enough!" shrieked the blacksmith. He reached with manacled hands, dug fingers into his own flesh, and ripped wide the wound. "Here is your Legacy!" Out tumbled the glistening items.

Dumbfounded, Karn caught them one by one in his imploring hands. Even as the blacksmith crumpled, dead, beside him, Karn saw that he held not just the items of the Legacy, but also a great, wet gem. The Touchstone, one of the few magical devices with the power to shut him down. And this one worked on contact.

The rage was suddenly gone. Even the fear. Even the despair. Karn was shutting down. Desire was draining away. Sensation followed quickly after. Vuel's mocking laughter dissolved into silence. Karn was defeated. He was deactivating.

In one final exertion of will, Karn clutched the grisly Touchstone tighter, irretrievable, within his silver grip. Warriors rushed him as they saw what he did, their hands clawing at his implacable fist, but they were too late. Already, he was as still and dead as stone.

The rest of that night—the rest of the next decade—he experienced in fleeting, fragmentary impressions. The world moves all too quickly when one is a statue.

Karn felt Vuel prying futilely at his hands of silver.

Karn saw warriors standing in dejection and defeat.

Karn glimpsed fires—torches—born by villagers, and oars and gaff hooks; shouts and splashing waters.

Vuel and his mercenaries were driven off the docks into the lake.

The slain figure of the blacksmith was born away.

Daylight came, and darkness after that, and daylight again.

The smith was brought back, this time within a great sepulcher, and a shrine was made in his honor at the foot of the silver golem statue. They were inseparable then, the metal Karn and the fleshly Karn, each in his time a bearer of the Legacy, each emptied now of what had once made him great. It was in gazing at that sarcophagus that Karn made his pacifistic vow, never again to fight or slay. Perhaps it was only the conviction of a moment, but as the sun circled above, the thought became cemented into an eternal vow.

And Karn stood. It was his final refuge.

At first, the townsfolk remembered him as the strange silver man who had come to rally the people of Albiuto and drive out the army of Vuel. Later, they remembered him to be a mere statue of that man. Last of all, he became only a public perch for cowbirds and swallows.

To be deactivated so long grieved Karn, of course. He agonized over the fate of Gerrard. Vuel's attack on his father's village must have been somewhat successful. Neither Gerrard nor Kondo nor any of their warriors had come seeking Karn. Perhaps they were all dead. But Vuel's success could not have been complete, either, since he himself had never returned. All Karn was left with, then, was worry and days. It became the pattern for his life, a tempest of emotion wrapped in a cold, still shell.

At least, deactivated, he could not kill again.

Tarnish and bird droppings and various substances conveyed upon the questing fingers of children conspired to make Karn almost unrecognizable by the time he was at last discovered. Even then, it was not Gerrard, or Kondo, or even Vuel that strolled into the public square and, arms clasped, surveyed the immoble silver golem. It was Sisay, captain of *Weatherlight*, a ship that was one more piece of Gerrard's lost Legacy.

She bought the shabby old statue and hauled it into the cargo hold. Still, she could not awaken the slumbering giant, who held the Touchstone in his grasp. So, Karn had been rescued from a sunlit public square only to stand, immobile, within a dark, wooden hold. There he remained, outwardly as still as a statue but inwardly ravaged by sorrow, guilt, anger, dread, and rage.

At long last into that storm of emotion came a new impulse—joy. It came at the touch of a crew member, a man in a white shirt, brown waistcoat, and black pants. The man had dark hair and a neatly trimmed beard. Something like mirth danced in his sharp eyes as he scrubbed the grime away from the golem.

"Hello, Karn. Remember me?" he asked, blowing a stream of dust from the silver collar. "I'm the kid that got you into all of this." The man placed a hand on the Touchstone. It shimmered, huge in the lantern light of the hold. Gerrard, trained in magic by the maro-sorcerer Multani, put forward what power he possessed, focusing on the Touchstone, knowing the trick of the thing, positioning it to reactivate the golem.

Metal shuddered as life surged back in. Joints creaked and limbs moved, trailing great curtains of grit.

"Wake up. I've come back to get you out."

"Gerrard," Karn said. His voice sounded metallic and hollow after so many years of silence, but there was a world of feeling in that one word. "*I'm* supposed to rescue *you.*"

"Yes, my friend, but sometimes flesh is stronger than metal."

* * * * *

"Wake up. I've come to get you out." It was not Gerrard who spoke this time, but a Phyrexian guard, a creature whose flesh was stretched and hypertropic beneath webworks of steel and bone.

Karn shifted, his gaze swinging toward the hideous figure in the open doorway of his cell. The woman's bald skull terminated in a jag-tipped sagittal crest, and the base of her chin sported a bare jutting bone. Karn had seen this guard before, had seen her chin-horn strike daggerlike into Tahngarth as she escorted him to his cell. The edge of the mutated bone was still stained with the minotaur's blood.

"Where are we going?" Karn asked dully.

The woman's lips drew back from filed teeth, and an expression that could not be called a smile stretched her neck muscles like steel cables. "It's torture time."

After his long stillness, Karn's body felt profoundly heavy. With an effort of will, he took a step back and turned around. "I must request mercy for my comrade, the minotaur," Karn began, his metallic voice tremulous. "He is captive only because of my—"

"Too late," the guard said curtly. She gestured toward the corridor outside, where three more Phyrexians and a passel of shoving, chattering mogg goblins clustered. "We've already moved him. If you'd like to see him, to give him a word of encouragement. . . ."

"I would very much appreciate that."

"I'll take you past his torture cell . . . on the way to yours."

Karn moved out among the clutching goblins and wondered what other torments awaited. Watching his friend's suffering and death would be the worst torture Karn could think of, but Phyrexians were artists of pain, and their violent imaginations were boundless.

The group escorted Karn into a dank and tortuous tangle of passageways, as rank as the bowels of a leviathan. Karn reflected that this was, in fact, a kind of digestive system for the empire. Each cell along the twisted hall contained a creature that had been swallowed by the vast war machine, and thereafter subjected to knives, teeth, acids, and fire and slowly dissolved away, the components of his flesh and fragments of his mind and rags of his pain borne outward to nourish the ravenous Beast. The same end would come to Tahngarth, too. His body and soul would go to power the mustering monster of Phyrexia. His flesh would be food to them, his agony would be their wine.

The procession of goblins and Phyrexian guards came to a halt, and Karn drew himself from his reverie. The guard with the sagittal crest gestured to a stout, round door of flowstone, bolted tight to the curving walls. Crimson and hot, the door seemed a valve leading into another organ of the leviathan. The guard set her hand on a slide in the door and drew it back, careful to keep her eyes away from the corruscating orange light that stabbed out from the space. With the light came roars of agony and rage.

"Tahngarth," muttered Karn, a frisson of dread moving through him.

The guard grabbed Karn's hand and drew him toward the slot. "You had something to tell your friend?"

Karn leaned inward. The light that glowed across his eyes seared like flame.

The chamber within seemed a smooth-walled, high-ceilinged oven. It was bathed in a fiery glow that originated from a single, dancing beam of light that stabbed down from the ceiling. Wherever the ray passed, it blistered the flowstone floors and walls.

Tahngarth fled that stabbing light. He leapt up a sloping wall to escape its stabbing ray. The beam swept just beneath his hooves, melting and scarring the flowstone. Tahngarth slid back to the floor, gathered his feet beneath him, and dived from the returning shaft. It struck him even so, in a diagonal line from hip to shoulder. The flesh caught in the wake of the beam mounded and roiled. Tawny fur turned white.

Tahngarth released a roar of anguish and scrambled away from the beam. He fetched up against the opposite wall and panted raggedly, his eyes glowing as he watched the beam sweep once again toward him. Launching himself along one side of the chamber, he struggled to skate past the ray, but it veered and lashed across his face. His horns, once thin and straight, began to thicken and twist. Reddish-brown eyes suddenly glowed yellow, like a pair of candle flames.

Blinded, Tahngarth clutched his face and crumpled, his body bucking involuntarily. Another furious shriek erupted from him.

Karn was shrieking too. He realized it only when the guards, all three, shoved him back from the doorway. He had felt each stabbing pass of that mutagenic ray as though it had struck his own body. He had twitched and swayed with each dodge and jump the minotaur took. He had screamed with every scream of Tahngarth.

Guilt. Rage. Shame. Hatred. Fury . . .

Karn's arms trembled, aching to crush the goblins around him as if they were grapes, to paint the walls with the blood of the Phyrexian guards, to smash down that door and free Tahngarth. Yes, he would do it. The storm of desperation mounted within him. Yes, he would kill them, and then he and Tahngarth would flee through the citadel, side by side, metal and machine, slaying whatever got in their way. They would leave a trail of bodies and blood. They would die, yes, but die fighting.

Karn's silver hands drew into fists, and he swooned, hungry for blood.

"I cannot blame you if you reach within me and draw forth what is yours."

The storm of hatred did not abate, but Karn pressed down upon it, sealing it away once again. He staggered, almost overcome, and turned to face the guard.

"Wh-what's happening? What are you d-doing to him?" Karn implored.

"Improving him," the guard replied vindictively. "He'll have to be considerably stronger, a bit more bloodthirsty, and a damned sight more submissive before he can be Greven *il*-Vec's second."

His second! Tahngarth's misery was only beginning. He

would not merely be turned into a hideous monster, but then also be suspended on strings, a puppet in the service of evil. It was Tahngarth's greatest fear, realized. Greven was doing to Tahngarth what Volrath had done to him.

"Your master's hatred must be great to do such a thing," Karn hissed.

"I'll pass along the compliment," the guard sneered. "Let's go."

As Karn pivoted to follow, a thunderous pounding came at the door.

Tahngarth's yellow eyes glowed feverishly on the other side, and wisps of acrid white smoke drifted up from his battered head. "Kill them, Karn! Kill them, and open this door!"

Gazing piteously back at his friend, Karn dropped his head in sorrow.

"Kill them! You must act, Karn! You must do something—" the shout dissolved into a shriek, and Tahngarth crumpled down, out of sight.

"I am sorry, my friend," Karn whispered. "Anger is fleeting; remorse is eternal."

One of the Phyrexian guards slid the slot closed, and the band moved their prisoner forward.

Karn shuffled along, devastated, his hide ringing hollowly with each step. He could not imagine greater torment than what he felt now. His vow of pacifism had not only brought about Tahngarth's capture, but had also made impossible his rescue. The minotaur would die, or he would be so altered he would wish he were dead.

What greater torment could await?

"Here is your cell," said the woman. She gestured toward an open doorway that led into a bare cube. There were no furnishings, no windows, no port in the ceiling for a mutagenic ray—only four red-glowing walls, a floor, and a ceiling. "Get in."

Karn gazed for one long moment at the blank space—

his solitary hint of defiance—and then moved quietly inward. His silver shoulders scraped the door frame as he pushed past. Mogg goblins clustered about his feet, intent on herding him within. The walls gave back the echo of Karn's ponderous tread as he marched to the center of the cell and stopped.

"Get in there!" shouted one of the guards, and three more moggs came skidding in among the others. Then, the door slammed and locked behind them, closing nearly twenty of the despicable beasts in with Karn. The slot in the door whispered open, and Karn pivoted to see who looked in.

"You should still be able to hear your friend's screams here," the woman said. A moment's pause confirmed the prediction.

Karn hunched down, miserable. "You torture him with action, and me with inaction. How fitting. You blaze away his body, and kill both of us in doing it. And you lock me away with these, these—" he gestured to the goblins climbing up his legs, gnawing on his fingers, fighting to scramble onto his shoulders "—reminders of the last creature I killed. You twist Tahngarth's body, and you twist my soul."

The guard seemed to shrug. "You could have stopped it. You could have killed us and stopped it. You could kill these moggs even now."

"I want to. Believe me, I do, but then you would surely have won," Karn said, patiently plucking away a goblin that had been playing his head like a drum. As Karn stared at the wriggling, cursing creature, the tempest of guilt and fury welled up in him again. "This way, I may be tortured, but I will not be damned. As long as I stand here and endure, I am still not yours."

"Oh, really?"

"Yes. I am very good at standing and waiting. I have stood and waited while the years crawled all over me, and

I can stand and wait again here, with these pests, too. I will not be goaded into violence. You cannot make me kill again."

"We'll see about that."

That was when the floor tilted, suddenly, violently. Karn was thrown off his feet amid a spinning cluster of goblins. They all simultaneously struck the tipped surface and slid quickly down to smash against one of the flow-stone walls. Even as Karn's body rang with the impact, goblin blood sprayed out from beneath him. The floor rose back to level, and Karn staggered up. Behind him, he left three broken bodies, crushed with the prints of his silver frame.

"Damn you," Karn growled as he stood, his feet slick with gore. It was as though the Phyrexians had read his mind. They had stolen away his last refuge against the chaos around and within him. Now he couldn't even stand. They had taken away his one salvation. Now, his very existence meant killing. "Damn you."

"We'll bring more moggs when you've gone through these. They breed like roaches. You'll probably go through a hundred or so a day." There was a vicious tightening of her eyes—that same non-smile—just before the slot slammed closed.

And the floor toppled again.

Here ends the Tale of Karn

A Dark Room

"Gods, that's horrible!" Ilcaster stared at the librarian, appalled, his mouth open. "What a fiendish torture. How long did it go on?"

"Long enough," replied the old man grimly. "Long enough to almost drive both Tahngarth and the golem mad. It was the clever cruelty of Volrath to find that element in both prisoners that would be the greatest torture to them: for Karn it was the denial of his pacifism, and for Tahngarth it was the destruction of his looks." He leaned forward and patted the boy's shoulder. "Never mind, lad. In time I promise you they were both rescued by Gerrard and his friends.

"And did they find her as well?" asked Ilcaster.

"Who?"

"Sisay, of course! After all, that's the person they came to Rath to find."

"Ah, yes. Well, as you've already seen, lad, the search was not simple. But yes, eventually they found her."

"Good. I was worried she'd be dead by the time they got to her. Or worse."

"No, Sisay was alive. But Gerrard was forced to wonder if finding her hadn't somehow been part of Volrath's plan.

"After they left the map room, Gerrard, Starke, Mirri, and Crovax continued on their way, climbing ever higher in the Stronghold. They found it increasingly necessary to cross bridges and walkways formed of flowstone. At last they came to a tower that Starke identified for them as the prison tower. There were no guards about it, but it could only be reached by a long, narrow flowstone bridge without rail. Below was only blackness; Gerrard knew that somewhere down there *Weatherlight* waited for him.

"Gerrard, ordering the others to stay behind a moment, set one cautious foot after another on the bridge. As he did so, ropes and tentacles of stone formed and flowed toward him, seeking to ensnare the intrepid adventurer.

"Hastily, Gerrard beat a retreat. He thought for a while, as his companions stood silent, near to their goal yet separated by an apparently unbridgeable gulf. Then, chuckling to himself, Gerrard disappeared back into the tower as the others stood wondering. He reappeared in a few minutes, bearing with him the body of the shapeshifting creature killed by Crovax. When he hurled it onto the bridge, the ropes and tentacles rushed at it, and as they were busy crushing it and pulling it to pieces, Gerrard and his friends quickly crossed to the tower.

"Within they quickly, and with little trouble, found the cell containing Karn—"

"Good!" interrupted Ilcaster. "So they stopped the torture?"

"Yes, of course. Those Moggs still alive within the cell fled shrieking into the darkness while Gerrard comforted his old friend.

"Farther down the same corridor, Gerrard found and freed Tahngarth, and though the minotaur was ashamed of his newly bulked and twisted body, he joined them in their search for Sisay, the final object of their quest.

"At length they came to a laboratory, clean, cold, and indifferent to their presence. There, at last, they saw the body of their long-sought captain, imprisoned within a strange glass cylinder. With some difficulty they freed her from the glass jail. She stared at them, seemingly unaware of their presence. Then Mirri, who was holding one of her arms, hissed in alarm."

"What was it?" cried the boy. "Was Volrath coming?"

The master shook his head. "No, something much worse. Before their horrified eyes, the body of Sisay swayed and changed into an armored guard."

Ilcaster brought his hand down on a small table, raising a cloud of brown dust from its surface that floated in the yellow candlelight. "Then it wasn't Sisay at all!"

"No," agreed the librarian. "Just one of Volrath's many tricks. The guard fled the laboratory, and the companions were left alone again.

"Now, bewildered, they agreed to Starke's suggestions to search for the Dream Halls. But since the way led back across the flowstone bridge they'd crossed earlier, Gerrard suggested they should seek a different path. And so they did."

Crovax's Tale

Kij Johnson

This is Crovax's tale, though he is not the one who tells it.

But there is no one else who will tell it, and so it is left to me, Orim, to make sense of what has happened to him. My people believe that each life is a tale, and further, that to tell the story of a life properly would take as long as the life itself. And so we do not often tell stories of this sort. And yet there are lives that should be recorded. Crovax's is one of them, though his tale is not finished yet.

Like all tales of this sort, the story is as much about me as about Crovax. For this I must crave the indulgence of my listener. Mine is an unimportant story. Listen and think only of Crovax and his guardian angel.

* * * * *

We came to Rath willingly but reluctantly, each of us for our own reason: rescue, loyalty, anger. I came because *Weatherlight* was my ship. Sisay captained it and then Gerrard; and Hanna understood the alien clockworks of the ship itself better than any of us. But a ship's heart is its people, and I was the one who kept them well and listened to their secret hurts when they felt inclined to speak of them.

Crovax came for the angel Selenia, walking already under a shadow I could not see. He held his secrets closer than a lover, but even he spoke sometimes, to me or to Gerrard. Selenia was a construct, a thing of raw mana and spells, created from an artifact to watch over his family. The brother had used some sort of artifact to craft her. When we found Crovax, the angel was long gone, perhaps captured by Volrath. In her absence, his family had been destroyed by Volrath's people. Perhaps revenge drove him to Rath, but strangely, he never spoke of this, only of Selenia, his guardian angel, trapped by Volrath for unknown reasons.

Rath was a horrifying place. I am used to the many forms life takes in our world, but Rath was horrible—a place where rock flowed like tortured boneless flesh, or heaved like a beached cuttlefish dragging itself back to water.

The sky was no infinite space of air and light over our heads; it was low and heavy, sullen blues and purples that heaved less like clouds than like restless magma. Having gotten to Rath, we were unsure exactly where to go next, and so *Weatherlight* drifted high over a strange choppy sea of purple-black waters, along a coastline shrouded in misshapen trees. I went below to my cabin. I had one small porthole, and my possessions, my journals and medical books: Rath would not seem so overwhelming there.

To distract myself, I read an old herbalist's manual I had acquired in Jamuraa, trying not to think about the gray-purple tone of the light that seeped in through the port-hole. From the corner of my eye, I caught a flicker of brown and white and black, of feathers and steel. I glanced up, but it was already gone. Odd, I thought. We had seen no birds or flying things in the hostile skies of Rath, and whatever it was I had seen did not linger in my memory as something easily dropped into a familiar category: bird or bat or drake or great insect. I frowned, trying to recon-struct what I had glimpsed.

The sudden cries on deck startled me. There was a tone of panic unusual for any regular maneuver. I hadn't even registered what was wrong when I heard a thundering, like cannons in a fight on the sea. There was a flash of indigo-white light past my porthole in the hull, and the scream-ing noise of an electrical bolt tearing the air. Both were gone before I had time to realize what they were and jump back. I dropped my manual and looked out the porthole. A ship, a flying ship like our own, swept at us from above and behind, like a drake driving an eagle to ground. But it did no such thing, just matched its pace to ours and settled overhead, so that I had to crane to see it through the port-hole, and then it was no more than a huge dark shape overhead, hiding the brooding sky from my view.

Weatherlight's movement stopped suddenly, as if it had snagged in a web. I fell to my hands and knees, then jumped up, grabbed my knife and slammed open my cabin door to pause for a moment in the passageway. One crew member—Csaba, hair still wet from washing and twisted into a dripping knot—ran toward the aft hatch, strapping her sword belt as she came.

"What's happening?" I asked, but she said nothing as she passed, only threw me the savage expectant smile of battle fever.

I turned to go to the infirmary. One cabin door was ajar, waving open and closed with the rocking of *Weatherlight*. It was Crovax's room, and from inside I heard a keening sound, like the cry of a tortured animal. With one foot, I shoved the door open, knife ready.

Crovax was there and the terrible hurt noise was coming from him. He clutched his head as if he had been stabbed there, and staggered across his room, slamming into furniture and walls as if he had not seen them. The only light in his cabin came from his porthole—the same bruised color that made me shiver.

"Crovax!" I cried and caught his hands. "You're wounded?"

With the shriek of a madman, he pulled free and hurled himself away, into another wall.

"Crovax!" I said more gently, fearing concussions, head injuries, damaged eyes. What pain could cause such a sound as this keening? I carefully touched his shoulder. "It's me, Orim. Let me see."

He seemed to calm then, and let me pull his hands away from his head. The keening quieted to a barely audible moaning, carried on each of his panting breaths.

Only then did I see his face. He was not injured, at least not by splinter or blade or any physical thing. But his expression was one of torment and betrayal and loss and horror. And, strangely, something else: love. It is the nature of a healer to view pain, even the pain that destroys souls, the pain of loss; but I have never seen such despair. This is not true. I have seen it once since. There will come a time for that in this telling, as well.

"What is it?" I whispered.

His voice was as raw as an infected bite. "I saw her. Selenia. The angel."

"She's here?" More screams aboveboard. I had to go, but I could not leave Crovax like this.

"She led them here. She—" His voice broke on a sob.

"What?" I said. There were noises in the hatchways now, but he continued as if he hadn't heard.

"This is Volrath's attack. She is Volrath's creature now."

His voice trailed into silence, but his lips formed another word. *Betrayed*.

He spoke as if watching his life's blood drip to the deck, but there was no wound. And others above decks *were* wounded, perhaps dying. The cabin door had swung shut, but I heard bare feet pattering along the passageway now. There were too many feet, and too small to be crew. His sword in its sheath hung over his cot. I snatched it down, unsheathed it and forced the dark-hilted blade into his hand. "Save your life, Crovax. And fight for us. We will talk later."

I pushed open the cabin door. Everything in Rath seems an oversized twisted version of something in Dominaria: the corridor seemed filled with goblins, but they were what Starke called moggs, oversized goblins ugly even by the low standards one brings to judging goblin appearance. They raced past, ignoring us. I led Crovax to the forward hatch. "Up!" I shouted at him. "Fight!" Obedient as a child in shock, he climbed and I followed him. I hoped the fighting would bring him back to himself.

I am no warrior. Others can tell the tale of the battle between *Weatherlight* and *Predator* better than I. My first and only impression was of total chaos. *Predator* hung over us, linked by scores of grappling hooks and lines. Moggs swarmed down the lines and across the deck. Several *Weatherlight* crew members were down. I cast a hasty ward over those crew members closest to me, and braced myself against the railing near Crovax. Though he held his sword at the ready, his dark face was blank, as if surprised by a stab wound.

My people were falling, slashed on knee or belly or chest by too many mogg blades. I tied tourniquets and held pressure bandages, and threw spell after spell at those I could not reach to help: even so I lost Vidats, and Ineka Termuelen and my countryman Ozel son of Suk, their lives slipping through my fingers, sand in the hot wind of Rath.

And still the moggs came. I wept with anger as they killed and killed again. I had to use my knife three times against moggs who attacked me. I hated the feeling, the slide of steel into flesh, the slight resistance of tendon or the sudden halt against bone, and the sickening feel and sound when I pulled the blade free. I hated it but I did it: if I did not stop these creatures, I would not be there to hold my wards or heal my people's wounds.

Predator fired on us again. My ward had been set, and it glowed in my mind's eye, but it was not enough. My hands trying to stop the bleeding from Bariel's severed arm, I closed my eyes and prayed.

There was the huge noise of *Weatherlight's* metal hull torn by the electrical attack. The ship shuddered and slewed to one side until it hung nearly sideways. Crew members slid along the vertical deck, catching whatever they could. I lost my grip on Bariel and felt myself falling. There was not even time to scream before I felt a warm arm tight around my waist. I opened my eyes. With one hand Crovax had caught me in the crook of his sword arm; the other clung to the railing. For an instant our faces were inches apart: his eyes no longer had their drowned look. *Weatherlight* righted herself and he released me. "Careful, healer," he said in his low voice. "They need you."

I started shaking. There was a shout from *Predator*, and the moggs returned to their ship, pouring from the hatches and swarming back up the ropes, loaded down with artifacts. One paused to swing his ragged blade at me but Crovax's sword skewered the mogg, and he vanished from my sight. The lines that had connected the two ships cast free; but Tahngarth hung from one, swinging wildly.

Even as I did what I could, I could not stop shaking. Crovax no longer looked numb, but his expression was more frightening, more horrible, than it had been, for now his eyes were the eyes of a damned man.

They need you, he had said. As if he were saying: but I will not.

* * * * *

We crashed in the Skyshroud, a forest of tall twisted trees and roots sunk deep in the ugly waters of the sea. The survivors came then, as they always do, those who could not walk carried by friends who left them in my infirmary and rushed back to their posts to do what they could to secure the ship and prepare for any attack that might come. There were not enough: some of the injured had fallen from *Weatherlight* when she had tipped to the side. But I cleaned and stitched shut ragged cuts and listened. The survivors struggled to make sense of what had been at the time no more (or less) than instinct and courage and fear. There was horror and the potent joy that comes from being alive when so many others are not. As I always do, I said the things that would help and comfort: time enough later to face the darker feelings, the shame and guilt that comes from survival.

When I had done what I could, I walked on deck for a moment, longing to stretch my muscles and ease my eyes—longing for fresh air. I had forgotten the heavy sky, so close overhead it seemed I could touch it.

Crovax stood by the rail, staring out at the trees that surrounded us. I think he had not moved since saving my life. I saw his profile only. The planes of his face caught the colors of Rath. One hand held his ribs absently like a man suffering from heartburn, but blood dripped between his long fingers.

"Crovax!" I said. "You're wounded."

He glanced down as if surprised. I pulled his hand from his side and showed it to him palm-up. He frowned when he saw his blood.

"When did this happen?" I asked. It had been some hours now.

He shrugged.

"Come to the infirmary. I will heal this."

"No," he said.

"Then I will look at it here," I said. He stared out at Rath, but did not try to stop me as I eased off his leather and scale mail and the black-and-red silk tunic beneath. A ragged gash as long as my thumb angled along his torso; fresh as it was, its edges were already puffy. "What did this?" I asked.

"A mogg."

"Then it's infected. Goblin blades are always filthy; I can't imagine the moggs are cleaner." I always carry a flat jar of salve tucked into my belt. I pulled it out, and scooped up some of the green ointment. It smelled fresh and sweet and sharp, of calendula and bite-weed, of bright meadows a long way from Rath. Perhaps the crisp scent of more familiar lands awakened Crovax from his trance. He began to speak as I smoothed the salve into his cut.

"Selenia." he swallowed. "I loved her and never wanted to be away from her. How could I not love her?" He said, and his eyes blazed at me, anger and anguish in equal measure. "She was my angel, *mine*. I should have given her to my brother to guard the family, but I kept her with me. My guardian angel." He laughed once, a single sharp noise like a crow when a hurled stone connects. "She watched well: no harm came to the family in the time she watched over us. But then she was gone. And I watched my family die, because she wasn't there. They blamed me for it."

I sat silently. The fire in his eyes dulled. "I loved her. We talked, we were friends. She had no memories, so I gave her mine. And then this."

The only sound was the air hushing past *Weatherlight's* hull: a sound so familiar to us that it was silence. I pulled a clean bandage from one of my pockets to tie over the wound.

"I had hoped—I did not want a guardian," he said finally. "Or not her. But she was lost to me. Stolen. But she is here!" He caught my hand as it finished tying, caught it between his blood-stained fingers, hard enough to hurt. I said nothing, only met his dark eyes as he looked down at me. "Can you understand? She was like light, like half my soul, guardian and companion and friend and true love. And she is here."

"Yes." I pulled my hand free.

And I did understand, though perhaps he did not yet.

* * * * *

We traveled across Rath, on our way to Volrath's stronghold. We had lost Tahngarth, dragged behind *Predator* and we did not know if he lived or died. I had not seen it, but Gerrard had fallen from *Weatherlight* during the battle with *Predator*; Hanna and Mirri retrieved him in the Skyshroud Forest, the interminable dark woods in which we crashed. We fought and then forged an alliance with the elves that lived there. The ship was damaged by the crash. We could still fly, but Hanna said the crystal that drove the ship would not be able to planeshift away from Rath. We took *Weatherlight* to a portal we had been told about, the only place that might permit us to escape. Ertai and I inspected the site, and he chose to remain there to open it for us. We sailed on through the Cinder Marsh, followed a plume of ash to the Furnaces of Rath. We were struck by an arc of lightning there. I fought to save the crew members injured by the explosion, but I lost them all. The Furnaces fought my healing spells, and when I tried to save Kadve, too injured to be removed from where she lay, creatures of shredding sinew and bone killed her and cornered us.

Crovax carried a strange rage inside him. When he fought (which was often, for Rath is a hard place), he fought as if for his soul. I said nothing of the angel, but there were occasions, weary moments of waiting between disasters, when he came to sit with me in the infirmary or on deck. In difficult times, I find it soothing to take bright-colored silks and spin them into threads as fine as spider web; perhaps he found watching it as calming, for he seemed to seek me out just to watch the whirling of my heavy silver drop spindle.

He never looked at me, but he would speak, confessing his secrets to the silver and silk as they spun. Sometimes he spoke of his estate, hidden in the shadowy swamps of Urborg: a proud but decaying place, haunted now by the spirits of his many ancestors who (he said) even in Rath whispered to him sometimes in the night, warning him of an undefined but horrible destiny.

He also spoke of his father and his brothers. There is a poetry style in my land, where only half the poem is written down and the reader must speak aloud the missing lines as she believes they should be. There is great skill to reading this poetry, just as there is in writing it. I listened to his words, and spoke in my mind the lines he withheld from me. His father was distant and cruel; as his family died, one by one, they blamed him for their destruction. There were other secrets in his family, and I could imagine some of them.

There were times he talked of the angel. He remembered her laugh, low and sweet as a bell, and her perfect face, wrinkled as she learned a game he tried to teach her. His face softened when he spoke of her. Perhaps he longed too much for her, or in the wrong way. Angels are made of magic and destiny, not flesh and blood.

He never asked about my life, my family or past, too trapped in the misery of his memories to think of another. I did not mind—my old master would say that a healer's strength is not in her mouth but in her ears. So I spun and I listened and gathered his tale to me, like the cold comfort of a thin blanket in a frozen time.

* * * * *

The Furnaces were a maze of stalactites and stalagmites that clung to the low stone ceiling and the rough stone floor. *Weatherlight* slid between great pillars as broad as we were long and fought whatever came to us. After a time, the ceiling began to lift and the rock shapes grew less common. The sky of Rath had seemed heavy, but now we knew what true weight was. Whatever I did—even in battle, when lives hung perilously on my actions—I could not escape the unimaginable weight of stone hanging overhead. At times it seemed to squeeze the air from my lungs. We all felt this, all but Crovax, whose life focused down to a single blinding point: his angel.

Even a league and more away, we could see Volrath's stronghold. The roof over our heads raised still more and showed us that we were in the heart of a great hollow mountain. Pale cold light sifted down from above to silhouette the vast mass of the stronghold. The crew clustered on deck, swords and cutlasses ready for whatever trouble might come. We drifted forward, but no enemy ship rose to greet us. No one seemed to see us at all. We ghosted closer, and closer.

The Stronghold loomed, a shape like claws and bones and teeth, like the standing tendons of someone pulled on the rack. Gerrard's face was pale but set. Others faced their fear in whatever way they could. But Crovax stood by the deck railing, his lips pulled back to expose his teeth. It might have been a smile.

The organic shapes began to make a little more sense. I recognized what might be walkways, and a bridge of spun stone that looked as fragile as a spider web. Closer, closer.

Hanging in the outrigging, Mirri saw the guard before any of us. We were bare yards from the Stronghold's side, looking for something we might tie to, a ledge or gangplank of some sort. Without warning, Mirri leapt across the space between *Weatherlight* and the Stronghold, sword pulled out, teeth bared in a nearly silent snarl. She landed on a narrow walkway—an arm's length from a startled guard. The guard died before he had time to cry out.

This was as good a place to land as any we'd seen. Hanna secured *Weatherlight*'s engines as Tice threw a rope across to Mirri. She tied off the ship, then leapt back. She showed her sharp-toothed smile to Gerrard. "Best thing to hear from a guard? Nothing."

Gerrard sighted along his sword blade, then slid it back into its sheath. "Now we go in. Starke, you're the only one who can lead us to Sisay."

The man flushed. "And my daughter. You won't forget my daughter."

"We won't forget her," Gerrard said gravely, showing considerable restraint, I thought. Gerrard did not like Starke much, I knew. "Mirri?"

She snorted, slapped her sheath. "Of course."

Crovax had not spoken to Gerrard lately. He had spoken to no one but me, really, but now he caught Gerrard's arm. "Take me," he said softly.

Gerrard nodded. "Four is good."

I stepped forward. "I also will go, Gerrard."

He laughed that sardonic laugh of his. "Bloodthirsty, Orim?"

I bit my lip. "What if someone is injured? Sisay, or you, or—"

"No, four is bad enough. Sorry, Orim, but you're no tracker. You would not get a thousand paces before you would hear some goblin screaming and run off to find out why."

I flushed. "Yes, but—"

"You have an infirmary full of people."

"Only three—" I began.

"No," he said, suddenly captain. "Orim, you remain here with the ship."

"I understand," I said, and stayed. I suppose it made sense. There were only four braving the Stronghold and over a score on the ship. But it was Gerrard and Mirri and Crovax leaving (and Starke). I was not happy with the decision.

* * * * *

They entered Volrath's Stronghold cautiously. Starke said he had been there before, and had warned them of certain predictable risks. He knew of mogg platoons pacing the Stronghold's corridors, and certain magical traps he knew of. Starke went first, beside Gerrard, with Mirri and Crovax close behind. The halls were irregularly shaped, as if they had grown from Rath's rock, and the torches that lit the corridors flickered in strange warm air currents, so that the walls and ceilings seemed to alter in the inconstant light. Sounds trickled down the halls, echoing until they were unrecognizable, even as voice or scream or clockwork.

They entered a large corridor, broad enough to walk four abreast, with a roof that soared into shadow far overhead. It seemed directed toward the Stronghold's core, and so they walked along it, checking each branching hallway. For the heart of an empire, the place seemed empty, despite the noises.

Mirri stopped suddenly. "Wait."

"What?" Starke said nervously, but she only gestured impatiently, ears swiveling and nose twitching.

"There." She pointed at an odd outcropping on the wall, pulling her sword. "There's a *thing* there."

The section of wall she had pointed out jumped forward. It was no wall, but a living creature. Its misshapen body might once have been that of a mogg or an elf, but its limbs seemed poorly attached and unmatched, like a child's bad drawing. It crouched on the ground, narrow unformed head lashing from side to side as it looked for an escape. Mirri darted past it, trapping it. When it tried to rush past, she slashed at it. "I don't think so."

It bared its ragged teeth and recoiled. Gerrard stepped closer, sword in his hand. "So what are you: animal, vegetable, or mineral?" he said in a conversational tone. The creature looked around again, then up, for the first time seeing the soaring ceiling.

Like paint in rain or clay under invisible hands, its body began shifting, to become a woman's slender torso, clad in the shadow of armor and silk. Limbs resolved themselves into arms with long-fingered hands and legs ending in slim booted feet. Flesh shifted: a face formed, that of a helmeted woman with cold pure features, eyebrows shaped like the twisting of a falcon's wing. And then came the wings themselves. Pulling from the creature's shoulders, perfect feathers made of layered flesh beginning to fill out shapes like the wings of birds—or angels.

"Selenia!" Crovax gasped.

"No," Gerrard said. "It's some sort of shapechanger. Perhaps we can—"

Gerrard never finished. With a howl of rage, Crovax hurled himself at the creature. She whirled, half-formed wings flaring.

His sword came down where she had been, but half-fledged, she leapt an incredible jump that took her over Mirri's shoulder and into the corridor beyond. Crovax knocked Mirri out of the way, and bolted after the shapechanger, bare sword in hand. Mirri, Gerrard, and Starke ran down the halls after them, but Crovax and the shapechanger easily outpaced them.

Crovax caught up to her in a huge room filled with seats like an amphitheater around a mysterious device. There were several doors out of the room, and this is what killed her. She paused to choose, and in that moment, Crovax threw himself at her. He caught her by one slender arm. She screamed wordlessly at him, and bared her teeth, clawing at his face. Teeth and nails began to lengthen, shaping themselves to a fiercer function. He slammed his fist into her changing face, and again. She clawed at him, but he caught her hand in his, and twisted her arm until he heard a cracking noise. He grabbed one strange flesh-feather wing in his hand, bracing his other hand against her shoulder. She screamed again. He bared his teeth as he ripped the wing from her body, black-red blood pumping into his face.

Gerrard and Mirri ran in to find him tearing the shapeshifter's limbs free. She still bore the angel's form, but she was melting as she died.

Crovax cursed as she died, slamming his fist into the remains of her face. "My family died! Where were you, when Volrath's people came to the estate, killed them, one by one? Here?"

There was no answer.

Gerrard and Mirri looked at one another in horror; it was Gerrard who at last approached Crovax where he knelt in the ruins of the shapeshifter. She was not much more than rags of flesh, smears of blood. The fist he kept pounding into her was hitting the floor now, splitting his knuckles so that his own red blood splashed over the thick darker blood of the creature. "Crovax," Gerrard said; then, when Crovax did not stop, more loudly. Gerrard laid a hand on Crovax's shoulder. He whirled, eyes drowned in madness, and raised a gore-smeared fist. Gerrard dropped back a step. "Crovax, come back to us."

The madness ebbed. Crovax blinked and shook his head, raised a hand as if to rub his face and stopped when he saw the mess. He stood quickly, looked down at what he had done.

"It looked like Selenia," he said, swallowing heavily

Gerrard shook his head. "It was a shapechanger. It saw her and took her form, that's all." Their voices dropped into the immense space without an echo, like a coin dropped into a bottomless well.

"It should not have taken her form." Crovax's hands were shaking now. He pressed them against his thighs, leaving glossy prints on his leggings.

"What happened, Crovax?" Gerrard gestured at the shapeshifter's remains. "You could have just grabbed it."

Crovax's voice caught as he tried to respond. He cleared his throat and tried again. "I had to kill it. It belongs to Volrath. It would have betrayed us."

"You didn't have to kill it like this."

"I saw her," Crovax said finally. "Selenia. When *Predator* attacked us, she was there."

Gerrard frowned. "I know. That doesn't explain this." He looked at Mirri, who shrugged and shook her head.

"She was there. I think she led them to us."

"Why?" Gerrard said. "I thought she was your guardian angel."

"I thought so, too," Crovax sobbed. "I thought she did not save my family because she was imprisoned in some way. But now—"

"Still," Gerrard said, "the shapechanger was not your angel."

Crovax said nothing. Mirri and Starke watched, silent.

Gerrard watched him for a long moment. "I don't think you're a good risk for this. You ran off without thinking about safety, and then—" he gestured to the wreckage on the room's floor. "We're still close to *Weatherlight*, Crovax. I want you to return there."

"No." Crovax frowned. "No, I can't. She's here, Gerrard. I have to find her."

"Why? So you can rip her to pieces, pull her wings off?" Gerrard took an impatient pace away and turned.

"No, we can't risk it."

Through clenched teeth, Crovax said, "No. The shapeshifter had no right to her form, that's all. You need me. Selenia was created to watch over my family; she is vulnerable only to the members of my family. Do you want to have her kill Mirri here? Maybe yourself?" Mirri opened her mouth to speak. Crovax continued, "I am the only one who can stop her. And I must."

Gerrard stroked his beard.

"Please let me find her," Crovax said, in a voice as raw as a wound. "The Legacy is your destiny, Gerrard, but Selenia is mine. Do not deny me this."

Gerrard tipped his head back and sighed deeply. "Very well. But control yourself, Crovax. The deeper into the Stronghold we get, the longer your walk back to the ship will be."

* * * * *

I was not there. I was at the ship, patient Orim, waiting and spinning and clearing the last crew members from my infirmary. But I know Crovax and Gerrard. These are the words they would have said, the gestures they would have made. No one knows Crovax better. He spoke to me when he spoke to no other, and I, trained to see illnesses of the soul as well as of the body, heard the things his words did not say.

* * * * *

The room they were in was vast, big enough to float *Weatherlight* in. The walls were green glass clinging like soap film between brassy supports, but even large as it was, it was dominated by the mechanism in its center. Strange mechanical jaws extended from ceiling and floor; suspended between them was a huge sphere, like a giant pearl in a deformed setting. Gerrard was the one who recognized it as a map of sorts, a spherical map of all of Dominaria—home. Mirri and Gerrard puzzled it out between them: Volrath was planning to invade us, and this was his guide. Starke contributed little, obsessed perhaps with rescuing his daughter. And Crovax said less, only wiped his hands on his leggings again and again, as if trying to remove the stains from them.

The four of them traveled through the mountain's heart. Many things happened, but though he was there they are not truly part of Crovax's story. They crawled through narrow passages, crept across arching bridges. They found Karn. His gentle nature had been ravaged by Volrath, who forced him to kill. They found Tahngarth, his form changed by Volrath's tortures. They found Sisay trapped in a crystal cylinder, but when they freed her she was just another shapechanger. Crovax did not fall into the killing frenzy again, but he was silent, grim-faced. I think he spent much of the time thinking about the angel.

They still searched for Sisay and the Legacy and Starke's daughter. Starke thought perhaps they were in Volrath's Dream Halls, and so he led them to yet another stone bridge.

Created of ragged stone that looked as though it had splashed and frozen in place, the bridge was a slender arch, without a railing. The crew members moved cautiously onto it, forced by its width into single file. Starke knew where they were going, so he was first, followed by Crovax, then Mirri, then Karn and Tahngarth silent and shaken from their tortures, and Gerrard at the rear. Only Crovax and Mirri had swords out; if Volrath's people saw them and chose to kill them, it would be a simple matter to destroy them from a distance, with arrows and crossbow bolts. What good would a sword do? And the path was narrow, except for Mirri (who had the perfect balance of her kind), and Crovax (too driven by his destiny to fall), everyone used both arms to balance themselves against the strange hot air currents that blasted them.

* * * * *

They were halfway across when the attack came, but it was not arrows. Buffeted by a sudden wind, Starke lost his balance and fell to one knee. The rest of the party paused for a moment, to let him catch his breath. They watched both ends of the bridge, looking for signs they had been detected.

The scream overhead took them all by surprise. It might have been a woman's voice raised in wordless pain, or it might have been a falcon's killing cry. It was neither and both—it was Selenia, the guardian angel.

She attacked from above, diving like a great hawk, dark wings spread wide. She held her sword in both hands over her head like a giant dagger ready to plunge down. Her pale face was beautiful in the way a well-made knife is beautiful, and colder than steel.

She aimed directly for Crovax. And Crovax, armed though he was, stood stunned and watched her drop toward him, like a rabbit under a raptor's claws.

Mirri snarled and jumped forward. From the end of the line, Gerrard shouted "No!" but Mirri was already in motion, sword arcing up to intersect the angel's downward sweep. Unable to get through the defense, the angel changed targets. Her blade ran with the reflected colors of Rath's skies as it sliced sideways. Mirri screamed as the blade connected. The cat warrior dropped her sword and fell to the bridge, hands pressed against a deep wound across the abdomen, from hipbone to hipbone. The angel fluttered back from the bridge, then ducked in again to kill Mirri.

But Crovax's sword stopped her this time. Steel against steel, angel in air and man braced on stone, they hung.

"Please don't do this," Crovax cried in a voice barely human.

"I must," she replied. Her voice was like a broken bell. Tears glittered in her eyes. With shrieking of steel, the swords slid apart. The angel's blade struck the stone of the bridge, and sparks showered down.

"How can you do this?" Crovax shrieked as he swung overhead at her. The angel danced backward on the air just out of reach before whirling forward again. The swords met over Crovax's head, crossed steel. Tears blinded him. "You were my angel, mine!"

"I wish you had not come to Rath," she said. The ice in her face seemed to melt, and she sobbed. "Why didn't you stay safe on Dominaria, safe at home?"

"'Safe?'" Crovax swung again. "You left us, and my family were killed. I am the last of my line. Where is the safety there?" He swung blindly, to keep her out of range until he dashed the tears from his eyes and could see again.

"Please don't make me do this," she cried. "I don't want to hurt you."

"And now you betray me." The final word ripped into an inarticulate roar, and he jumped forward at her, inches from plunging off the bridge's side.

"I had no choice!" Her sword flicked out and caught him. With a cry he stumbled back, blood blooming from a cut along his cheek. "I am what I was made," she said. "Why did you not stay away?"

"Because I loved you," he answered through clenched teeth.

"Then you were twice fool," she said bitterly and swung again. "Once for coming to Rath, and once for loving an angel."

"Don't do this!" Crovax blocked and thrust. "If you feel anything for me, stop."

"Don't!" she cried. "I cannot stop your destiny—or mine." She attacked as if to silence him, flickering steel ringing between them. He fell back to one knee.

Starke was gone, of course. He had bolted for the bridge's end as soon as the attack had begun. Karn watched, paralyzed, still dazed from Volrath's tortures. Behind Karn, Tahngarth cursed and pounded on his back, but there was no way past the golem, no way but the one Gerrard found. He dropped to his belly and snaked between Tahngarth's and Karn's legs to get to Mirri. Her abdomen was slashed open; he saw gleaming tissues inside in the second before he pressed both hands against the wound, trying to stop the bleeding.

The fight continued between Crovax and his angel, in silence now. They each wept as they fought, and the tears on Crovax's face mingled with his blood. Selenia's tears slipped ignored from her face, and shone as they dropped into the depths. Mirri's blood still leaked onto the bridge and ran along its irregular surface. Crovax stepped back and slipped, barely catching himself. As he fought for balance, the angel's blade flicked in again and sliced open his arm. Crovax was losing. It is impossible to fight an angel: she made her sword dance as easily as before, though his blocks grew slower and slower still.

"You should not have come," she said. "I would do anything to save you, but I cannot." She raised her sword one last time and froze, as if listening to an unexpected voice calling her name. Half-blinded and exhausted, Crovax gathered himself and thrust wildly. And it connected, piercing her heart, or where it would have been, had she been woman and not angel.

She did not die, or not exactly. She arched up into the air above Crovax, wings a great shadow over him. She looked down for a moment with great black eyes and whispered, "I'm sorry Our destinies are completed. We are both doomed." Then her stabbed body shattered into countless glittering shards.

Crovax was lost in a blizzard of flakes of feather and

blood that shifted to white and black crystals and then back. The shards that had been Selenia burst out into a huge sphere, but whirled like a cyclone back together, a funnel of light and dark, of light and shadow, forming and reforming the shape of wings as they fell onto Crovax. Her great sword clattered to the bridge beside Crovax. He cried out and the shards swept into his mouth, then gathered around him, thrusting themselves into eyes, ears, and mouth. He screamed hoarsely and clawed at his face. He shuddered as if struck while the crystals forced themselves into his body.

And then they were gone. After the screaming and the whirlwind, the space seemed filled with ringing silence. The only sound was Mirri's panting as Gerrard pressed against the gash in her belly.

Crovax stood unsteadily.

"Crovax, are you all right?" Gerrard said.

Crovax said nothing, took a step toward the bridge's edge.

"Crovax, you had to kill her," Gerrard said. "Karn? Tahngarth? I can't let go of Mirri."

Karn still did not move. With a grunt, Tahngarth vaulted over him and leapt across Mirri and Gerrard. He caught Crovax just as he stepped off the bridge.

"Let me go," Crovax croaked.

"No," Tahngarth said. "I can live through this; you can too."

Their eyes met for a long moment, and then Crovax collapsed to the bloody stone of the bridge. He cuddled the angel's sword to himself, and wept.

* * * * *

Tahngarth brought Mirri and Crovax back to me, one over each shoulder as if they were sacks of grain. I heard his voice and ran up the gangway. Tahngarth, hideously misshapen, was lowering Mirri into the arms of Davved and Zinaida. At the change in position, Mirri murmured incoherently and struck out at Davved, who caught her clawed hand easily as he took her weight onto his shoulders. Blood dripped onto the deck from a stained bandage around her belly. "Into the infirmary!" I shouted. I touched her face as Davved carried her past; she was hot to the touch.

Tahngarth lowered the other body. It was Crovax.

"What happened?" I said. Crovax was conscious but his skin was as pale as the dead. He breathed the fast shallow breaths of an animal.

Crovax said nothing. Tahngarth said only, "He is ill. Do what you can."

"Crovax, talk to me." I tipped his head up to check his pupils for signs of concussion. He pulled away. I bit my lip, trying not to cry. "Crovax, come downstairs."

He followed me, but I do not know why.

* * * * *

Mirri lies on her cot, swathed in bandages. She had the beginnings of fever, which I brought down with herbs from home and a spell taught me by my old master; now she sleeps, with the near-silent breathing of her people.

Crovax sits in the infirmary, face in his hands. He has no major injuries from his fight with his angel, and yet there is blood on his lip and his glossy dark skin is pale and lightless. I remember his face, when I tipped it to the light up on deck. He snapped away, but not before I saw that his eyes had changed color, from brown to a sick yellow-white without pupil or iris. And not before I saw that his teeth had grown pointed and pierced his lip.

Something happened when the angel died. She entered him in some fashion. A guardian angel is meant to be good, but with her death she is changing him into something different, and I do not think it is good.

Mirri is the injured one, and yet for some reason, I feel Crovax is the one I am losing, to a disease I cannot name, unless I call it damnation.

I would do anything to heal him, but I am powerless. A healer grows used to losses, even horrific and incomprehensible losses such as this one. But even a healer feels despair when it is one she loves.

Crovax loved the one he thought of as his guardian angel. But he did not realize that in the end, it was not Selenia who watched over him and longed for his happiness and fought for his life.

And I failed.

Here ends the Tale of Crovax

IV

EXODUS

A Dark Room

The old man had left his seat and was poking among the papers stored in a large oaken cabinet set to one side of the hall. Dust rose from the piles he disrupted in little spurts and clouds.

"We're almost done with this bit," he said with some satisfaction. "This corner of the library has been undisturbed in decades. Now perhaps scholars can get some use out of it." He rubbed his hands on his robe, cleansing them of dust.

The boy shifted impatiently. "So what happened next? Was Mirri badly hurt?"

"Oh, yes." The master bent his face to read one ancient parchment on a table. His nose seemed to smell the paper before he flicked it aside to join a heap of other scraps on the floor. He turned to look at the student, his head slowly oscillating from side to side; like some strange creature, the boy thought, and for a single shocking moment he seemed to see the white-haired old man as something horrible and alien. Then the moment passed, and he repeated his first question.

"So what happened?"

The master sat down once again, resting his chin in his hands. "Mirri and Crovax were both injured. Mirri was bleeding heavily from a slash across her abdomen. Gerrard and Starke bandaged her as best they could, but they knew time was growing short. So Gerrard, seeing no alternative, ordered Tahngarth and Karn to return to *Weatherlight* with the two injured companions."

The master shook his head sadly. "It might have turned out better if they had left them there. Or at any rate, if they had left one of them . . ."

"Which one?" The boy broke into the master's thoughtful silence.

"Which one? Which one?" The master turned back to his listener. "Haven't you been paying attention? Isn't it obvious which one?"

The boy considered for a long, silent minute. In the stillness of the library, the rumblings from beyond the walls sounded louder.

"Well," he said at last, "I suppose something horrible was happening to Crovax. So maybe if Gerrard had just left him, he would have died." He looked up, eyes round. "But Gerrard wouldn't do that! A real hero never leaves his companions behind!"

The old man looked at him. "You think not?" he said at last. "Well, maybe being a hero is something more than helping your friends. Maybe it has something to do with responsibility, with seeing a bigger picture. Maybe that was the problem that plagued Gerrard all along, all through those years when he ran from the Legacy."

The boy screwed his face up in thought. "Maybe," he

said after a time of intense concentration. "But how can a hero just leave his friends behind. I mean, Crovax and Mirri were hurt. Gerrard couldn't abandon them without abandoning his honor."

"And do you think that's what heroism is about? Is it about honor?"

"Well, Master, honor is at the heart of—"

"Honor can be just as dangerous as cowardice," the old man interrupted harshly. "Gerrard had to learn that to cling blindly to honor, to value friendship above the fate of the world, that is fatal. To be a true hero is to recognize one's own place in the world and to rise to the challenges that fate throws in one's way. Up to now Gerrard had always rejected those challenges. But in the Stronghold, in the heart of Rath, he was once again forced to choose, and this time he chose the right path."

"And what was the path he chose?"

"Well, listen.

"Gerrard ordered the minotaur and the golem to carry Mirri and Crovax back to the ship, while he and Starke continued the search for Sisay and Takara. Tahngarth and Karn reluctantly agreed and began the tortuous journey back to where Gerrard told them *Weatherlight* lay waiting for them—not, however, before the minotaur mate had extracted from Starke a detailed explanation of how he might rejoin the two searchers once he'd relieved himself of his burden.

"The two companions carried their friends through the twisting tunnels of the Stronghold. At every stage they checked and rechecked the directions given by Gerrard. At last Tahngarth sensed they must be drawing near to the ship. But suddenly he was halted by a call from Karn. The silver golem stood in the tunnel, swaying back and forth."

"Why, master? Was he wounded?"

"Little could wound the golem. But he told Tahngarth that he somehow felt the nearby presence of the Legacy.

Volrath had evidently secreted it somewhere quite close by. Hastily the golem passed the body of Crovax to Tahngarth. 'You must carry them both to the ship,' he told the minotaur. And then, without another word, he was gone."

"Gone! Where?"

"Ah, well, Tahngarth didn't know either. But he trusted the silver golem, and so, hefting the bodies of Mirri and Crovax in his mighty arms, he stolidly resumed his journey toward *Weatherlight*.

The
Weatherlight's Tale

Francis Lebaron

Deep in the heart of the ship, a glowing crystal hums softly, its light washing over the wooden beams and struts of the lower decks. The light is fragmented and distorted by a long crack that runs through the crystal from top to bottom. At the heart of the crystal, almost as if it were contained within that fracture, gleams a single point of light, so brilliant that a star might have descended from the heavens to illuminate the darkness. Above is the clatter of feet, the thump and grind of human activity. A long scraping noise as something is dragged across the deck and thrown down; then the feet are off again, racing along the boards on an urgent errand as a clear female voice shouts a word of command. Footsteps resound on the ladders, and there's the hum of ropes vibrating in the unnatural winds that sweep across Rath. But here, in the sheltered center, the crystal glows serenely.

Hanna stared about her in the dim light, seeking out the tiny figure of *Weatherlight*'s cabin boy. "Squee! Where's that rope?"

"Here. Rope. Nuthin' else you need? Good." The goblin's body shivered as he glanced about them. "I'm goin' down below decks."

"Oh, no, you're not." Hanna grabbed him and twitched him away from the open hatch. "I need those grappling hooks brought forward from the aft port side. Move it, Squee! Or would you like to explain to Gerrard when he gets back why you spent your time cowering below?"

The little goblin disappeared in the direction the navigator had indicated, not before Hanna heard a muttered, "*If* he comes back. . . ."

She pushed away the thought as quickly as it had come and returned her attention to the scene around her. Everywhere crewmen struggled with recalcitrant canvas or brought forward bundles of spears and swords, working at feverish pace to make the ship battle ready. Hanna sighed and allowed herself a momentary glance toward the brooding darkness beyond the ship's decks that she knew was the Stronghold. No! She would not think about it. Right now she had a job to do. Best concentrate on that, and that alone.

"Stivale! You and Grifel reef the port sail! Step lively! We've not got all day! And while you're at it, try to make a bit less noise."

She turned to give another order and suddenly staggered back. Before her, a lithe figure appeared on the ship's deck, forming out of thin air. There was a sudden silence, as if every crewman had been frozen for a split second in action; then, with a low cry, Hanna drew her sword and sent it whistling through the air. It slashed through the figure's midriff, but met no more resistance than the air.

The woman—if she was, in fact, a woman; the figure was sufficiently androgenous that it was difficult to tell—

stared blankly at Hanna for a moment, and then spoke.

"Ertai and Barrin!"

"*What* did you say?" Hanna stopped in astonishment, her sword already drawn back for another blow.

The woman calmly stepped forward. Squee, who had reappeared from his errand, dropped a bundle of ropes he was carrying and stared at her, open-mouthed.

"I am Lyna of the Soltari." The voice was low and gentle, but with a hint of steel behind it. "I have been speaking with Ertai, your wizard. He suggested I speak his name to you, as well as the name of your father. Ertai is a very . . . capable man. " From her tone, Hanna almost felt the woman was laughing to herself. "I have informed him that the portal he guards may lead to many destinations," the woman continued. "Some may be places where your ship will find refuge. I and my people will help Ertai open the portal. But you must hurry." There was a subtle change in the tone of her voice, a new note of suppressed urgency.

Hanna shook her head. "We can't leave yet. We have companions who are not yet aboard."

Lyna looked at her unblinkingly. "Time grows short. You must prepare to leave."

She waved her hand at the staring crewmen. "Unleash the lines."

"Now just wait a minute!" Hanna spun on her heel and gestured angrily to the crew. "Belay that! No one is going anywhere on the say-so of someone we've just met. We'll stay here until Gerrard returns, or—"

Her words cut off abruptly as Lyna stretched out a hand to Hanna's face. The fingers were long and slender, and the touch, though seemingly gentle, was hard as iron. The tips of the Soltari's fingers rested on Hanna's throat, and the thought flitted through the navigator's mind that if the other were so minded, she could—would—slay her with a touch. Lyna's voice, as well, was still gentle but brooked no disagreement.

"You must leave *now*. There is no time."

Hanna stared into the depths of the Soltari's fathomless eyes. "Yes," she murmured, more to herself than to the crewmen. "Now."

Jerking back, she turned again to the crew. "What are you waiting for? Cast off!"

"Wait!"

The shout came in quick answer to her snapped order. One of the crew, a tall, dark sailor named Javan, hung over the side of *Weatherlight* staring into the murky air. He turned back to glance at Hanna, then waved his hand to someone beyond her sight, someone who was now climbing onto the deck, sweat dripping from his flanks.

"Tahngarth!" Hanna cried gladly. Then, seeing him in the light of a flickering ship's lantern that swung from a beam, she gasped and repeated softly, "Tahngarth!"

The minotaur's features seemed strangely changed. His chest and shoulders were grown larger, muscles bulging beneath the skin as if swollen by some illness. Instead of proudly flaring from either side of his head, his horns were twisted and inverted. But to Hanna the most shocking change lay in the twisting and bulking of the great minotaur's bone structure. It was as if an invisible hand had reached inside of him, distorting his anatomy in a parody of what he had been. "Tahngarth," the navigator whispered. "What have they done to you?"

In each of his great arms the minotaur clasped a limp body. One, Hanna saw, was Mirri. Her tail hung limply and she bled from a great slash across the abdomen. The other—lamplight shone on the features of Crovax, and the navigator shuddered at the change she saw. His face was pallid, skin stretched tightly across the bones. His eyes were wide open, staring, red-rimmed, the pupils a sickly yellow. Blood trickled from one side of his mouth, and Hanna could see the white tips of his teeth protruding from his lips.

Hanna wrenched her eyes from the ghastly trio and yelled to the crew for assistance. Javan, stepping swiftly to Tahngarth's side, relieved him of Mirri, while another sailor gathered up Crovax.

The minotaur leaned against the rail, his breath coming in ragged gasps. Sweat dripped from his fur and pooled on the deckboards.

Hanna approached him and laid a trembling hand on his arm. She could feel the swollen muscles tense and tremble beneath the skin. The minotaur seemed to be fighting some inner conflict, as if he were forcing himself to stand still and rest before moving on to some larger challenge. He raised his head and stared at the navigator; she shuddered. It was as if someone had wiped a damp sponge across a painting, blurring some features and obliterating others.

"Did you find Sisay?" she asked.

Tahngarth shook his head. "I don't know. They were still searching for her when I left. Gerrard ordered Karn and I to carry these two back to the ship, but the golem left me; he claims to have found some clue to the whereabouts of the Legacy. We fought Selenia, and Crovax killed her, but Mirri was hurt."

"Take them below," Hanna instructed, turning to the crew who had clustered around to hear the minotaur's words. "And somebody get Orim to tend their wounds. You, also." She turned back to Tahngarth, but the minotaur was already on the side of the ship, poised to leap back to the Stronghold's balcony.

"I'm going back to Gerrard," he called over his shoulder.

"Wait!" Hanna shouted. "We have to leave *now*! Tell Gerrard to meet us at the Gardens."

"The Gardens," he flung back over his shoulder. "Where are they?"

"Starke gave directions to Gerrard before they set out. He can guide you. Tell Gerrard to get there as fast as he can."

Tahngarth nodded, leapt, and was gone.

Hanna turned back to Lyna, who, during the exchange with the minotaur had stood silent, unnoticed in the shadows.

"Well? Satisfied?"

If Lyna noticed the hostility in the slender woman's voice, she gave no indication. She bowed her head in acknowledgment and said calmly, "Very good. I shall return to Ertai. Who knows? He may need my assistance in opening the Portal, despite his tremendous native ability." Hanna thought she detected a half-smile on the Soltari's face. Then, with the same ease with which she had boarded the ship, the woman faded and was gone. Hanna ran to the side and stared into the thick, fetid air, but she could see nothing. She shaded her eyes. Surely that was something moving in the dark passage that emptied from the balcony? No! Yes! Yes!

A cry came from the Stronghold. Hanna grasped a coiled length of rope and hurled it from the ship. A moment later she and two sailors were hauling on it with all their force. Slowly, the end came up, bearing with it the bulky form of Karn. One massive four-fingered hand gripped the rope. The other clasped a device the navigator had never seen: a seemingly senseless twist of metal.

"What is it," she asked, as soon as the golem was safely over the side.

Karn could not precisely shrug, but the silver golem looked as though he would have, had he been able. "The Skyshaper. I retrieved it, along with other pieces of the Legacy, from the Sliver Queen."

"The *Sliver Queen* !"

"Yes. She was the guardian of the Legacy, set to the task by Volrath himself. And now I have recovered it."

Proudly the golem gestured to his chest. "It lies within here." He turned back to the Skyshaper and stared at it thoughtfully. "But this belongs to this ship. It *should* make

Weatherlight go faster, in fact. I wonder . . ."

"Time for wondering later." Hanna spoke more brusquely than she had intended.

"We need to go. We're to meet Gerrard and the Gardens, and we haven't much time."

She turned to go, adding over her shoulder, "Take that thing down to the engine room. If it helps the ship go faster, we may well need it soon enough."

* * * * *

The light in the heart of the crystal sparkles and flames, as if in sudden anger. Around it there is a sustained groaning and creaking, as if some giant beast were stirring from a long winter's sleep. Then, steadily, a gentle hum fills the air. The ship backs away from the side of the great fortress, graceful as a dancer, pivots, and in silence streaks into the darkness. From above a great wave of air surges down to fill the void where a moment ago the ship stood poised, like some giant insect by the side of its hive. There is a resounding boom that echoes and reechoes in the giant chamber that encloses the fortress. Here and there in the looming blackness of the Stronghold, lights gleam and glitter before they slowly dim and disappear. And now the only noise that fills the silence is the slow, everlasting cry of the tortured earth. Yet far away, almost out of sight of someone standing where the ship had stood a moment before, an observer might have seen a faint river of light, as if an army carrying torches was surging up to the Stronghold's entrance. And then, through the musky air, deadened by the immense distance, comes the roar of faraway battle.

But Weatherlight *hears none of these things.*

* * * * *

Karn stared from the skyshaper to the complex of bumps and depressions on one side of *Weatherlight*'s engine room. He remained in that position for so long that the crewman who stood near him finally cleared his throat. "Karn?"

Karn looked up slowly, and, as always, the crewman experienced a slight sinking sensation in the pit of his stomach, as those grave eyes refocused and contemplated him.

The golem shook his massive head. "I cannot understand it. This seems to belong here, but there is no proper place for it." His fingers, delicate in their gestures, probed the engine assembly, while his other hand twisted the Skyshaper as if fitting it into an invisible port. "It *must* fit, Tomalan. But where?"

Tomalan nodded sympathetically. "Yes. But perhaps it's meant for a different kind of ship?"

Karn looked at him unblinkingly. "No. It is part of the Legacy. And I know it belongs with this ship, just as the Legacy belongs with Gerrard." He turned back to the engine and moved methodically along it, nearing the complex that housed the glowing Thran crystal that was at the heart of the ship. Then, suddenly, his hands seemed to slip, and he stumbled, almost falling. Tomalan fell back against the opposite wall as the ship gave a start and a drunken lurch. From the deck above came a general shout, torn from a dozen throats.

"Attack!"

Tomalan recovered his feet and rushed across the swaying deck to Karn. The golem had risen and without apparent haste was continuing the search the engine. Then came an even more violent start, as if the ship were trying to tear itself apart. Tomalan once again lost his footing and fell against the golem. His hands, clawing for support, grasped the Skyshaper.

There was a click and a loud hum. A panel slid back, revealing a hidden recess. Karn looked at the fallen crewman.

"Congratulations, Mr. Tomalan," he observed quietly. "I believe you've just solved the puzzle." He glanced about the engine room and turned back to his assistant. "You'd better get above decks. You're more needed there."

Tomalan needed no second order. With a leap he was at the ladder leading upward. In a second more his head thrust above the deck level, and he emerged into a scene of steel and fire.

The deck pitched beneath him, and he almost lost his footing again. At the prow, Hanna shouted orders, while crewmen rushed too and fro. Some few lay fallen on the deck; one, whom Tomalan recognized as a young riggings rat, was lying on his face near the mast, a pool of blood around his head.

A dark shadow, a deeper blackness spread across the deck like ink. Tomalan glanced up and saw a sight he'd earlier tried to put out of his mind: the sleek, hulking shape of Greven *il*-Vec's ship.

Predator.

There was a flash and a roar from the dark ship's side. From its guns sprang long snaking lines tipped with steel bolts. Two of them hammered into *Weatherlight*'s deck, while one buried itself in the rail, binding the two ships together.

Almost simultaneously, two sailors lifted cutlasses and slashed at the harpoon lines on the deck. The ropes parted. Then *Predator* pulled upward, and the remaining line went taut. *Weatherlight* jerked, and its timbers seemed to cry out to Tomalan. Another violent jerk from *Predator* hurled most of the smaller ship's crew headlong. From deep within the bowels of *Weatherlight* came a sudden cry, as of a great beast in torment. Another jerk of the line. Tomalan could almost hear a faint echo of the manic laughter he'd heard in those first horrible hours when they entered Rath.

The laughter of Greven *il*-Vec.

Tomalan clenched his fists. That laughter, louder now, seemed to freeze his heart, to shred it, cut through it to the core of his being with a surgical indifference. In a frozen instant, he saw everything about him with absolute clarity. Hanna stood before him, her face streaming with tears of helpless rage, clinging to the ship she loved. And in that instant, Tomalan knew that he too loved the ship, that he could not let it die. With a cry, he drew his own cutlass and leapt forward to the rail. He raised the gleaming blade above him to cut the line. Dimly he heard another roar from above and felt a tremendous blow. He stared stupidly from a moment at the steel harpoon sticking through his chest. And in the instant before his heart burst and darkness claimed him forever, he brought his blade down in a whistling stroke that severed the harpoon line.

Hanna shrieked as Tomalan was jerked from the ship's deck by the line still implanted in his body. At the same moment, she saw that *Predator*'s cannons had planted other ropes in the smaller ship. She could see moggs on board Greven's ship frantically cranking winches, trying to draw *Weatherlight* closer, to ready it for the killing blow.

Clutching the rail, she yelled a frantic order to the steersman. In response, *Weatherlight* suddenly shifted and turned, pulling *Predator* behind it.

All right, thought the navigator grimly to herself. If he wants to play this game, that's just what we'll do. She shouted further commands, as *Weatherlight* dodged and wove. Behind her she could hear goblin screams from *Predator* as it smashed into the Stronghold's foundations. Cannon roared again, and Hanna realized that the larger ship had used its firepower to destroy a part of the Stronghold directly in front of it. She set her jaw, and stared into the dark air before her.

* * * * *

The crystaline hum shifts upward an octave, two, three, then intensifies to an agonized shriek. The boards are trembling, and throughout the ship lights dim and flicker in mourning for a lost soul. Above the crying crystal can be heard the deep-throated roar of its foe as it falls back, leaps forward, pounces, and is dragged behind with the crack of a whip. The crystal murmurs in triumph, and now it seems to feel something else, something resting near it, not yet active but prepared to aid it, should need arise. The humming is more confident now; the ship laughs at its opponent as it twists and tears through the air.

Far away the armies of the Vec, Kor, and Dal are assaulting the mighty fortress. The powers that hold Rath in sway slowly give way, stumbling back, staining the stone halls and stairways with their blood. And before the elven armies, Eladamri gives a cry of triumph as he sees victory in his grasp.

* * * * *

Hanna saw the flash of fire above and behind her. For a moment she waited, cowering, for the blow from *Predator's* cannons. Then, in growing astonishment, she realized that the flames were on the other ship itself. Tendrils of orange ran up and down *Predator's* rigging. A goblin caught in the inferno blazed suddenly and fell shrieking into the abyss below. Looking at the scene, now lit with the ghastly light of blazing ship and burning moggs, Hanna thought she could see the dark form of Greven gesturing furiously, shouting orders to those of his crew still standing. *Weatherlight* veered again, dragging the now-captive *Predator* behind it. Then, suddenly, Hanna felt her ship leap forward, as if released from a great burden.

She turned again. Greven's goblins had slashed through the lines that bound the two vessels together. The ship was free.

Even now *Predator* was falling behind. Hanna almost laughed aloud.

An odd thumping sound came through the air, and she saw two ornithopters—clumsy flying machines—swoop up from Greven's decks. Moggs clung desperately to the fliers' delicate structure. Each had a bundle of round objects in his hand.

Goblin bombs. Hanna's heart beat hard and fast in her chest. Gerrard had told her what these devices could do. They could shatter *Weatherlight* once and for all. The battle was far from over.

Hanna clawed her way along the deck and plunged onto the bridge. Here, too, was chaos: Sarmiane the steersman fought to control the vessel, other crewmen rushed about, shouting contradictory advice and instructions to him, while almost unnoticed, the green form of Squee shivered convulsively in a corner.

Hanna grabbed Sarmiane's shoulder and dug her nails into his flesh. He winced, but kept his eyes on the path of the ship.

"Rise," she snapped in an urgent whisper. "Climb faster than you've ever climbed in your life. Because if those ornithopters get too close, this will be all the life you'll ever get."

There was a muffled squeal from Squee, and the other crewmen grew silent, drawing together behind Sarmiane and the navigator. Hanna reached to one side of the great wheel and flipped open a panel, revealing a small dial and a bewildering variety of switches and levers.

Sarmiane glanced at the array. "What's that?" he grunted. "Never seen that before."

"It's something new," Hanna returned briefly. "Turn and face the ornithopters."

"*What!*" Sarmiane almost lost control of the wheel, and the ship lurched drunkenly to port. "Are you insane?" he shouted harshly.

Hanna drew herself up. "That is an order, Mister! Don't argue with me—just do it! Now!"

Sarmiane glared at her for a moment. Then he shrugged. "Oh, well. It's been fun. Stand by to come about!"

Weatherlight turned, wind whistling through her rigging. Squee, flung from his hiding place, went rolling across the bridge and bounced into the wall. Hanna paid no attention. Her eyes were on the ornithopters, as she delicately turned the wheel this way and that. A small beam of light shot out from the center of the ship's wheel and focused on the nearest ornithopter.

"Sarmiane, try to hold us steady for a minute." Her fingers were busy with the other controls. Then she flipped a lever, and suddenly, without a sound, the light beam intensified into a blinding flash. The lights throughout the cabin dimmed simultaneously, and the crew cried out as one man. Some turned their heads away, while others clutched their eyes, tears spilling between their fingers. Hanna alone seemed unaffected by the beam, though Squee, peeping cautiously out, also seemed not to mind its brightness.

The ornithopter on which the light was focused wobbled violently, spilling its goblin pilot. He fell with a scream, and a second later the bombs he'd been carrying blew up as his body struck an outcropping of the Stronghold. The explosion shook *Weatherlight*, and Sarmiane almost lost control of the wheel. A few seconds later, there was a second, greater explosion, as the empty ornithopter ploughed squarely into the side of *Weatherlight*..

Hanna felt her feet go out from under her. Her head struck something hard, and awareness ran away from her, like water dripping from a stone.

She was asleep in her old bed at home. Her father was calling her name. No, no, it was her mother, long dead and nearly forgotten. "Hanna, Hanna! Time to get up! Come and have your breakfast, child!"

"Hanna!"

"All right, mother. I'm coming." Hanna sat up, and immediately sank back down into the arms of Orim. Squee crouched before her, his wrinkled goblin skin next to hers. She could feel its dry, slightly scaly texture rubbing her arm, as he furtively stroked her. She smiled, and felt a wave of unexpected tenderness toward the little goblin. Then a wave of nausea swept over her, and she turned to one side, retching and choking.

"All right, Hanna. That was a bad knock." Orim's fingers were busy pulling, poking, exploring Hanna's head. She pressed carefully in several places, and the sharp pain and nausea receded, leaving only a dull, throbbing headache. Hanna looked up at her friend, then slowly, carefully, rose to a fully sitting position.

"What's happening? Where's the other ornithopter?"

Sarmiane, still at the wheel, glanced at her and smiled broadly. His eyes still seemed slightly glazed, from the effects of the light beam that had destroyed the one flier. "It's still there, but a good ways back. I think we can outrun it, if we need to. But right now, it's hanging back. Probably wondering what we did to its friend." He paused a moment, and cleared his throat. "By the bye, what *did* you do?"

Hanna shrugged off Orim's protesting arm and got to her feet. "It's a new weapon. I concocted it by jury-rigging the lighting system. I've experimented with it, but I never had to use it against anything before." She brushed a hand against her aching, bruised forhead, feeling the place where she'd struck against the wheel casing. "As far as I can tell, it uses the same mana source that powers the lights on the ship. It just takes a tiny beam of light, focuses it, and makes it into a giant beam of light. The goblin on that ornithopter probably never knew what hit him. It must have been like staring into a thousand suns at once."

Sarmiane glanced behind him. "You want to use it against that fellow back there?" He gestured toward the distant ornithopter.

Hanna shook her head wearily. "No. One time's all it's good for, at least for a while. It seems to need to recharge after every use." She looked ahead. "Steady on, Mr. Sarmiane. Steady on."

* * * * *

The tiny crystal, calmer now, sends out its light to illuminate the recess where the golem, whose silver skin shines dully in its light, has placed the Skyshaper. The light caresses the new device, stroking it, kissing it, welcoming it on board. And yet at the heart of the tiny gleam's warmth, there is a hint of adamant, one that will admit no challenge. The golem steps back in satisfaction, staring at his work. "Yes," he whispers to himself. "Now it is complete."

* * * * *

"By the way," asked Hanna, as Orim turned to leave, "how are Mirri and Crovax?"

Orim stopped, her teeth worrying thoughtfully at her lower lip. She hesitated before speaking, and Hanna turned to look her full in the face.

"Mirri is recovering. The wound was serious but not life-threatening. She will be fine, given time and rest. Crovax . . ."

"What about Crovax?" Hanna asked quickly.

Orim shook her head, as if puzzled. "Crovax has undergone certain changes. I do not understand them. He was not wounded, yet he sleeps as if he were. And he seems a soul in torment. He has called out several times in his sleep to Selenia. And whenever he calls her name, his face burns as if with fever." She sighed. "I must go now. Others need my help as well."

She passed out of the bridge, and Hanna returned her attention to the murky way before them. Another crewman entered the bridge and stepped to her side.

"M'am, with respect, Karn the golem says he's got the Skyshaper in place. He's not sure what it'll do, but he says if you want to try it, he'll figure out how to get it started."

Hanna hesitated for a moment, then shook her head. "No. Let's wait. We don't know exactly what help it will give us. Perhaps it's better to wait until we've recovered Gerrard and the others. We may need it on our way to the Portal."

"Speaking of Gerrard," Sarmiane broke in, "there's the Gardens ahead, if I'm not mistaken."

Beside the ship as it rose past the Stronghold, a space suddenly opened, as the steep walls of Volrath's fortress fell away. Below them, Hanna could see a series of terraces, on which trees and shrubs huddled together, seeming to shelter from the raging skies. She caught a glimpse of pools and streams of water flowing through the heart of the garden; paths and avenues wound through the greenery, looking incongruously domestic amid so much chaos.

Weatherlight swept lower, its keel brushing the tops of the tallest trees. Hanna stared into the shadows, straining her eyes for a glimpse of Gerrard. She caught a flurry of movement and bent farther over the rail, ignoring the restraining hands of the crew.

"There!" she cried, pointing.

"Look out!" The cry came at the same moment from Sarmiane, as he wrenched the ship hard to port. The pursuing ornithopter had finally caught up to them and swept past in a flare of beating wings. Hanna caught sight of the mogg's staring face, as he fought to control his machine. The ornithopter flashed into the distance, then swung around, readying itself for another pass.

Sarmiane was having a hard time steering his own vessel. Despite his best efforts, *Weatherlight* bucked like a frightened horse. Hanna grabbed it, her slender hands over his larger ones, struggling to control the ship. In the stronger light over the gardens, she could see the damage the first ornithopter's collision had done to her ship: the sails were full of holes, and parts of the aft hull appeared cracked and crumpled. The first midspar was entirely gone and the remaining spars on both sails were broken, hanging loose by a splinter. As Sarmiane lowered the ship toward the garden, it collided with trees, and Hanna shuddered to hear sounds of further tearing along the hull.

They were close enough now that the rest of the crew could see the figures racing toward them. A woman whose red hair streamed behind her helped Starke, who seemed to stumble as if blind. Behind was Gerrard, arm around a dark woman, staggering, dazed, but still alive: Sisay!

But Tahngarth? Where was the minotaur? Surely he had found his way back to Gerrard. Hanna opened her mouth to shout a question to the bearded young man running toward the ship; then, suddenly, she saw the first mate of *Weatherlight*.

He was climbing a tree, hand over hand, his beaded mane streaming behind him in the wind. Up and up he went, seemingly effortless. He grasped a high branch and swung his massive body onto it. The branch swayed and bent, but Tahngarth hesitated not a moment. He was at the highest point of the tree now, almost level with the deck of *Weatherlight* but some fifty feet away from it.

Hanna heard the ominous beat of the ornithopter's wings. In a flash, she saw what the minotaur intended. As the goblin steered the ornithopter toward the ship, Tahngarth jumped, an impossible leap for a man and a mighty one even for a minotaur. He landed full on the machine, and the ornithopter swayed and pitched from the unexpected weight. The goblin pilot spun around, looking for the source of the problem. The tiny flier jerked upward and suddenly the goblin was no longer on board. Tahngarth alone held on, pulling himself into the control seat.

Hanna stared in amazement. The mogg had vanished completely. Had he fallen, or, no! She stared in fascinated horror.

A protruding branch from a dead tree had plucked the mogg from his seat, pinning him neatly. His body writhed on the end of the point, arms and legs flailing in his death agonies. She heard his thin, dying squeal, and then the body went limp.

Tahngarth was obviously having a great deal of trouble controlling the tiny ornithopter. He was unfamiliar with the controls, and the flier was unfamiliar with his weight. It bobbed and wove, dipping and rising. The minotaur was trying to twist the course of the flier about to bring it down near Gerrard. The ornithopter, though, was fighting back as if it were a living thing. It swept closer to *Weatherlight*, passing above it in a rush of wings. Hanna shut her eyes. She knew that any moment she would hear a cry as Tahngarth was hurled from his precarious perch into the trees. There would come a long, drawn-out scream, followed by the horrid crunch of a heavy body striking the unresponsive earth.

Something thudded on the deck beside her, and her eyes jerked open. Tahngarth stood there, panting but calmly watching as the now riderless ornithopter spun in an ever-tightening spiral downward toward the far edge of the Garden. A flash of yellow and orange flame marked where it struck, igniting the vegetation around it.

Tahngarth turned and looked at Hanna. "Time to go home," he said.

* * * * *

The Thran crystal at the heart of Weatherlight hummed softly.

Here ends the Tale of Weatherlight

A Dark Room

The boy was frowning, one foot scuffing at the papers heaped before him. He made no pretense of trying to sort through them.

"Master, so many things are unclear. What happened to Volrath? Did Gerrard kill him? And what about Crovax—what was happening to him? Was Starke blind? And did Mirri get better?"

"Oh, is that all you want to know?"

"Well, no, not exactly." The boy shuffled his feet again. "I guess I want to know if Gerrard is really a hero."

"Well, the answer's complicated. But it's bound up with what happened next.

"Many things had befallen Gerrard and Starke since Tahngarth and Karn left them, bearing the bodies of Mirri and Crovax. Following Starke's advice, the two sought a passage to the Dream Halls through a twisted garden. But as they traversed its dark paths, they found shelter beneath a tree and Gerrard, looking at it closely, made a startling discovery: it was a Dominarian tree, ripped from Llanowar. Gerrard puzzled over what a tree from Dominaria might be doing on this plane. The conclusion he drew was not a comforting one.

"What was that, Master?"

"It was that Rath was actually *absorbing* parts of Dominaria, slowly insinuating itself into Gerrard's home plane. Now the map they had found earlier made more sense, and Gerrard began dimly to understand the shape of Volrath's ultimate plan."

The old man opened a drawer in a large cabinet and ran an experienced eye over the contents. Then he took the paper he'd been studying and inserted it into the drawer. Closing it and wiping his forehead with a wispy handkerchief that he drew from the folds of his robe, he resumed.

"Even as Gerrard made this discovery, he and Starke were attacked by spikes—sluglike creatures that fell from the trees to prey on them. The two retreated, finally finding their way back into the maze of corridors that led to the Dream Halls.

"At last they found the place they were seeking. But oddly, the tower that Starke claimed held the Dream Halls had no entrance. The only apparent way of egress was through the balconies that towered high overhead. Gerrard, his sword bound at his side, slowly began to climb.

"After struggling against the ever-changing flowstone, he reached the top. Pausing only to catch his breath, he entered and was blinded by an array of visions.

"All his early life came back to him. Gerrard saw he and Vuel sporting together as boys. He saw Vuel's rite of passage and his own struggle to save his blood brother's life. He saw Vuel's hatred of him growing, and the sidar's son's theft of the Legacy. The death of his stepfather at his own son's hands rose up before Gerrard. Once again he was at Multani's caves with Mirri and Rofellos. Then he saw Vuel, now surrounded by dark shapes, horned monstrosities that slowly divide and recombine into one terrifying creature, bestowing powers upon Vuel that transformed and corrupted the young man. All this Gerrard beheld with horror, and with sadness for the fate of his former friend and blood brother."

Ilcaster sat silent at his master's feet as the old man, a hand on the boy's head, spoke in a kind of chant, the sound of his voice rising and falling against the walls of the room.

"Gerrard also saw visions of the future—the future as Volrath wanted it: armies sweeping across Dominaria, Gerrard bound and cringing at the evincar's feet. Then, to Gerrard's amazement, these images began to speak to him in Volrath's own voice. The shape of the ruler of Rath appeared before Gerrard, standing, mocking him.

"Starke appeared suddenly behind Volrath and plunged a dagger into the evincar's back. But it had no effect whatsoever; Volrath plucked it forth, casually swatting Starke aside as his flesh closed over the wound.

" 'The warclan was my future from the moment I first opened my eyes,' declared Volrath. 'You took it all away when you saved me during my rite of passage. I never coveted your Legacy, even though *your* destiny became my father's primary passion in life. His service to your Legacy cost me a family, and you cost me a clan.'

"Gerrard could stand no more. He hurled himself forward at Volrath, his sword raised. The image retreated before him, and now two other figures came at him: a redhaired woman, sword raised, and Sisay."

"But *was* it Sisay, Master? Or was it just another shapeshifter?"

"No, it was Sisay, right enough, but now she was under Volrath's control. Gerrard fought desperately against she and Takara—for the red-haired woman was Starke's daughter—while trying to avoid hurting them. Starke cried out and lifted his arms to Takara, but she, unrealizing, slashed him across the face, blinding him.

"At last, after several moments of bitter conflict, Gerrard succeeded in disarming Takara and knocking out Sisay. Chasing after Volrath, who fled the chamber, he cornered the evincar just as Tahngarth, roaring in rage, burst into the room. Together the two friends slashed at Volrath, and Gerrard drove home the killing blow."

"So Volrath was dead." The boy breathed a final sigh of relief that seemed to go through his entire body.

The librarian looked at him apologetically. "Well, no. Just as the body fell to the floor, it shapeshifted into one of Volrath's experiments. The evincar had escaped Gerrard once again. In a rage Gerrard hacked at the corpse. 'Should I have let you die back then, Vuel?' he shouted. 'Would that have satisfied you?' But the minotaur pulled him away from the shapeshifter's body and brought him back to reason."

The boy shook his head in resignation. "Well, but at least they had Sisay."

"Yes," agreed the librarian. "They had Sisay and Takara, and with them they began the long journey to the Gardens where, they hoped, Hanna and *Weatherlight* awaited them."

The boy nodded. "I see. But you still haven't answered my question, Master."

"Bless me, boy, I've answered more questions tonight than I have in a decade. What question?"

"If Gerrard is a hero."

"Ah. A good question. I'm glad you've been listening, Ilcaster. There may be hope for you yet."

"So if there's hope for me, master, will you answer my question about Gerrard?"

The old man looked at him thoughtfully. "I don't know

if I can answer you, Ilcaster. Being a hero, it seems to me, is not something you *are*; it is something you *become*. Gerrard was not born a hero—but he might become one if he passed the challenges that fate put in his way."

Ilcaster wrinkled his brow. "Do you mean, Master, that a hero needs challenges?"

"I suppose so."

"Then wasn't Volrath really doing Gerrard a favor? Didn't Gerrard need the experience of fighting Volrath to become a hero?"

The master looked at the boy for a moment, a smile half-formed on his lips. "Yes," he said. "Yes, that's it. A hero needs enemies, needs monsters to slay, foes to outwit, mountains to climb."

"Or," said Ilcaster, "in this case, to enter."

The old man grunted. "Yes. Yes indeed. But the challenge is not enough; the hero must give up something."

"What do you mean?"

The master sat down on a box and put his chin in his hand. The boy moved closer, as the dim candlelight drove back the shadows around them. Far above, in the windows, the flashing light seemed to be slowing, and there were the first hints of true light, beneath which might be glimpsed roiling clouds laced with rain. But neither figure paid any attention.

"I must tell you, Ilcaster, that I am not entirely sure of this proposition myself. But it seems to me that a true hero is made not merely by the accretion of heroic deeds but by the shedding of part of his old self. Think of a snake in the spring, when the season turns and the new year is blossoming."

The boy nodded. "It sheds its skin."

"Exactly. And it emerges, clad in shining new armor, reborn into a new year. It has left behind something of itself, something it has grown beyond. Now, in my opinion, a hero goes through a similar process. He leaves behind something of himself at each stage of his growth. Gerrard had already done this. He'd lost his parents, his teacher Multani, his friend Rofellos, and his home in Benalia."

"I think I see." The boy tapped his fingers together in imitation of his tutor. "But what else was there to leave behind?"

"Something that capsulized his old life. Something that summed up all that he had been up to that point. Something that represented a choice he had to make, a fork in the road, so to speak."

Ilcaster thought again, then shook his head. "I'm sorry, Master, but I still don't see—"

"Of course you don't!" Something of the acerbity of his former tone had returned to the librarian's voice. "You have to be still and listen."

"Remember that Crovax and Mirri had been taken below when Tahngarth brought them aboard the ship? Well. . . ."

Mirri's Tale

Liz Holliday

The darkness was moving.

Mirri stared at the door that led from her cabin out into the crew quarters. Despite her pain-dulled senses, she was intensely aware of the pitching and yawing of *Weatherlight* beneath her, of the rasp of her breath in her throat, of the muted sounds of shouts above. It wasn't right. Her friends needed her. They needed her sword at their sides. Was it her imagination, or could she hear the sounds of battle? She had tried to tell them she was well enough to fight, but they hadn't listened. Rest, Sisay had said. Get well, Gerrard had said. We will need you well, for what is to come. And so they had put her here, in the darkness, like an Elder waiting to die.

And now this.

The shadows, moving. Her hands curled reflexively,

body tensed, sending little shockwaves of pain through her from the wound.

Probably one of the others, come to see how she was. Sisay, perhaps. Or Gerrard. She brightened at the thought, but she couldn't relax. Something smelled wrong.

The scent was tantalisingly familiar, yet she couldn't place it. Enemy, she thought. That was stupid. The pain wouldn't let her think properly. Animals smelled. People smelled. You could say someone smelled like an enemy you already knew. But animosity and evil had no stink of their own.

And yet whoever was watching her smelled like an enemy.

If she were wrong, best to find out now, and have one less thing to disturb her rest. If she were right . . . well, enemies were to be dispatched or neutralised, and injured or not she would do so.

"Show yourself," she called.

The darkness moved. A shadow detached itself from the deeper darkness behind it.

"It's just me—Crovax," said a voice. It sounded like him: weary perhaps, but certainly him. Yet there was that smell . . . "I was worried about you. The way Selenia cut you—"

"They're fighting up top," Mirri said. "You should be with them."

It was intolerable. She should be with them. Standing with Gerrard. Standing at Gerrard's back, in the only place where her life made sense.

Crovax shook his head. "There's no fighting, Mirri. You're imagining things. There's a lull—"

"I can hear them," Mirri said.

Crovax moved forward. He was swathed from head to foot in a silken robe of midnight blue, completely hiding his usual foppish clothes. Mirri struggled to sit up.

"Don't," he said. "Really, there's nothing wrong—nothing

you can do to help." He was by her bed now, looking down at her. For a moment his eyes looked golden in the candlelight, like a wolf's in the darkness.

She stared at him. The stench, the enemy stench, came off him like sweat. Coppery, it was, like blood.

"Stand back from me," she said. She felt the claws in the tips of her fingers extend, felt every muscle tense and her fur bristle.

"Mirri, what's the matter?" His voice was thick, his words slurred. His eyes. She couldn't stop herself from staring into his eyes. Golden eyes . . .

. . . and suddenly she saw Gerrard, his bright sword flashing as he stood on the foredeck of *Weatherlight*, though whether it was dream or memory or vision she could not have said. His face and arms were laced with blood—his or his enemies, Mirri could not tell. Three of Volrath's servants circled him, warily, keeping out of range of his blade. Circled like wolves, but he would tire, and they would close on him. They would bring him down like the dogs they were. There would be no help from the others: they had their own battles to fight, and besides, they did not . . . did not care for him as she did. They were not so loyal.

"He needs me," she murmured and began to rise.

Crovax's hand clamped over her wrist. "He does not. There is no battle, and it is his wish that you rest."

Mirri stared at Crovax. Something wrong with that statement, she thought. Gerrard was—Gerrard was . . . it was too complicated. Surely if he hadn't actually said she should rest, he *would* if only he thought of it.

But he had gone. Yes, she thought, and started to sit up. He wasn't on *Weatherlight*. Hadn't been. What was Crovax doing to her? She saw her cutlass on the shelf by her cot. She started to reach for it, but Crovax was somehow in the way. She stared at him for a moment. At those eyes, dark as night. She could not break away.

His hand caressed her arm. She sank back against the bed. It was easier. She felt a warm lassitude creep through her. "Should rest," she said. It was what he wanted. What *Gerrard* wanted.

"Yes," Crovax whispered. "Good Mirri. Gerrard knows you would go to him if you could." He stroked her face with the back of his hand. It opened old scratches. They stung, but it was nothing. She was doing what Gerrard wanted.

She saw him again, then. Saw him thrust and parry and feint and slice. Saw his enemies watching him . . .

There had been another time when she had watched him so. The yellow moon had stood full against the indigo sky, and he had fought for her. For himself, too, but for her.

He had won. He had saved her, but he had killed her too. Killed the heart as it beat within her.

A foolish child she had been. And he so beautiful, with his dark eyes and darker hair and smooth human skin.

They had been students together, learning magic from the maro-sorcerer, Multani. She had never spoken of her feelings for him. How could she—outcast that she was, what did she have to offer him? And then Multani had asked them to take a message into the Deep Country for him.

Cat people. He had not told them that his message was for a tribe of the cat people, only that he had thought Mirri would be best suited to the task.

Child that she was, she had leapt at it. To be of use to someone, to repay her debts. To have a place in the world that she had earned. And when Gerrard had offered to go with her—to stand at her back—her joy had redoubled. Alone with him, she had thought she would surely find the courage to speak of her feelings.

But she had not. They came at last to the border markings of the Chitr'in, and her shock had been intense. How their scent filled her senses—a scent she had not smelled since she was a kit, before she had been abandoned by her tribe.

"Be easy, Mirri," Gerrard said. "Don't let them see you afraid—"

"I'm not afraid," she snarled.

"Of course not." He patted her arm. "Angry, then. Upset. Diplomacy is like magic. As Multani would say, magic is best approached with a cool heart and fast thinking."

She nodded. The Chitr'in . . . she could not remember ever having heard of them, though that meant little. Her memories of her time with her tribe were scattered and sparse, a montage of playing in the dirt at catch-claw and sneakshot; and of drowsing by the campfires while the Elders discussed policy and hunting tactics, and the shamans drummed to bring the prey-beasts closer.

Soon her memories were irrelevant. The Chitr'in came, appearing as silently as smoke from between the trees. Warriors at the back, magnificent in dyed and painted hunting leathers, their arms and torsos scarified with kill tattoos and crisscrossed with weapons belts. And at the front, three elders.

"You violate our lands," said the middle one, in Trader-tongue.

"Speak," said the one on the right, who was dressed in robes and furs, rather than fighting leathers.

"Or begone," said the one on the left, when Mirri did not answer and Gerrard would not, because it was her place.

"We come in peace," Mirri said, and cursed herself. They would think they were dealing with puling weaklings. "To negotiate terms on behalf of our master, the sorcerer Multani, who would trade with you."

"I am the shaman of this tribe," said the robed elder on the right. "We know nothing of outland sorcery. We wish to know nothing."

"You are a *person*, girl," said the middle Elder, using the Catling word for person, which excluded humans and others from consideration. Mirri felt her ears go back, and fought to stop it. They must not know they discomfited her. "Are you a slave, to call another master?"

"I learn at his sufferance," Mirri said. "It is human custom to call their teachers Master, but he does not own me."

The elders consulted.

"It is well," the middle Elder said, but her ear twitched and Mirri knew she had not quite won the argument. "I am Seyen, Most Old of the Chitr'in. By my will, you will accept our hospitality tonight, and tomorrow tell us what this Multani wishes with us."

That night, the Chitr'in drummed while the great triple pipes as long as a man howled discords, and the warriors danced. The fires burned hot, sending wreathes of flesh-scented smoke into the cool night air. She had sat with Gerrard on her left. To her right, there was the Most Old Seyen, who said nothing more to her but from time to time burdened her with a glance or a long hard stare; and more often, he looked at Gerrard.

The shaman, who still had not named himself, was here and there, always watching them.

Most Old Seyen plans, Mirri thought. She sees advantage, and she wants it. Or she sees the possibility of disadvantage and wonders how it may be avoided. That was well enough. What else should a leader do for her people? But whether the Most Old was to be trusted, that was another question. And what her other elders wanted, that was another matter entirely.

All her life, Mirri had tried to live up to the code of the Cat People, the code she remembered only vaguely. How they had spoken of it, the warriors of her clan that she remembered. Proud they were, and vicious. And when they gave their word, they never were foresworn. So she said, and Multani agreed with her in that grave way of his. But was it so? Really so, or just the half-memories of an abandoned child, desperate for some great heritage to cling to; and the agreement of a wise old sorcerer, equally desperate to give her something to be proud of?

Their lives might depend on it. And she did not know.

The Most Old stood up, still lithe despite the graying fur showing between the straps of her leather armour and the strips of coarse linen that covered it. She moved to the centre, to the dance, and the warriors made room for her. Round they went, and up and down and round and down and up, while all the time the drumming beat the night and the drone of the triple pipes moaned an eerie counterpoint. Mirri found that her fingers were tapping out a rhythm of their own. Some of the tribesfolk who were not dancing were beating their hands against the packed earth. She wondered if it would be all right to do the same. She leaned across to ask Gerrard his opinion, but before he turned to her, the warrior seated on the far side of the Most Old stood up.

Keilic, he was called. He had introduced himself in halting Trader before the feast had begun. But Seyen had seen him and gestured sharply, and he had left them.

He took a pace. Two paces, and he was directly in front of her, rimlit by the dancing light of the flames, his fur gleaming as if it had been oiled. He began to dance, those strong legs stamping out their own rhythm, between and around the complex pounding of the drums, and she understood that he danced for her.

He was watching her. The vertical slits of his pupils were almost round in the darkness, and his eyes glittered like topaz. Dance with me, they seemed to say. Dance with me, by the fire, under the stars. Dance with me till morning comes.

But she did not want him. Did not want his fur, gleam though it might, or the strong exciting cat-smell of him.

She wanted a smile that put the world to rights and which revealed blunt white teeth, not sharp cat fangs; and pale skin, tanned to gilt by the sun; and round brown eyes.

So she stared up at him, but did not move. He wove a deep bow into the tapestry of his dance. "Dance with me," he said, in Catling.

"I do not want to," she answered.

Gerrard leaned toward her. "I think he wants you to dance with him," he said. Jealousy? Hope rose up in her.

"I don't want to," she repeated, but she thought, I want to dance with you instead.

"You should—they might be offended," Gerrard said.

The words hit her like a blow. "I do not *want* to," she said again. She stood up, unsure what she would do. He would give me to him, she thought. If it would help to get what Multani wanted, he would give me away.

It was more than she could bear. She ran, then, into the darkness.

Later, of course, Gerrard apologized. But that was after the cat warrior challenged him, and after all three of them took the spirit walk, and after he stood alone in the darkness drenched in blood, and Mirri foresaw his death. . . .

Drenched in blood. Pressed up against the wall of her cabin, with Crovax crouching over her, she whimpered, and then hated herself for her weakness.

"You should not overtax yourself, my dear," Crovax said. "You'll start your wound to bleeding again." He licked his lips. Whenever had his teeth been so sharp? Almost like a catling's Mirri thought.

His hand drifted toward her again. She did not want him to touch her. But he was a friend. A friend who smells like an enemy, she thought. His hand touched her neck. His face lowered toward hers—

She lashed out. Her claws connected hard with his cheek. Flesh rent under them.

He screamed and staggered back. His hands went up to

his face, then came away bloody. *Good*, Mirri thought. *Good*. The ship pitched violently. Crovax slammed back against the door jamb.

He licked the blood from his fingers. His tongue flickered across his dark skin, and now it was obvious that his teeth had become fangs.

Something's happened to him, Mirri thought. She rolled out of bed, and by the time she was on her feet, her cutlass was in her hand. The deck rolled beneath her. She struggled like a human to keep her balance. Pain from her wound jagged through her as she stretched.

She took a step forward. Another. Crovax moved backwards. Somewhere above, someone screamed. *Don't think of it*, Mirri admonished herself. *Don't think of the battle above, think of the fight here. Focus. Focus.* She strode toward him. One more pace, and he would be within striking range.

Saliva glinted on his fangs. He smelled of fear and anger.

What have you become? She wondered, but she did not say it. She knew better than to waste her breath during a fight.

Something like Selenia, she thought and knew then why Crovax smelled like an enemy. Like Selenia, who had almost killed her.

She would not give Crovax the same opportunity. She raised her cutlass. He barely seemed to move, but the jewel at his neck flashed and glittered in the lamplight. It gleamed in her eyes. Tears blinded her. When she could see again, he was gone.

There were so many places he could have hidden. On any normal ship, it would not be so, but *Weatherlight* was far from normal. Strange bits of machinery dotted the vastness of the lower deck, sculptural in the half dark. The area belowdecks was filled with pulleys and wires, pillars pierced with holes and strung with filaments and crystal prisms, clockwork mechanisms and things that might have been clockwork except that none of the cogs interlaced. All this was there, and the rolled and slung hammocks, the boxes and crates of food, and the bales of spare sail material that any great ship might carry in its hold.

And somewhere in here, Crovax waited.

Mirri inched forward, expecting attack.

Again, there was that faint scent of . . . blood. She had it now. Selenia, coming at her, dark wings iridescent by candlelight, sword flashing—

Something slammed into her back. She stumbled forward, momentarily unbalanced. Her incisors drove into her bottom lip, and she tasted blood.

"Don't fight me, Mirri," Crovax said. "This is my destiny. I *must* do this, as surely as you must yield to me."

She felt his hand on the sleek fur of her nape, and felt his breath on her cheek, as his other arm came round her neck to secure her.

"Enough," she shouted, and rammed her elbow into his belly.

He grunted. His arm locked round her neck and jerked her back. She couldn't breathe. For a moment, they were held there, as if frozen in time. Mirri's vision turned red. She bit down on Crovax's arm. Her teeth scissored through layers of cloth, into flesh.

He screamed. His grip loosened. Before he could regain it, Mirri reached up over her head and grabbed him by the shoulders, dropping low as she did so. She yanked him hard. Harder. Her muscles strained against the ripped fabric of her shirt. Pain seared across her chest and belly. She felt the stitches in her wound start to pop.

She ignored it all.

There was an enemy to fight.

So fight.

She yanked Crovax over her head and hurled him at the bulkhead. He slammed against the wall. Mirri stared at him. She was breathing much too hard, and the long cut across her belly burned like fire. The world swam in front of her eyes.

Finish it, she thought. Finish it before the wound finishes me. The darkness was encroaching, swirling round the edges of her vision so that all she could see was Crovax.

She went toward him. I ought to put an arrow through his heart, she thought. Safe. From a distance. But she had no bow, not even a throwing knife.

There was a blur of motion. Something swung at her. She got her arm up in time, but it clipped the side of her head.

She fell.

* * * * *

Darkness took her, and she was running through the forest again, fury powering her legs.

There was a noise behind her. She turned, and saw Gerrard crashing through the undergrowth. Quickly, she stepped behind a tree. She ought to speak to him. But there was no way to explain without telling him how she felt: what he meant to her, what she wanted there to be between them. And she couldn't. She would have fought the Great Wolf alone and unarmed before she would have told him any of it.

"Mirri!" he yelled. "Mirri."

A shadow slipped out from the tree behind him. "She is not here, human." It was the cat warrior, Keilic. "She has run from your enslavement."

"She isn't my slave."

"So you say," said Keilic. "But when you try to give her away, when she is unwilling, then what else is she, human?"

"She is here to accomplish a mission, as am I," Gerrard snapped. Mirri's ears went back. If she failed Multani because she could not control her wayward heart. . . . "Our master is depending on us."

Keilic's lips skinned back from his fangs. "I know you humans. He is not of your tribe. You would put his needs against your loyalty to your—"

"She's my friend," Gerrard cut in. "We are not of a kind, cat man. Would it please you if there were more between us?"

"It would please me if you treated her with the respect she deserves," Keilic said. "That you don't tells me you have no honor. You are not to be trusted."

"Speak softly," Gerrard said. "I'll not be insulted by the likes of you, cat man." Mirri noted to her horror that his hand was on his sword hilt.

"So much for your mission, human." Keilic stepped forward. His ears were flat against his head. Red lights glinted in his eyes. "You serve your master well."

Gerrard's sword hissed as he drew it from its scabbard. "I'll serve you better," he said.

Suddenly, there was a dagger, curved and white as horn, in Keilic's hand. For a moment, human and cat warrior faced each other. Gerrard shifted. Keilic followed him. Another pace. And then the cat warrior leaped, so fast he was inside Gerrard's guard before the man could react.

Gerrard went down, Keilic on top of him. The human's sword flashed in the moonlight as it tumbled away from him. Mirri saw his hand scrabbling at his belt for his poniard and saw Keilic's dagger-hand come up.

. . . and saw no more, because she was in motion. She leapt at Keilic's back, but by the time she landed, his dagger had slammed down and reversed, so that the pommel crashed into the side of Gerrard's face. A gash along his cheekbone wept blood. The salt smell of it enraged Mirri. She grabbed Keilic's scruff and hauled his head back.

"This is not your fight." Her heart slammed in her chest.

Keilic said something fast and hissing in Catling. Mirri did not understand. She tightened her grip.

"It should be your fight," Keilic said in Trader after a moment. "The human dishonors you."

"I make my own decisions," Mirri interrupted. She shoved Keilic away from Gerrard. "You talk of respect, but you do not respect that." Under her light armour, her fur was rippling with the adrenaline surge of anger.

Gerrard scrambled to his feet. "We are friends," he said. He glanced at Mirri. Friends, she thought, and strove to keep her face impassive. If it was all she could have, it would have to be the best she could have, she decided. No more dreams. No more wild thoughts of what they might have together. Friends. But Gerrard was still talking. "We study together. Work for the same aims, as the members of your tribe."

"You mean, she makes compromises," Keilic said. "Look at her. How blind are you, that you can't see what she wants?"

How dare you, Mirri thought at him. How dare you think you know my mind. She took a step forward, so that she was between the others. Her hand rested on the hilt of her sabre. "Enough," she said.

Keilic seemed not to have heard her. "It pleases you to let her near you! How pleasant to have a beautiful woman purring round your feet! And it pleases your master, for he can learn as much from her as she can from him. But in truth—"

"I said, enough," Mirri roared. She drew her sword. The blade glinted coldly in the moonlight. She turned to Gerrard. "You, understand that I do for Multani as much as I deem wise and fair, and no more." She swung round to face Keilic. "And you, understand that my tribe abandoned me when I was but a kitling. If my loyalties are other than—"

"But perhaps your loyalties are wrong," Keilic said. "Blood goes to blood, stranger. What's bred in the bone can't be denied. If you try to deny it, you'll lose yourself."

Keilic's words sent a shiver through Mirri. For a moment she felt dislocated from herself and from the scene around her. Then anger raged through her. "You speak in riddles and nonsense," she said. "I live my life. I am happy with my life."

"Are you?" Keilic's voice was soft, almost soothing.

"Yes!"

"Only your words say that. Your eyes don't. The way you hold yourself doesn't."

"You've had your answer, cat man," Gerrard cut in. "Go back to your fire and your dance before the Most Old notices you're missing."

"Oh, I will," Keilic said. "The only question is whether she comes back with me, or whether she chooses to live her life alone."

"I am not alone." Mirri's anger was fast being replaced by impatience. "I have my teacher and my friends."

"Is that enough, though? Will you live a loveless, joyless life among the humans? Do you think he'd ever accept one as different as you into his—"

"That's sufficient!" Gerrard stepped up close, to face off to Keilic. The scent of his sweat mingled with the resiny smell of pine. Mirri wanted him so much she almost ached. "What does she have to do to convince you?"

He didn't expect an answer; Mirri could tell by his tone. But Keilic gave him one anyway.

"Take the spirit walk," he said. "All three of us: let the shaman lead us along the path of the Great Cat, and we will see which path the ancestors think she should take."

Gerrard made a little sound of disgust. "What nonsense! Magic is magic, but this is just superstition."

Mirri stared at him. For a moment, he met her gaze. Then he looked away. "Is it?" she demanded. "Is that what you think of my people's beliefs: just nonsense to be dismissed?"

"They aren't your people."

"But we could be," Keilic said.

There was an instant in which Mirri barely knew who she was. A cloud slid in front of the moon. The darkness was absolute. Everything changes, she thought. Nothing's forever. Perhaps it's for the best.

"Tell your shaman I will walk the spirit path," she said.

* * * * *

The rough wood of *Weatherlight*'s lower deck bit into Mirri's cheek. For a moment, the half-dream held Mirri. Something about the spirit walk . . . something she must remember. But the ship lurched under her, and up above, people were shouting across the sounds of the lurching ship.

"Crovax," she muttered. The stink of him—blood and sweat and that indefinable smell of enemy—was everywhere.

Mirri hauled herself to her feet. He had meant to kill her. If he hadn't, it could only be because he had greater harm in mind.

How long had she been unconscious? Not very long, she thought. She looked round for her sword, but it was gone. Either he'd taken it or it was lost somewhere in the jumble of lashed down crates and barrels that packed *Weatherlight*'s underdecks. No matter. She swung her head heavily from side to side, trying to sense a difference in the density of the smell. Nothing. But on the decking was the most minute of scuff marks. There were a few drops of blood on the deck a little further on. She rubbed her thumb against them. They were still damp. She hadn't been out for very long, then.

Cautiously, she made her way between the boxes and crates of *Weatherlight*'s supplies. There was too much cover here. Crovax could be anywhere. Mirri's ears flickered at a faint sound. He was up ahead then.

"Damnation," she muttered. There was a companionway up there, and nothing much else. Despite her pain, she hurried on, pushing her way through the crowded hold, not worrying now about ambush.

She got to the bottom of the companionway just in time to see Crovax's dark leggings whisking up through the open door at the top of the ladder. She went up the rungs three at a time, ignoring the agony that screamed through her with every extended movement.

She clambered onto the upper deck. *Weatherlight's* mighty wings beat the air, causing a wind that clawed at Mirri's face. All over the ship, the crew leaned over the railings, staring at the scene beneath them. Overhead, an ornithopter swung back and forth erratically. Even as Mirri watched, a form came hurtling down from it to land on the deck: Tahngarth. The abandoned ornithopter shot past the ship and disappeared in the foliage a way beyond in a cloud of flame.

Mirri stared around wildly, looking for Gerrard. Surely, surely he had returned to the ship by now with Sisay. Surely he'd drawn *Weatherlight's* captain from the dark and awful center of the Stronghold. Gerrard was never one to walk away from a battle. Again she had that flash of memory, of the Spirit Way they had walked together, of his blood-drenched figure slumped against a spire of rock. She shook her head. Spirits be damned; she had to concentrate. But he was nowhere in sight, and she realized that they must not yet have picked him up.

That must be why they were hovering here instead of running for the portal and the waiting Ertai.

But where was Crovax? She clambered onto the companion housing to get a better view. She turned and saw him. He was up near the bows, about one hundred and fifty feet away. He had his back to Mirri, but she could see that he was fiddling with something, apparently undisturbed by the fighting going on all around him.

Mirri leaped off the companion housing. She landed lightly enough, but the impact still sent pain tearing through her. It was nothing, she told herself fiercely. She ran toward Crovax, leaping over bits of the ship's superstructure that had broken in their various battles. What was he doing? She had never paid much attention to the working of *Weatherlight*. Now she wished she had.

She slammed into him and grabbed his heavy coat in both hands. He turned in the loose folds. She glimpsed an open hatch behind him, and a complex mass of cogs and wheels and rods.

The sails, she thought. The housing covered the mechanism that transferred power directly from the Thran stone to *Weatherlight*'s great wings. Wreck that and the ship would plummet into the tangled Gardens below.

"Tschakren," she yelled at him. It was the worst catling oath she knew.

He didn't answer, just slipped from her grasp and danced away. Blood glistened on his cheekbone and on his arm, where she had bitten him.

"Don't try to stop me, beast woman," he snarled. The voice was no longer Crovax; it was deeper, stronger, somehow alien to everything she remembered about the nobleman. "You could have joined me," he continued, "but it's too late now. My destiny is fulfilled. You had your opportunity, but it's past."

"Then I won't try," Mirri said, and launched herself at him. "I will simply do it." As she yelled the last word, she crashed into him.

The force of her attack sent him staggering back. She went with him. There was no chance now to use her sword. Instead she rammed the heel of her hand up into his face. His head cracked back, and she she drove her fist into his gut. He flailed at her, connecting with the side of her head. But the battle rage was on her, and she hardly felt the blows. She tried to loop her leg round his, seeking to unbalance him. She failed, and he grabbed her free arm and started to force it up. She jabbed at his eyes. He yanked his head back, and her fingers met cold flesh instead. She hit hard enough to force him back again, and now they were hard up against the taffrail. Just beyond them, the great wings stirred.

Mirri was tiring fast now. She could feel blood from her leaking wound soaking the thin fabric of her tunic, gluing it to her skin. He was pounding at her now, slamming his fists repeatedly into her face, chest, belly—anywhere he could. If she were ever going to finish it, it had to be soon.

She let his next blow move her back. Just a little. Then she rammed her knee hard up between Crovax's legs. He screamed, and folded up. As he went down, she slammed her open hand into his face, catching him under the jaw.

For the space of a heartbeat, she fumbled for her dagger before she realized she wasn't wearing it. The mistake cost her dear. Crovax bellowed. He leaped at her, face contorted in rage and agony. Before she could react, he had grabbed her. He lifted her bodily off the deck and swung her round. For a sickening moment, she hung suspended over the side of the ship, with nothing between her and the jungle below except a patchwork of the overlapping sails of *Weatherlight*.

His hands loosened. She clamped her hands 'round his wrists. She fell, then stopped with a jerk, anchored by his weight. But the momentum of her fall was too great. Slowly—so slowly—he tumbled forward. A section of the taffrail came away with him, and then with a shriek of tortured wood they were falling.

Then they were in free air, with the green canopy of the Garden rushing up to meet them. Mirri tried to spread her arms and legs and tail out, hoping to slow her fall. But Crovax was thrashing around, sending them tumbling. Loosening her hold was the easy option, but it would have meant possibly having him free on the ground, free to run to Volrath's creatures, or attack from behind. There was Gerrard's raiding party to consider. She tightened her grip, and was rewarded with a look of pure hatred.

He screamed something, but she couldn't work out what it was. The moment seemed to stretch out for ever; everything was happening very slowly. The fall was taking forever.

The world spun around her, green of the jungle, blue of the sky, green, blue, green, all smeared through the tears that the wind whipped into her eyes, while Crovax jerked and flailed, so that her arms felt as if they were being pulled from their sockets. Her chest burned with the effort of breathing.

And then there was no more time for worrying about anything, because the canopy of the jungle was rushing up to meet them.

Crovax was under her. She let go of one of his wrists and managed to get her arm up in front of her face before she smashed into the trees, only glad that it was Crovax that was breaking the path for them. She plummeted through a chaos of branches and vines. Leaves as sharp as blades tore at her. Thorns stabbed her. The sweet smell of putrefaction was everywhere, threatening to overwhelm her senses.

Crovax slammed into the solid branch of one of the trees. He screamed. Mirri pivoted on the fulcrum of his arm and crashed into the thinner end of the branch. It broke beneath her weight, and her fall continued. But, by reflex she had clenched her hand still tighter round Crovax's wrist; now they fell much more slowly, and Mirri was underneath. Each new impact with a branch or leaf sent new agonies jagging through her.

She reached out to grab a branch—anything to stop herself falling—but it was impossible. She twisted round as they slammed into the ground.

* * * * *

Consciousness slipped away from her. She fought to hold the world in place, but it seemed to her that she was no longer in the jungle fighting Crovax. Instead, she was on the Spirit Way with Gerrard and Keilic. The dark path: it was night, and by starlight she saw a path lead up onto the stony side of a hill. Somewhere in the distance, the Chitr'in were drumming. The potion the shaman had given her to drink was bitter on her tongue.

She was dressed in the fighting leathers of the Chitr'in, and in her hand was one of their razor-edged horn knives.

"Now?" she said, bewildered.

"Now," Keilic said from behind her. "You find your spirit beast and defeat it, and in the defeat know the path your fate lies upon."

"And you?"

"We are your choices. Where else should we be but at your right hand and your left?"

Mirri glanced behind her. Sure enough, Keilic and Gerrard were behind her. Keilic was dressed in the full panoply of the Chitr'in warrior, his fur and leathers brightly painted, feathers and beads at his ears and throat and wrists. Gerrard was dressed simply, in his rough breeches and white shirt. Neither of them were armed.

This is my fight, then, Mirri thought. She led the way up the hillside. If there was a choice to be made, she could not see it. The path led up between a cliff on one side and a sheer drop on the other, all made of black rock, without a vestige of plant life.

Ahead of her, there was a cave mouth. Plainly, she was meant to enter. She wished she had her sword to hand instead of just the dagger.

Warily, she approached. Behind her she could hear Gerrard's soft footfalls and Keilic's, softer yet. She paused at the cave mouth. After a moment, her eyes adjusted to the deeper darkness within. Shadows were layered upon shadow.

One of them moved.

Instantly, Mirri dropped into a fighting crouch, knife held low and ready.

The shadow uncurled and became a vast black cat. Its tail swept the floor. Twin coals burned in the pits of its eyes. Its mouth stretched open, revealing yellow fangs as long as daggers. The stench of rotting meat rolled over Mirri.

"Am I to fight you?" Mirri asked. It was a stupid question, yet nothing was clear to her.

"Defeat me and I will kill whichever of those two you choose," it said—or thought; Mirri could not entirely tell if the voice echoed in her ears or in her mind.

"Suppose I do not wish you to kill either?"

"Then you will not defeat me. I am your destiny. Make your choice, or let the Spirit Way take you where it will. But I will feed on the choices you leave aside."

"Choices, yes. But those are people—"

"They are on the Spirit Way," the cat said. "They are mine." And it sprang at her.

Instantly, she was ready for it, braced and with the knife ready to plunge into its soft underbelly. Its claws raked her cheek, but she ignored the pain and sliced up into its belly. She felt the blade graze a rib, and ripped backwards. The cat screamed with pain. Blood and slime splashed over Mirri.

And then, somehow, the cat twisted into nothingness and was gone. Only a faint hint of mist remained. But before Mirri could move, the mist coalesced, and once again the great cat sat regarding her, now completely uninjured. Something glistened on its forepaws. Her blood, Mirri thought, and knew it for truth. Even as the certainty grew in her, the cat raised its paw to its mouth and began to lick it clean.

After a moment, it lowered its head, averting its eyes. "I am defeated and yours to command," it said.

"This is too easy," Mirri said.

"For you, perhaps. What would you have me do?"

"Let me go, and them."

"You must choose."

"I will not."

"I am the Spirit Way," the cat said. "I will choose for you."

Again, it launched itself at her. But this time, it leaped over her head, and landed between her and the two men. It crouched there, tail swishing, head weaving back and forth, back and forth as if it were getting their scent.

Choosing.

Faintly, in the distance, there was the sound of the Chitr'in drumming. This is the Spirit Way, Mirri thought. Nothing hear is real. Our bodies sit entranced by the fire. We cannot be hurt, not here. Yet the claws of the great cat had felt real enough when they raked her. Nothing here is real, she insisted to herself. Probably.

The cat stretched itself out and began to smell Keilic, from feet to head and back again, letting its face come right up to his. He held perfectly still. So did Gerrard, when his turn came, though Mirri could tell by the way he held himself that he found it hard.

"She would have much honor, in the way of your tribe, if she stayed with you, Chitr'ini," the cat said at last. "And when her fighting days were done, she would give you many fine cubs. Your line would be strong, aye these many years. And yet, she would yearn always for the soft-skinned one, and for knowledge of the world and adventures of a kind you could never give her."

"I would give her all it is fitting for one of the Chitr'in to have," Keilic protested. "She would be happy—"

"After a fashion," the cat agreed, and turned its attention to Gerrard. "If she goes with you, she will be your strong right arm, ever at your back. She will give you more than you can ever, waking, know. All her loyalty, all her heart."

"Yet she will be incomplete," shouted Keilic.

"Be silent, catling," the cat roared. "You have forgone your right to speak." Mirri looked away. "Yet I tell you," the cat went on, in a milder tone, now addressing Mirri directly, "you alone will remember what transpires here—of those who live."

Mirri nodded. The great cat turned back to Gerrard.

"All her heart," it repeated. "Yet in giving all that she has, she will lose who she is. How can it be otherwise, when you will deny her her heritage?"

"She could learn the way of her people," Gerrard said. "She is my friend, my closest ally. How can I give that up?"

"Your friend, yes," the cat said. "But you have her heart. Do you hold it gently?"

"I—"

"Do you want her?"

Now Gerrard looked away. "I love her as I would love a sister," he said at last. "How can it be otherwise? We are too different."

Mirri felt her heart die within her. It was as she had feared. The world turned to ash and saltwater around her. The great cat turned to her. It stared at her for a moment. She did not speak, but perhaps something in her stance gave her thoughts away.

The cat turned back, and in a single fluid motion, sprang at Gerrard. Unarmed and ill-prepared, he went down before it. He screamed as it slashed at him with his front paws. It scrabbled at his belly with its strong back claws, seeking to rake and gut him open. The mouth opened. Saliva glistened on the yellow teeth. It roared fury to the world.

All this in the space of a heartbeat. In the next, Mirri threw herself against the beast. It was too heavy to knock off balance. She pushed back and raised the horn knife in both hands. It would be a difficult blow, for the cat's soft parts were protected by its thick coat and rib cage. She struck once, but it twisted lithely away, and the knife did no more than scratch it. It ignored her, and swung back to Gerrard. Its jaws opened, and it snaked its head out to tear out his throat. Before it struck, Mirri hurled herself forward and down, then shoved the dagger up into the soft tissue of its throat.

It thrashed around, digging its claws into Gerrard spasmodically and causing even him even more damage.

"How many times," Mirri said, panting with the exertion of driving the knife home, "do I have to kill you, cat?"

Suddenly the beast went limp. Mirri pushed it off Gerrard. He fell forward. She caught him. He was slick with his own blood, and there was more pumping out of the deep wounds in his chest and belly and back.

"So you have made your choice, catling." It was the cat's voice, from behind her. Mirri turned. Fiery eyes regarded her.

"I love him," she said.

"He does not love you."

The words were like a slap across the face. "After his fashion, he does."

"After his fashion," the cat agreed. "Though you will come to find it is not enough."

"No."

"After you have died a little each day, watching him, knowing he will not hold your heart, you will come to find it is so."

"If that's the price, I'll pay it," she said. "You may know the hearts of your catlings, but you do not know the hearts of men, and I was never yours."

"No," the great cat agreed. He swung his great head to face Keilic. "Chitr'ini, she has made her choice. Will you accept it?"

"I would have given her my life. How can I do other than accept her choice?"

"Then stand ready."

Mirri watched, horrified, as Keilic dropped to his knees and threw back his head, exposing the soft flesh of his throat. The cat padded over to him.

"Wait!" Mirri said. "You can't—"

"You have rejected him. He is mine."

"Yes, but—"

"This is the Spirit Way. There must be choices."

"I do not wish anyone to die."

"This is the Spirit Way," the cat repeated. "The only death here is the death of the life you might have had."

"Mirri?" Gerrard called. His voice was weak.

"Go to him," said the cat. "He is your life now."

But Mirri couldn't move. The cat turned back to Keilic, who was waiting still as stone. Without saying anymore, it sliced down with its huge fangs and tore out Keilic's throat. Blood spurted across the cave, drenching the cat and the stone behind it.

Keilic's body disappeared into the mist and did not reappear.

"I am done here," the cat said. "Attend your loved one, catling. For I tell you, your time with him will not be long, and when his end comes, it will come at your hands." And with that the cat moved back into the shadows. For a moment, its eyes of flame watched them. Then those, too, disappeared.

* * * * *

A great weight was pressing down on Mirri. She opened her eyes. Crovax's face was inches from her own. His thumb moved across the side of her face. She tried to shove him off, but he had pinioned her hands behind her back, and he had his knee across her thighs.

"Sweet Mirri," he whispered. "Foolish Mirri, you shouldn't have resisted me." His hand continued to caress her, along her face, her jaw. Her neck.

She thrashed around, trying to get free, but the hand under her and the knee across her were too strong. "What we could have together. . . such burning power you have never tasted," he said. He brought his head down toward her. Immediately, she arched upward and sank her fangs into the side of his throat. His blood tasted bad. Putrid. She wanted to spit it out, but instead she hung on, wishing only that she had managed to strike true into a large artery.

He moaned, and for a moment went limp against her. Then he jerked back, at the same time slamming the heel of his free hand against Mirri's face. There was a terrible rending sound, and he was free. Some of his flesh was stuck to Mirri's teeth. She started to spit it out, but he covered her mouth with his hand, driving his thumb up into the base of her jaw to keep it shut.

"You will join me," he gasped. "You will stand by my side. Together we can rule this world."

He bent his head to her neck and drove his fangs deep into it. She gasped, and lashed her body around, trying to get free. It was no good. Besides, the blood was burning round her body, bringing with it a glorious warmth and exhilaration.

How had she had resisted this? Why?

Crovax removed his hand.

"You see?"

"Yes," she said, staring into his liquid eyes. "Yes." She drew his head down to hers, and began to suck at the wound she had made in his neck. No longer did it taste bad: rather, it was the sweetest nectar she had ever drunk.

"Mirri!" The voice came at her out of the fire that her world had become. She ignored it. Nothing mattered, nothing but slaking her thirst. "Mirri!"

She knew that voice. It burned into her, burned brighter than the searing delight that coursed around her body. She looked up.

Gerrard was fighting in the Garden beyond her. She could see him; she would have known him anywhere. He was fighting . . . battling the misshapen one who had attacked *Weatherlight* when first they entered Rath. Greven. That was his name. Greven *il*-vec.

Even as she watched, he slashed at Gerrard and opened a wound in his shoulder.

Rage poured through Mirri. Her Gerrard. His blood was hers. She had rescued him from the Spirit Way for this? No!

"See," Crovax murmured. He rolled away from her, and pointed up at the fight in the upper branches. "See, he spurns you. He gives his blood to another. He is not the chosen one."

"Yes," she said. Gerrard should be hers. That was right. That was what she had been promised on the Spirit Way.

She remembered the breath of the great cat on her, rancid with rotten meat, and warm. Your time with him will not be long, and when his end comes, it will come at your hands.

She stared at her hands. The fur was matted with Crovax's blood and her own, and there were shreds of flesh under her claws.

Her claws, tearing into Gerrard's flesh, she thought. It was hard to think, with the warmth still pulsing through her, burning out logic, searing her senses with its white-hot power.

How it had hurt. Crovax had hurt her. He would have killed her. He would make her hurt Gerrard.

"No!" she screamed and rolled away from him. Crovax was smiling now.

"Will you hurt me, now? When I've shown you the way to power? You can have anything you desire, Mirri. You can have Gerrard."

It was hard to think. Gerrard's face. Gerrard's eyes. Gerrard laced in blood, slumping in her arms on the Spirit Way.

His end, when it comes, will come at your hands.

If thinking was too hard, then she must not think. She launched herself at Crovax, in a fury of slashing and biting and punching.

It was sweet, his blood on her tongue. But not as sweet as Gerrard's would be. No reason she couldn't have both. The trick was not to do what Crovax told her, but to do those things that pleased her anyway.

"Mirri!" It was Gerrard's voice, calling her again. He'd seen she and Crovax battling. Now *Weatherlight* was dropping ropes to haul up those who'd emerged from the Stronghold with Gerrard: Sisay, Starke, and a red-haired woman who Mirri did not recognize. All that stood between Gerrard and his ship was Greven *il*-Vec.

And all that stood between Mirri and Gerrard was Crovax, and he was nothing, nothing at all.

But from the edge of the Gardens, a shadow emerged, black against the deep purple of the sky. *Predator* was coming. Mirri saw that it was almost upon *Weatherlight*. In a moment it would be alongside the smaller ship, and this time, Mirri knew in her heart, there would be no escape.

Mirri saw Gerrard beat down Greven's sword and kick Volrath's commander away. The twisted features of *Predator*'s captain were contorted with rage; Mirri saw his lips moving as he shouted commands to his ship, though it was still too far away to hear them.

Crovax slashed at her with a bit of broken branch he'd got from somewhere.

Suddenly, Mirri understood. He was trying to delay Gerrard. If Crovax couldn't kill him, at least he could slow *Weatherlight* down long enough for *Predator* to catch her.

If Gerrard remained, Mirri could have him. How sweet

it would be, to finally possess him. And then there would be the others on *Weatherlight*. Perhaps even on *Predator* as well.

* * * * *

Gerrard's blood. He had fallen into her arms on the Spirit Way, coated in his own blood. But when they had come next to the fires of the Chitr'in warriors, there had been no blood on him. Nor on Keilic, who was also unharmed. Shakily, she had told the shaman her decision. He had nodded slowly and had taken off the mask of the Great Cat he had worn throughout the ceremony.

Bitter smoke from the fires billowed about them. Gerrard, remembering nothing, strode off toward their tent; Keilic, more subdued, also went his way. Mirri considered following him. She was doubting her decision now. If anything in the ceremony held true, all of it did. Gerrard would die before long, at her hands.

But as she started after Keilic, the shaman's hand shot out and grasped her wrist.

"You are troubled, child. The Spirit Way is often troublesome to those who follow it."

"I am, Father," she said. She could not look him in the eyes. The amber glints in them burned too bright, reminded her too vividly of the embers of the great cat's eyes. "If I follow my heart, I will never have my love, and he will die before his time, at my hands. So said the great cat."

"The great cat knows the hearts of his Chitr'in," the shaman said. "But he does not know the hearts of men. And you were never his."

Mirri started, remembering what she herself had said on the Spirit Way.

Before she could say anything, the shaman said, "Which worries you more: that he will never love you, or that you will kill him?"

"That I should kill him," Mirri said. The shaman glared at her, implacable. "I will have what love of him I can," Mirri finished at last.

"You are wise enough," the shaman said at last. "Though I would have it that you had learned other lessons from the Spirit Walk. A Chitr'in without her heart is no Chitr'in. Nevertheless, I say to you: if you will pay the price, you can step away from the path the Spirit Way has decreed."

That was it, Mirri thought. That was what she had striven to remember.

All she had to do was pay the price.

* * * * *

Gerrard was beyond her, between her and the rope leading to *Weatherlight*, hesitating. Another heartbeat and he would come for her. *Weatherlight* would be lost. The Legacy would be gone forever.

She stepped forward toward Crovax, her paws down, her neck bared.

He came toward her.

"Mirri!" Gerrard called from somewhere far off. Burning gold pumped through Mirri's veins. She struggled to keep her eyes open.

Damn, she thought.

As through a red mist, she saw Gerrard's face; he stared at her for an eternal moment and somehow read the message in her eyes.

He turned and leapt for *Weatherlight*'s ladder.

Go, she thought. Go with my love.

Here ends the Tale of Mirri

Dawn

Beyond the high windows of the library, the soft light of dawn steadily grew. The rumbles of thunder seemed now no more than a distant backdrop against the morning. Amid the piles of manuscript and tremulously leaning books, Ilcaster sat silent, tears streaming down his face. His breath came in short, sobbing gasps. Before him the old man also sat in silence. His face, as he gazed at the young man, was filled with compassion, yet there was in it as well a kind of watchfulness, as if he were waiting for some thought, now barely stirring, to burst into full flower.

The light brightened slowly, and Ilcaster's sobs grew softer. At last he sniffled, pushed the damp hair from his face, and looked at the librarian.

"Why?" he asked, his voice cracking with emotion. "Why did she have to die? Why didn't Gerrard save her?"

The silence again lay between the two, until the old man laid a hand on Ilcaster's shoulder. Beneath the parchmentlike skin, the boy could see the veins, blue as sapphire, and the slender bones, worn and brittle with age. Yet he also saw, for the first time, an inner strength that he had not before recognized.

"I told you," the librarian said quietly, "that a hero is not just an accumulation of deeds. He is also one who has sacrificed, who has given up something profoundly important to him. For Gerrard, Mirri's death was the last step on the first stage of his journey. In that horrifying instant, as he stood caught between *Weatherlight*'s safety and the life of his friend and companion, in that moment he *knew* for the first time in his life where duty lay, where his road pointed. It was not a road he had chosen, but it was one that had been picked out for him long before he was even born. And now he knew that to take it would mean more pain than he had ever imagined."

Ilcaster snuffled again, wiping his nose on his sleeve. "So what happened after . . . after Mirri died? Did they get out of Rath through the portal?"

The old man nodded slowly. "Oh, yes. But again, it was not a victory without cost.

"The ship sped over the Gardens. Gerrard, looking back, glimpsed the still body of Mirri lying on the ground, while Crovax, now only a shadow against the grass, flitted back toward Volrath's Dream Halls. The ship gained speed, but Gerrard and Sisay, clinging to the rails, could see behind them the looming shape of *Predator* hurtling in pursuit.

"Gerrard shouted to Hanna to put on more speed. The navigator frantically clawed at the ship's controls, but it was obvious that the larger ship must shortly catch up to them. Hanna gestured for Sisay to take the wheel and fought her way through the shrieking wind to Gerrard's side.

" 'We've got one chance,' she shouted in his ear. 'The Skyshaper. Karn's fitted it into the engine. I don't know what it'll do. . . .'

" 'But it can't make things any worse,' finished Gerrard. 'Go ahead and activate it on my mark.'

"Now *Weatherlight* plunged across the barren landscape. In the distance, the crew could see the steep walls of the canyon wherein lay the portal—and, perhaps, safety.

" 'Gerrard stood at the prow of his ship, hair whipped back by the wind. His face was wet with tears for Mirri— and for Rofellos, for Crovax, for all the souls lost to help him gain his Legacy. But now within his heart there was no more doubt.

" 'Now!' he shouted to Hanna, and the navigator bellowed down into the deep recesses of *Weatherlight,* 'Now!'

"The ship gave a great shiver, as if a giant hand had seized it. Then it shot forward, in a blinding burst of speed. The landscape rushed by, and now Gerrard saw the portal, light swirling within it. As he gazed, he seemed to see a ghostlike parade of figures flitting through, escaping the dark prison of Rath. Above the portal, clinging to a rope that swung from the arch above the portal, was the slender, blond, boylike figure of Ertai.

" 'Slow down so we can get Ertai!' Gerrard shouted to Hanna.

" 'I can't! she yelled.

"*Weatherlight* seemed to be moving even faster. Behind them, *Predator* had also accelerated. Gerrard even fancied for a moment he could hear the shouts of Greven *il*-Vec, demanding vengeance for his defeat. He looked up, and for a drawn-out second that seemed to go on forever, he saw Ertai's face—white with fear, or anger—and then the ship shot through the portal."

* * * * *

"That's it? That's the end? What happened to *Predator*? What happened to Ertai? What about—"

The old man held up his hand. "Quiet, lad, quiet. There's more to the story, of course. But perhaps now you should get some rest. The night is over, and the dawn is breaking." He looked out the window. The clouds were beginning to break up. He nodded slowly, as if to himself. "The storm is passing," he said quietly. "But it is not yet over. There is another yet to come, one mightier than any we've yet seen. But for today, it has passed. Rest now, lad. Rest while you can, that you may be more ready for tomorrow."

Ilcaster yawned tremendously. "Perhaps you're right, Master," he muttered. "I do feel awfully sleepy. Maybe just a little nap, just a little . . ." His voice trailed off as his head sank on a pile of books. He stretched his cramped limbs out, and a whiffling snore came from his throat.

The librarian smiled to himself and, poking in the distant recesses of a dark cupboard, came forth with a moth-eaten blanket, which he spread over the sleeping youth. Then he stretched as well, moving his neck about to work out the kinks. The library was brighter now, and soft motes of dust drifted in the early morning sunlight. The old man turned to go when one more paper caught his eye. He lifted it, studied the archaic script, and read softly aloud to himself.

"*Weatherlight* passed from Rath through the portal to a place unknown. Even as the wizard Ertai let go the rope above the portal, he saw, to his horror, the gateway slam shut. A split second later *Predator* slammed into the archway, its decks cracking and splintering with the impact. The arch crumbled and fell. Ertai tumbled downward, landed on something solid with a resounding thump, and gazed up into the angry visage of Greven *il*-Vec.

"High on a hillside overlooking the place where the portal used to be, Lyna of the Soltari stood. Beside her was a hooded figure, tall and silent. His face was hidden, but a beard bristled in the shadows of his cowl.

"Lyna turned to him. 'It was good luck the portal closed when it did,' she said.

" 'Yes,' he agreed, and turned away."

At the very bottom of the manuscript, in fading ink, the librarian read, "And so *Weatherlight* passed from Rath. Of its further adventures . . ."

The handwriting ended at the bottom of the page.

The rest of the manuscript was missing.

The librarian stood gazing at it for a moment or two. Behind him he could hear the gentle breathing of Ilcaster the pupil, who lay dreaming of heroes and quests, of brave deeds and sorrowful deaths, of tragedies and of triumphs.

"After all," he said thoughtfully to himself, "what matters are memories."

He let the last manuscript page of *The Rath Cycle* slip from his fingers and flutter gently to the floor. Then he turned his back on the rest of the library and walked through the doors into the sunlight.

Here ends the Rath Cycle

When you pick up a **Magic: The Gathering®** product, you hold the key to a world of strategy and imagination.

Magic® products are now rated for the level of strategy they represent, making it easy for you to find the right cards, whatever your experience.

Recommended for new players.
Look for *Portal Second Age™* in June!

Recommended for players who want more game options.
The *Fifth Edition™* trading card game features specially built decks for two players. *Fifth Edition* decks and booster packs are great for deck building and for sealed deck play.

FIFTH EDITION™

Recommended for advanced players who want to experience the highest level of strategy available.
Look for *Exodus™* in June, and *Urza's Saga™* in October!

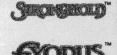